The Girl Behind The Fan

Also by Stella Knightley

The Girl Behind The Mask
The Girl Behind The Curtain (September 2013)

About the author

Stella Knightley is the author of twenty-six novels published under other names. *The Girl Behind The Fan* is the second of three books in the *Hidden Women* series, which blends the daring stories of historical women of note with an erotically-charged contemporary love affair which will delight the fans of *Fifty Shades*. Stella grew up in the west of England and now lives in London. You can follow her on Twitter at twitter.com/StellaKnightley.

STELLA KNIGHTLEY

The Girl Behind The Fan

First published in Great Britain in 2013 by Hodder & Stoughton
An Hachette UK company

First published in paperback in 2013

1

Copyright © Stella Knightley 2013

The right of Stella Knightley to be identified as the Author
of the Work has been asserted by her in accordance with
the Copyright, Designs and Patents Act 1988.

All rights reserved. No part of this publication may be reproduced,
stored in a retrieval system, or transmitted, in any form or by
any means without the prior written permission of the publisher,
nor be otherwise circulated in any form of binding or cover
other than that in which it is published and without a similar
condition being imposed on the subsequent purchaser.

All characters in this publication are fictitious and any resemblance
to real persons, living or dead is purely coincidental.

A CIP catalogue record for this title is available from the British Library

Paperback ISBN 978 1 444 77707 9
Ebook ISBN 978 1 444 77706 2

Typeset by Hewer Text UK Ltd, Edinburgh
Printed and bound by Clays Ltd, St Ives plc

Hodder & Stoughton policy is to use papers that are natural, renewable
and recyclable products and made from wood grown in sustainable
forests. The logging and manufacturing processes are expected to
conform to the environmental regulations of the country of origin.

Hodder & Stoughton Ltd
338 Euston Road
London NW1 3BH

www.hodder.co.uk

To Helen Cutler and Emma Lloyd, who encouraged me to think this just might work . . .

I

Paris, December 6th, 1846

There was a full house that evening at the Salle Favart of the Opéra Comique. The gilded auditorium brought to mind an aviary, filled as it was with the very best of Parisian society, looking like a charm of hummingbirds and chattering like a murder of crows. That evening's performance was to be the premier of Berlioz's new *Damnation of Faust,* but with moments left until the lights were dimmed and the curtain raised on the composer's self-styled '*legende dramatique*', the audience awaited the beginning of an altogether more interesting display.

Suddenly a murmur went up and all eyes were trained on a hitherto empty box to the right of the stage. Ladies and gentlemen both were transfixed as a footman helped a slender young woman to her seat. The woman was dressed in the most opulent fashion, in a deep-red silk dress that complemented her hair, so dark and glossy it was almost black. An Indian shawl fine as a cobweb slipped from her daringly bare shoulders. Her long neck was wound with a triple string of pearls fastened with a solid gold clasp studded with diamonds. Two more diamonds as big as quail's eggs glittered at her ears. She was alone. Her companion – the owner of the booth

– was absent for the evening, but everyone knew who he was and, by extrapolation, they knew the beautiful young woman's profession. But how confident she seemed. How comfortable in her fine clothes and fancy jewels. How arrogant, some of the other women whispered.

'I'd be arrogant too, if I was wearing those pearls,' said the mistress of the young Prince Napoleon.

The girl sitting alone in the best box in the house was Augustine du Vert, born plain Augustine Levert in a fishing village in Brittany some twenty-three years earlier. The owner of the box was the Duc De Rocambeau, forty years her senior and wealthier than all the other men in the opera house put together. Augustine was his mistress.

She played the moment well. Augustine knew how to position herself to best effect. Picking up her opera glasses, she leaned forward over the velvet-covered barrier on the pretense of examining the stage, while in reality she was setting out her fine décolletage like a shopfront, the better to show the women her pearls and the men the fleshy assets that had captured the heart of one of the city's wealthiest aristocrats. The women hissed at her brazenness. The men knew better than to say anything at all. Still, they gawped when they thought they would not be noticed and, when Augustine put a hand to her delicate white throat, more than half the room sighed with her.

Augustine du Vert held the audience so captivated that the first few bars of the opera went almost unheard. For the next two hours, some people paid no attention to poor Faust whatsoever, as they wondered instead what devilish sort of deal Augustine had struck to earn her earrings. When the curtain came down, Augustine applauded the artists and then, while the audience was still clapping, she got to her feet and looked around her as though she too deserved their congratulations. She cast her gaze around the stalls, taking in her friends, her rivals and those who disapproved of her all with the same steady smile. Until, that is, her eyes fell on a box almost opposite her own, and the young man inside it and the pretty blonde woman by his side . . . The young man looked back at her. He held Augustine's gaze with an angry stare that spoke of his impotent fury.

Augustine steadied herself with one hand on the rail. With the other hand she brought out her Spanish-lace fan and quickly covered her face. Never had she seen such hatred as she saw in those beloved brown eyes that evening. Never had she felt quite so despised. He hated her. The man who once claimed she meant more to him than anything in the world had glared at her as though he wanted her dead. Augustine's exit from the theatre was far less composed than her arrival. She picked up her skirts and half ran from the lobby to collapse, coughing hard, into the arms of her driver. Thank goodness the Duc had given her a carriage, with heavy velvet drapes at the windows for warmth and privacy.

As the Duc's horses hurried Augustine back to her new home near the Champs Elysées, her only comfort was to know that there can never be true hatred without there first having been love.

2

Paris, June, last year

The Friday afternoon Eurostar from London St Pancras to Paris Gare du Nord had the atmosphere of a party on rails. In my carriage alone there were two lively gangs: one of stags, one of hens, heading over to France to help their friends bid goodbye to the single life in style. They were starting early; passing around plastic tumblers filled with champagne (the girls) and vodka mixed with Red Bull (the boys) before the train even left the station. By the time the train manager announced that we were entering the Channel Tunnel, the two groups had become thoroughly intermingled and no one would have been in the least bit surprised if another marriage two or three years hence was the result.

Though the hens offered me a swig from their champagne bottle, I kept myself to myself. I settled into my seat by the window and got out my laptop, opening it like a shield. I had plenty of work to do. But it was hard to concentrate, though not because of the revellers. I had quite a bit on my mind.

I was in the process of putting the final polish to a doctoral thesis I had begun some three years earlier. My subject was Luciana Giordano, an eighteenth-century Venetian noblewoman whom I had discovered to be the real author of a notorious anonymous erotic novel called *The Lover's Lessons*. My research had taken me to Italy, of course, and there began a whole other story.

At the beginning of the year, I had spent almost two months in Venice, studying Luciana's personal papers in the library of the Palazzo Donato, a spectacular private house on the city's Grand Canal. I had expected to find confirmation of the erotic novel's authorship there and I did. It turned out that the novel had much in common with Luciana's diary and letters. They were definitely by the same hand. I had not, however, expected to find myself embroiled in my own curious epistolary love affair with the private library's owner, Marco Donato, playboy heir to a vast shipping fortune. Rich, intelligent and handsome as any male model in the photographs I found of him online, Marco Donato was every woman's dream of a lover, which made it all the more exciting that he seemed to be interested in me. Me! A Great British bluestocking.

Thinking about my time in Venice with four months' and several thousand miles' distance behind me, half of me wondered whether I had imagined the increasingly flirtatious emails and messages between me and Donato that had culminated with – I blushed to remember it – me agreeing to have virtual sex at the library desk, using a vibrator he had left there for me to find, while he sent instructions to my laptop. After that – and before that, actually – I had pushed hard for a face-to-face meeting but none ever came, despite his promises. He always seemed to be busy elsewhere. 'Away on business'.

All this time later, I still oscillated between shame and embarrassment – convincing myself that Marco had got what he wanted when I stripped off and played with myself for his distant pleasure – and anger mixed with sadness. You see, I also had reason to think that Marco's reluctance to meet me face to face was less about his having got everything he wanted without having to meet me than about his being afraid of *my* rejection if he did. There were aspects to the way things ended between us that quite simply didn't add up.

I didn't get to the bottom of it while I was in Venice. Perhaps I never would. I had not heard from Marco in all the time I'd been back in London. In any case, I had plenty of other business to grapple with. I had a thesis to edit and I was on my way to Paris to begin a new job. I'd been commissioned to complete some research for the producers of a historical movie. It was an exciting assignment that I hoped might lead to more interesting work in the film industry. That's why I needed to get my thesis polished and sent off before too long.

While the stags and hens partied on, I turned my attention back to the glowing laptop in front of me. Having read her personal diaries so closely, I had grown to love my subject Luciana, but that evening, with so much change right ahead of me, reading the diary passages I had translated back in Venice couldn't help but make me melancholy. When Luciana talked about the Venetian courtyard garden of her lesbian lover's house, for example, I could picture it only too clearly, because that house was the Palazzo Donato, where I had spent so much time. And when I thought of the Palazzo Donato, I couldn't help but think of Marco. Or at least the image of him that still lived in my heart. An image based on old photographs and encouraging words blinking on a screen.

Closing my laptop again, I gazed out of the window at the vast flat expanse of Northern France, speeding by at 175 mph. But I wasn't really seeing the farmland and the pretty provincial church spires that punctuated the endless fields of green. My mind's eye saw only the courtyard garden in Venice. I was remembering plucking a single white rose on my very first trip there and how that petty theft had led Marco to tease me into telling him how I lost my virginity. A rose in exchange for a defloration.

I told Marco Donato more about myself than I had ever told anyone. Over those weeks when we wrote to each other

– sometimes dozens of emails a day – we shared our childhood joys and pains. I shared my hopes for the future. My deepest fantasies.

And though we had never met in the flesh, I felt as though Marco knew my body intimately. Long before we had cybersex together, he had infiltrated my dreams. I'd stared at photographs of him for long enough to be able to imagine him well. And in my dreams, Marco was my ideal lover. He was dominant but always careful and tender. Sometimes he asked me to do things I wasn't sure I wanted to do, but I always found that I enjoyed myself when Marco took control. I liked to imagine the strong grip of his hands round my wrists or my ankles, holding me in place as he forced me to take my pleasure, teasing me with his soft lips and his warm tongue on my nipples or my clitoris until I could take it no longer and begged him to enter me while my entire body vibrated with desire. When I imagined him inside me, it was as though fireworks had been lit in my head. I couldn't get enough of him. I would grab his buttocks with my hands and try to force the pace. I wanted to feel him flood me with his passion. I wanted to see him be as swept away by the moment as I was. I wanted him to give in to me and buck and thrash with an energy he could not conquer. I wanted him to be mine.

I had never had such strange dreams or such strong orgasms as I did when I thought about Marco. But of course it never came to anything more than that strange moment in the library. And now he was gone. He had retreated back into his private world, leaving me wanting more and without a hope of getting it. You can see why he had perhaps turned me slightly insane.

Soon the train was pulling in to the Gare du Nord. I got up quickly, grabbing my bag and heading for the door before the drunken stags and hens could start blocking the corridor. I was among the first off the train, walking quickly up the long platform and racing for the taxi rank. Compared to the bright new station at St Pancras, the Gare du Nord seemed old-fashioned and even slightly sinister. There was no one there to meet me as there had been in Venice, when Nick Marsden, my university colleague, came to take me to my flat in the city's Dorsoduro area. This time I had just an address on a scrap of paper and the promise that the concierge would be there to give me a key. Providing I turned up in good time, that is; I'd been warned that the concierge wouldn't hang around on my account.

Reaching the front of the taxi queue, I showed the driver the street name. He nodded curtly and plugged the details into his satnav before resuming a conversation on his mobile phone. There was none of the friendly banter that was standard with the water-taxi drivers of Venice. Neither was there anything like Venice's astonishing beauty to look at on the way. We drove through streets that were far from the picture-book fantasy of Paris to a grey-looking square in the second arrondissement. Standing in front of my new building with my luggage, I wondered for a moment whether I should have stayed in London.

What kind of adventure would Paris turn out to be?

3

Paris, 1838

No girl had a more wonderful childhood than Augustine Levert. The only child of doting parents, she made it to the age of seven without considering for a moment that the world was run for anyone's pleasure but her own. The Levert family lived in a small hamlet near the sea in southern Brittany. Augustine's father Jean was a fisherman. Her mother Marie, a seamstress. Marie and Jean were childhood sweethearts, desperately in love with each other and utterly enthralled by the one small girl who was the result of their passionate attachment.

But good fortune was not to stay long with *la famille Levert.* Two weeks after Augustine's seventh birthday, her father went to sea and did not come back. An unexpected storm had taken six vessels with almost all hands. One of only two survivors explained that Augustine's father died trying to rescue his brother, so Augustine lost an uncle as well. Every family in the region was affected. The entire village was in mourning for months. Theirs was a close-knit community and people were always keen to help each other, but, like a sudden war, this storm had taken too many of the men. Poverty came hot on the heels of grief and soon everyone had to look out for him or herself again.

Marie Levert had not really worked since her marriage. In those short years of bliss, the real world had changed greatly. There was no work to be had in the village. Her elderly mother could not feed two more mouths for any length of time. There was nothing to be done: Marie and her daughter would have to go to Paris.

Augustine detested Paris. She had grown up knowing the freedom of village life and the refreshing breath of the sea. In Brittany, the Leverts lived in a cottage. In Paris, they lived in a single room: a stuffy *chambre de bonne* – or maid's room – on the top floor of a big house. Marie had already lost her sunny smile when she lost her husband, and living in Paris seemed to leach the very colour from her skin. Seeing her mother so sad made Augustine determined that one day they would leave this wretched city and go home. She hated to have to live in a hovel with no view.

Neither did Augustine enjoy her new school. The city children teased her for her country accent and her unsophisticated manners. But it was more than that. The other girls were jealous. Augustine was as beautiful as an angel. Her brown hair was as glossy as the mane of a thoroughbred horse. Her skin was as smooth and even-toned as a porcelain doll's face. Her eyes were a bright summer sky-blue, intelligent and alert. Even as a child, she aroused the envy of grown women, who spent hours at their toilette to impersonate Augustine's natural glow.

Five years after leaving Brittany, however, Augustine was beginning to feel like a real Parisienne. She had the accent. She knew the slang. She knew the places to avoid. She didn't talk much about Brittany any more. The only trace of that life that remained in their new existence was an oil painting of a fishing boat on calm seas. Augustine's father had painted it as a courting gift for Marie. It hung above the bed mother and daughter now had to share.

'If he hadn't been a fisherman, he could have been a great artist,' Marie often mused. 'If he hadn't been a fisherman then perhaps he wouldn't be dead!'

Marie could have married again. She had her offers and there was no doubt that it would have made her life easier, but one of the things Augustine admired most about her mother was her fidelity to Jean Levert's memory. Theirs had been a love truly worthy of the word 'toujours', which was engraved on the inside of the wedding ring that Marie would never take off.

Marie Levert often talked with pleasure about the day she and Jean would be reunited in a better place, but when she finally made the journey to Heaven, she would find the way there long and arduous. She died of consumption, over a series of many painful months. Her anguished coughing became more familiar to Augustine than her voice. When Marie finally died, Augustine was relieved. At least now she could remember the mother who had laughed and played, not the mother who only coughed and sobbed.

But now Augustine was an orphan. She had no one to turn to in the world and nothing to her name except the little seascape and the sewing skills she had learned from her mother. Well, perhaps that wasn't the entire sum of her assets; but her most significant blessing, her beauty, was not to be without its downside.

The orphaned Augustine's plight raised pity in the heart of her landlord, Monsieur Laurent Griff. Though he could not afford to let the young girl pay no rent, he was able to help find her a job with his brother, Claude, who had a garment atelier nearby. Augustine was good at sewing; she could make stitches as small and neat as a spider's. Moreover, she was diligent. She was neat and polite. She was always on time. She kept her mother's small-town ways in that respect. It was important, Marie had always told her, to make the very best impression. You never knew who might be watching.

Unfortunately for Augustine, the person watching her most closely at the atelier was Delphine Griff, daughter of the proprietor. Delphine had seemed friendly enough at first, but that soon changed.

Claude Griff was a little too effusive with his praise for Augustine's sewing. Delphine – who considered herself to be the best seamstress in Paris – found it hard to believe her father had been moved to such loud admiration by Augustine's embroidery alone. She got it into her head that her father had fallen in love with the teenager from Brittany. She told her mother. An argument ensued and Augustine found herself out of a job.

It got worse. Monsieur Laurent Griff's wife put pressure on him to ensure that not only did Augustine lose her job, she also lost her lodgings. It would not have been seemly for them to continue to house the girl who had tried to wreck his brother Claude's marriage. They had to stand by their family. The girl would be fine on her own, said Madame Griff. She clearly had an aptitude for gold-digging.

And so Monsieur Griff informed Augustine, with great regret, that she would have to leave the room she had shared with her dying mother. He was about to offer Augustine a return of her last month's rent to help her on her way when Madame Griff arrived and insisted on watching Augustine pack her bags.

Not that Augustine had much to take with her. The furniture in the room, like the room itself, was rented. Her mother's finest clothes – and some of Augustine's – had already been sold to pay for Marie's funeral. Augustine had just two dresses, both plain and sober as a nun's. She had her rosary. She had her hairbrush. She had the small seascape her papa painted all those years ago. She packed these few things into the battered leather bag that had once belonged to her grandfather.

Madame Griff – who was every bit as jealous and fearful of Augustine's beauty as her sister-in-law had been – put it about that Augustine left the building spewing curses. In fact, Augustine left quickly and quietly, with an undeserved sense of crushing shame. She found it hard to believe that people could be so cruel without provocation and thus assumed that she must be somehow at fault. She thanked Monsieur Griff for all his kindnesses and apologised for causing him trouble. While Madame Griff was busy crowing about the steps she had taken to avenge her sister-in-law, Monsieur Griff found time at last to press a few sous into Augustine's hand.

News of her eviction had come upon Augustine so unexpectedly that she had not the slightest idea where next to go. She knocked on some doors advertising rooms to rent but was turned away from them all; Madame Griff's unfair opinion of her had already spread far and wide. After seven or eight knock-backs, Augustine took herself to a café. She counted her money beneath the table and tried to calculate how long she might survive. If she found lodgings, she still had the problem of finding employment. How would she find employment without her last employer's recommendation? She could hardly go to Claude Griff and ask him for a letter. Not now.

Augustine came to the conclusion that the only possible course of action open to her was to return to the one place she had truly called home. She would go back to Brittany, where people knew her and would think the best. She thought her grandmother was still alive, but if she was not able to take her in, then surely a cousin would. Family was the most important thing in the end. Augustine's travails were simply God's way of letting her know that truth. The more she thought about it, the more appealing a return to Brittany seemed.

Augustine finished her modest meal and laid a few coins on the table. It was growing dark. She must make her way to the station at once. She went to ask the café proprietor if he could point her in the right direction. It was while she was asking for the quickest way to the station that one of the café's other customers lifted her purse. Poor Augustine was quite unaware until she came to buy a ticket.

A weaker-hearted girl might have given up at this point but Augustine was resolute. She would walk to Brittany. She did not care how long it would take. She would beg her way home if she had to.

By midnight, Augustine had found her way as far as the Bois de Boulogne. She spent the night shivering beneath a tree, too scared of what might happen to dare to sleep. In the morning, however, exhaustion overcame her and she could stay awake no longer. She curled up with her bag beneath her head and fell into dreams.

Augustine dreamed that a horse was gently prodding at her with its big warm nose. Its breath gave her a welcome blast of warmth in the coldness of the early day. Augustine touched the velvety muzzle. It felt like kindness itself. The horse snorted, warming her with its hay-scented breath.

'Is she dead?' came a human voice. High-pitched. Female. Cultivated.

'I don't think so, Madame.'

'Then for goodness' sake, Jean-Aude. Don't let Alphonse eat her.'

The horse's nose was duly pulled away.

Slowly, Augustine opened her eyes to see a pair of shining boots right in front of her face. Looking up the legs attached to the boots to see a man she did not recognise, she sat up suddenly and clutched the bag that contained all she had left in the world to her chest.

'It's all right,' said the man. 'I'm not going to hurt you.'

Augustine scrabbled along the ground until she had her back against a tree.

'She's not dead. Thank heavens,' came the female voice again. 'It was so cold last night. She must be absolutely frozen. What are you doing here, girl?' The woman, who was speaking, or shouting, from the window of her carriage, addressed Augustine directly. 'Did you sleep in the park overnight?'

Confused and fearful that she would not find the right answer, Augustine struggled for words.

'You don't look like a street urchin,' the woman continued. 'Are you lost? Where are you from?'

Augustine gave her address. 'Until yesterday, Madame. I had to move out. All of a sudden.'

'I know what that's like,' the woman said. 'Where are you going?'

'I'm going to Brittany.'

'Ha! Brittany!' The woman in the carriage let out a peal of laughter, as though that were the funniest thing she'd ever heard. 'On foot?'

Augustine nodded.

'Well, you're heading in completely the wrong direction. Not to mention the fact it will take you three weeks at the very least to get there and I don't think you've the wherewithal to survive another day. Have you any money?'

Augustine shook her head.

'Come closer. Let me have a proper look at you.'

Augustine got to her feet and walked up to the cab. Getting a proper look of her own at the woman for the first time, Augustine decided that she had a kind face. Very pretty. She had softly curling fair hair and a generous smiling mouth. She was beautifully dressed in the very latest fashion. Augustine knew about fashion; she had stitched a very similar bodice just a couple of weeks earlier. In fact, the dress the woman was wearing so well might have been the dress Augustine herself had made.

'Not bad,' said the woman, when she'd finished her appraisal of the waif. 'But you seem very young to be on your own in the world.'

'I'm fifteen,' Augustine confirmed. 'My mother died last year.'

'You poor thing. And your father?'

'Years ago. At sea.'

The kindly woman shook her head. 'An orphan! How terrible. What can you do? Have you ever been in service?'

'I've been a seamstress.'

'I often have need of a seamstress.'

The woman held out her arms to display her beautiful quilted sleeves as though they were ragged and in need of mending. 'Come with me, little Breton girl. I think there is room for a girl like you *chez moi.*'

Augustine was too tired, cold and hungry to question the beautiful woman's kindness. Instead, she allowed herself to be helped into the carriage, where she was seated next to the woman like a well-loved friend. When the driver had climbed back into his seat and they were on their way back into town, the woman, who said her name was Arlette, offered Augustine a share of her picnic. Augustine tried hard to remember her manners when faced with the food offered her, but it seemed like a feast after the past few months of grief and dry bread. She could not help gobbling. She let the food run down her chin.

Arlette smiled indulgently as she handed Augustine a napkin. 'My poor child,' she called her. She had Augustine tell the whole story of her downfall from the very beginning. When Augustine explained why she had lost her job, Arlette said, 'I'm not surprised in the least.'

Augustine was offended, until Arlette explained the reasoning. 'I'm not saying that you led the man on, dear. Far from it. But you are a beautiful young woman,' she said. 'Not only are you beautiful, you have the freshness of a newly opened flower. Every sensible woman should be envious of you. Have you not noticed men staring at you in the street? You are exactly what they want. And you are a virgin?'

Augustine was astonished and affronted at the question. 'Of course I am,' she exclaimed.

'Then you're all the greater prize.'

'I don't think of myself that way.'

'I will have to see to that. Come along.' She took Augustine by the hand. 'You must have a bath and go to bed. Your new life begins tomorrow.'

The woman in the carriage confused Augustine. Arlette dressed like a wealthy woman – every finger sported a jewel as big as a cardinal's ring – and yet she said she was unmarried. She was not old, perhaps twenty-five, but when Augustine asked whether Arlette's father would mind her bringing a stranger home, Arlette simply laughed.

'I am my own mistress,' Arlette explained. 'I will entertain whomsoever I please. Would you care to stay with me?'

When her other choice was the street, Augustine had to accept this stranger's generosity. At Arlette's house on the Rue de la Ville L'Evêque in the eighth arrondissement, Augustine was installed in a *chambre de bonne.* It was a tiny room, but it was a far better place to spend the night than on the road to Brittany. Over tea, Arlette persuaded her that her plan to walk all the way to Concarneau was as realistic as planning to fly to the moon in a Montgolfier balloon. Far better that she stay in Paris for a while, work as a housemaid for Arlette and save her wages. That way she would stay safe, warm and well-fed until she could afford a train ticket. If she still wanted to go, that is, Arlette added with a smile.

Augustine was certain she would still want to go back to her home town, but just a couple of weeks later, she was less sure. Living at Arlette's house, she saw a side of Paris she had never before experienced. Here near the Palais Royal the streets were clean. The houses were well-kept. Some of them even had gardens. The other girls who worked in the house were kind to her. There were several; all were without family and very young. Arlette sometimes called the house her very own convent. That would make everyone fall about with mirth.

At first, Augustine thought Arlette must have come from a very wealthy family. Like the girls she employed, she had no parents, Augustine knew that. But she had a great many friends and Augustine's eyes popped out of her head when she saw the names on the visiting cards of some of her employer's visitors. Arlette entertained dukes and princes. Once, she even entertained Prince Napoleon himself.

'How well-connected Arlette's father must have been,' Augustine remarked to Elaine, who was Arlette's general maid.

'Her father? Well-connected?' Elaine snorted. 'Are you trying to be funny? Arlette doesn't even know who her father is. Neither did her mother, more to the point.'

'But . . . The visitors?' Augustine voiced her confusion.

'You are a weird little thing,' said Elaine. 'You don't know why they come here? You're having me on. You never heard of Arlette before you met her? Honestly? You really never did?'

Augustine had to admit she knew nothing of her mistress but the stories Arlette herself had told her.

'You're as green as your namesake! Come with me,' said Elaine. 'Walk on your tiptoes and don't say a word.'

Augustine followed Elaine through the labyrinth of corridors to the *chambre de bonne* on the very top floor of the house: the room that had been made up for Augustine. Not speaking and taking care not to make the floorboards squeak, the two girls entered the room. Elaine motioned that Augustine should help her roll back the worn silk rug. There, in the centre of the floorboards, was a hole where a knot in the wood had been knocked through. The hole sent a shaft of light into the dingy maid's quarters. Augustine had never noticed it, though of course she had rolled up the rug when she was cleaning.

Elaine got down on her knees and put an eye to the hole. A smile spread over her face.

'Just in time to see the finale.'

She indicated that Augustine should lie down on the floor beside her and take her turn. When Augustine was in position, Elaine slapped her playfully on the bottom.

'Look, you goose. Here's the reason why all them notable gentlemen come to pay their respects to our Arlette.'

The room beneath swam into focus. It was Arlette's bedroom, the paradise of gilt and silk and chinoiserie that Augustine loved tidying most of all. Augustine let her gaze find the bed. It was a four-poster, with diaphanous muslin curtains, but Augustine could see that Arlette was sitting on the edge of it, with her legs dangling freely. Her stockings were round her ankles and her skirts were pushed up her naked thighs, white and smooth as alabaster. Between Arlette's open knees knelt the general Augustine had admitted to Arlette's salon an hour earlier. He had his face buried in Arlette's mound of Venus and was making a great deal of noise as he busied himself with bringing her to a climax.

Augustine sat up and asked in anguish, 'What on earth is he doing to her?'

'What do you mean, what's he doing? He's licking her cunt!'

Augustine covered her mouth – open in shock – with a hand.

Elaine was delighted by Augustine's horror. 'He loves it. Can't get enough of it. It's all he ever wants to do. Can only get an erection if he's nose-deep in her pussy.'

Augustine kept her hand clamped over her mouth.

'Arlette says that's why he's one of her favourites. She only has to lie back and let him get on with it and while he's getting on with it, he can't bore her stupid with his war talk.'

Elaine laughed and continued to elaborate. 'The one she really hates is Girodin.' This was the politician who had called the day before. 'He's the opposite of the general. As far as he's concerned, it's all about his cock. Which would be fine if he ever got a proper stiffy, but sometimes she sucks his prick until she's got lockjaw and the bastard still refuses to come. And then he takes it out on her, of course. He gets angry and then he gets vile. Tries to stick it up her arse and ends up slapping her for being too tight. She'd have stopped seeing him ages ago but if he gets angry, afterwards he gets ashamed of himself and when he's ashamed of himself, Girodin brings her pearls.'

Augustine sank back against her narrow maid's bed for support. To think all this might have been going on right beneath her as she said her rosary before sleeping.

'Don't look so shocked,' said Elaine. 'It's just the way of the world. And it keeps you and me safe and warm. Men want what Arlette's got. All three of us – you, me and our mistress – want the money they give her in exchange.'

'But . . .' Augustine couldn't begin to find the words to express her dismay. She didn't have time. From downstairs, a bell rang to announce that Arlette had yet another visitor.

'Arse,' said Elaine. 'That'll be the poet. And the general still hasn't gone. He's taking his own sweet time today. I better go downstairs and keep the poet busy while the old warhorse finishes her off.'

Straightening her apron, Elaine returned to duty, leaving Augustine alone in the *chambre de bonne.* Augustine continued to sit against the bed for a moment, half paralysed with shock as she tried to take in the truth of the situation. Her mistress was a prostitute. She was living in a common prostitute's house! It went against every moral teaching Augustine had ever heard. She could end up in the vile book – the police chief's list of immoral women and their associates. And yet Elaine was right. Arlette's sin had been Augustine's salvation. Arlette had shown her great kindness and Augustine had come to love her as a small child loves an older sister.

What should Augustine do? For the good of her soul, she knew she should leave at once. She had saved a little money. She could catch a train halfway to Brittany at least and perhaps find work along the way. But how could she expect anyone to hire her when her last reference came from a kept woman?

Unable to articulate what moved her, Augustine paused in her fretting and put her eye to the peephole again. In the room below, the general was still hard at his labours. Augustine could see Arlette's be-ringed fingers twisting in the general's thin grey hair. She could see Arlette's tiny feet – still in their elegant satin shoes – flexing and pointing with increasing agitation. She could hear the sounds of Arlette's excitement floating up from below.

Augustine put her hand to her own breast. Much as she hated to admit it, something about the scene was stirring to her. She felt a curious blossoming begin to take place inside her. Though the sensation was very strange, it wasn't in the least bit unpleasant. The skin of her décolletage was suddenly covered in goose pimples. Her nipples puckered underneath her chemise. She felt her own breath quickening in time with Arlette's.

'Oh! Oh! Oooohhhh!' Arlette cried out.

Augustine was transfixed.

'Augustine! Come on! I've been ringing the bell for ten minutes!'

Elaine was back at the door, panting with the exertion of having run up all the stairs.

'For goodness' sake. Stop peeping. I need you in the kitchen. The poet has brought a friend with him. They want us to get them some dinner.'

Augustine quickly rolled the rug over the peephole and followed Elaine back downstairs.

4

London, last year

So, what happened between Venice and Paris?

I left Venice in something of a hurry. Towards the end of February, Marco had arranged a Martedì Grasso ball. I had expected to meet him face to face for the first time that night. On the one hand, it seemed odd to choose to make our first meeting so public. On the other hand, I couldn't help but think it was a rather romantic idea. I imagined it like the ball scene at the beginning of Baz Luhrmann's *Romeo + Juliet*, where Leo DiCaprio and Claire Danes find a quiet moment away from the revelries to discover each other properly and press their palms together. Hand to hand. 'Holy palmers' kiss.' Wasn't that the line? Everyone else just faded away. That was what I wanted.

In the event, it wasn't like that at all, though the ball was amazing. The usually gloomy Palazzo Donato looked like the glittering set of a Hollywood fairy tale. Bunting hung from the gallery around the courtyard garden. There were liveried servants and a string quartet and blazing torches illuminated every corner. It was as though a wand had been waved over the place, bringing it back to life in a way that hadn't been seen for a decade, according to the rumours around the city. The guests added to the evening's enchantment. In their finery and their masks, everyone was beautiful and elegant. They seemed to find more poise as they left behind their modern cares and were transported back in time.

To make the evening more special still, Marco had sent me the most beautiful Christian Dior dress to wear. It was the most wonderful gift. The dress was made of pewter silk with a tight bodice that fitted exactly to my curves, flowing into a full skirt that fell like a waterfall of feathers. But he had also sent me a *servetta muta*, a type of masquerade mask that has no straps but is instead held in place by a button, which the wearer must clench between her teeth. I wasn't sure what Marco had meant by sending me a mask that would render me unable to talk. That's partly why I decided to let my friend Bea wear the Dior instead, disguising herself as me, while I put on the vintage red dress she had found in the dusty corner of a tired old dress agency.

I'd wondered ever since if that was the decision that changed everything: my swapping costumes with Bea so that Marco might mix us up for just long enough for me to observe him as a stranger. You see, later that evening, Bea had an unexpected encounter in the library of the palazzo with a man she thought might indeed be Marco. When she introduced herself, however, he claimed he was just the gardener, dressed up for the party. Not believing what she heard, Bea made a playful grab for his hand, only to discover that it was horribly burned and disfigured. She failed to disguise her shock; I knew all this as I had watched everything from the door.

Bea fled the room in tears but I caught up with her in the corridor. By the time she'd finished telling me the story, I was convinced that the stranger had lied to her and that he was Marco Donato after all. I raced back to the library but the stranger was already gone. How? I had no idea. There was only one door into the room and I hadn't seen him come out of it.

It was an odd moment, but it made perfect sense of the fact that Marco had been so mysterious throughout our email relationship and so difficult to pin down to a meeting. Had he been disfigured in some accident? Was that why he hid himself away? Only the master of the house could have known how to get out of the library without being seen.

It struck me some weeks later that perhaps I was meant to wear the *servetta muta* so that when Marco finally revealed himself to me, I would not give myself away with a sudden exclamation of horror as Bea had done. Having the button clenched between my teeth would have given me time to consider my reaction, potentially sparing both me and Marco the agony of a misplaced word. But in any case, after the ball Marco claimed he was not at the house at all that night. He sent me an email, with a photograph attached. The photo was a view of Hong Kong from a hotel window many storeys high. He'd been called away suddenly on business.

Because I was sure he was lying, for reasons that were perfectly understandable if my hunch was true, I couldn't see what choice I had but to pretend that I believed him and, after that, leave him alone.

But of course he had been on my mind constantly. I couldn't put Venice behind me. Not while I still had to work on Luciana. I thought about him every single day and, even when I wasn't thinking about him consciously, he still drifted into my dreams.

I missed our daily banter. I missed feeling that there was someone who cared to hear about the minutiae of my life. I wanted to tell him he need not be embarrassed if he was no longer the gilded Adonis of the 1990s photographs I had pored over for so long. It needn't stop us being friends. Or more.

I drafted emails to that effect but never got round to sending them. I told myself I was respecting his privacy, but perhaps the truth was that it *did* matter. Perhaps the difference between how Marco had looked in those pictures and the way he might look now was more important to me than I thought. And now four months had passed.

Then, out of the blue, I got an email from Nick Marsden, the fellow academic who had helped me find a place to stay and study in Venice. It was entitled, 'I think this one's for you.' It was a job description. His email continued:

> This came to our department today, from some big shot Hollywood film producer no less. Wants to know if we've got anyone who can help him develop a film about a Parisian courtesan: Augustine du Vert. Mean anything to you? I'd be all over it but I've just been promoted, don't you know? Don't have time to do anything much with all the paperwork that involves. Flying between Venice and Oxford every other weekend. I'm starting to feel like an air hostess. Bea has other commitments too. Not least of which is that security guard she had a thing for. Remember him? The one with the Neanderthal brow ridge and the intellect to match? She's meeting his mother this weekend. She's gone and bought a knee-length skirt for the occasion. Must be serious. Anyway, I digress.
>
> So, I thought of you. Have a read of the attached spec and tell me what you think. If you fancy a shot at it, I'll put you in touch with the producer at once. It would be great to hear from you anyway. How's life in the Big Smoke?

Life in London was really not all that – I was dossing on a friend's sofa. The weather was predictably awful – and reading Nick's email made me wistful for Venice. Nick and Bea may have been just colleagues at first, but they had quickly become very good friends and I missed the happy evenings we spent together in a little bar by the Ponte dei Pugni, gossiping over glasses of Venetian spritz. Bea had been a good sounding board for relationship worries. Nick had been something else. Though I wouldn't have admitted it at the time, his quiet attention had gone a long way to making me feel better about myself. I still wondered why I hadn't taken it further.

Actually, I knew why I hadn't taken it further. I was chasing an imaginary love that had appealed to my romantic heart far more strongly than the possibility of a nice sensible relationship with another historian.

However, the one thing that definitely wasn't imaginary in my life right then was my ever-increasing overdraft. I needed a job. I had a teaching post lined up in Berlin but that didn't start until September. I had been hoping to find some teaching work over the summer: tutoring bored teenagers at an A-level crammer college or something like that, but this was much more interesting. I decided I might as well find out more.

I wrote back to Nick at once, asking him to pass my details on to the producer. I told him it was indeed as though the job had been made for me. I'd just about finished my thesis, I had three months with nothing to do before Germany and I was wearing out my welcome on London's finest couches. A trip to Paris was exactly what I needed. I did a quick Google search of Augustine's name and quickly found some very juicy information. I had a feeling the project would be enormous fun. All I had to do was convince the producer that I was his girl.

Nick was true to his word and Greg Simon, the producer, called that very afternoon, as soon as Los Angeles was awake. Though we were unable to see each other face to face, even over the telephone we had an instant rapport. He assured me he didn't need to verify the details of my CV. As far as he was concerned, the fact I had been working with famous professor Nick Marsden was recommendation enough. He felt sure I would make an excellent go of it. What kind of fee would I require for the job? And how quickly could I start?

'You want me to name my fee?' I said.

Greg confirmed that was exactly what he wanted.

Fortunately, I had already run through this scenario with Nick.

'Think of a number, double it and add ten per cent,' had been Nick's advice. 'They can only beat you down.'

I named my price. It was enough for me to stay in Paris in a modest hotel or a furnished apartment (I'd spent some time researching both). I could also pay off some loans and replenish my savings. I was astonished when Greg agreed without a quibble. It made me wonder if I should have asked for more. But the package he offered me was already beyond my wildest dreams before he added, 'You know what? We made a movie in Paris last year and I think we still have a lease on an apartment someplace in the city. You want to stay in it? Save you looking for somewhere else? Means you could start right away.'

I couldn't say 'yes' quickly enough.

5

And so, in the course of a single phone call, I had a new job and my own Parisian apartment. The apartment was on the Place Boiledieu in the second arrondissement, Greg told me, right in front of the beautiful Opéra Comique. It would be ready for me as soon as I could get to the city. I made arrangements to leave London later that very week.

I travelled to Paris on the party train and arrived at the apartment building at around seven in the evening. The concierge met me with the keys and nodded me in the direction of the right staircase. There were four staircases altogether, set around a little courtyard. It was not unlike a college quad.

The apartment itself was exactly as I had always imagined my dream Parisian apartment. It was on the first floor – the equivalent of a Venetian *piano nobile*. A polished wooden staircase wound round a wrought-iron lift shaft. The metal doors to the apartment were huge and imposing, giving a suggestion of the luxury beyond where I found parquet floors and long shuttered windows, double doors and a fireplace with a huge baroque-style mirror above it. Two extravagant chandeliers hung from the ceiling of the salon but other than that and the mirror it was furnished relatively plainly. A large, white overstuffed sofa faced the fireplace. An iron bed that was already made up with crisp new linen dominated the bedroom. There was even a vase filled with camellias on the dressing table. I was impressed. Greg Simon must have called ahead and made sure they were waiting for me. They were a welcome touch; I felt just a little less alone at the thought of the unseen hands that had prepared the flat for my arrival. I wished whoever it was might have been there so I could thank them.

Having dumped my bags in the bedroom, I went back downstairs and caught the concierge just as he was leaving. I asked about local restaurants. He said he didn't have a particular favourite, so I went to the closest and ate a very ordinary *croque monsieur*. I was feeling too tired to go further than a couple of streets away.

It would have been better if I'd had friends in the city but the only person I knew in Paris at that time was, by a most unfortunate coincidence, my ex-boyfriend Steven, who was working at the Sorbonne. I wasn't going to be calling him. As a result, I was ready to go to bed by nine o'clock.

In the dark, I lay awake and listened to the building talking to itself: the hisses and creaks of old water-pipes and the squeak of ancient parquet as someone walked on the floor above. This was a grand apartment. I wondered who had been its first occupant. Who had slept in the bed? Who held parties in the beautiful grand salon beneath the twinkling chandeliers? What stories could this building tell? I would have to investigate the building's history when I'd finished finding out about Augustine.

I sat back up for a little while and scribbled a few lines in my notebook – the beginnings of a plan for my research – but eventually, the day's travel and anxious anticipation caught up with me and I drifted into sleep.

In my dream, I lay on a bed in another room. It was a room I felt I knew well, though it existed only in my imagination.

It was the bedroom on the first floor of the Palazzo Donato. The one where Luciana Giordano had spent many long, tumultuous nights with her lesbian lover Ernesta Donato, Marco's courtesan ancestor. Luciana had described the room in her diaries and I had adopted it for my own dreams, imagining that Marco was now the room's occupant. Luciana had talked about an impressive four-poster, with sumptuous red velvet curtains that brushed the parquet floor. The sheets, however, were of purest white linen, a virginal backdrop for such devilish debauchery.

I lay on those sheets. I was wearing a white nightgown. My long dark hair was loose. Outside, it was dusk. Not quite night-time. I watched the reflections of the last rays of sunshine on the Grand Canal play on the painted ceiling. I waited for my lover to come.

He arrived. He was wearing, as usual, a mask to cover the top half of his face but his mouth was uncovered and as he crossed the room to the bed, his lips formed the smile of someone anticipating a good meal or a long draught of cool water at the end of a dry, hot day. As he moved, he took off his jacket. He was wearing a white shirt and he unbuttoned it so that I could see his bare chest beneath; his tanned skin and the light covering of dark hair. When he was close enough, I reached up to him and pulled him down towards me so I could trace the curve of his lips with my fingers.

I told him that I'd missed him. He promised he would not be away for so long again.

He lay down beside me and we started to kiss. His mouth on mine was so familiar. His lips were warm and gentle. His delicious tongue fluttered against mine. I immediately felt my whole body opening towards him and pressed myself against him, greedy for his kiss and his touch. I struggled to open those buttons on his shirt that he hadn't already unfastened.

'Not yet,' he said, taking both my wrists and flipping me onto my back with my arms apart so that I was pinned into place. He nuzzled the side of my neck. The sensation was both arousing and ticklish. He kissed his way towards the dent between my collarbones. Sitting across my legs, he pushed my nightgown up to my waist, revealing my belly and the dark triangle of my pubic hair beneath. He smiled when he saw the neatly trimmed arrowhead. Glancing at the front of his trousers, I saw that he was already straining the front of them, as he grew hard in anticipation of what was to come.

He continued to push my nightgown further up my body. I sat up and raised my arms so that he could pull it off over my head, leaving me entirely naked. I flopped back against the pillows in a posture of complete abandon. Playfully, I hooked my little finger in the corner of my mouth and regarded him, daring him to do what he would.

Slipping from the bed to stand on the floor, he took me by both my ankles and pulled me so that my bottom was on the very edge of the mattress with my legs dangling freely. He knelt on the floor between my legs and kissed his way along the inside of my right thigh. The feel of his hot breath on my Venus mound was excruciatingly delightful.

'Don't tease me,' I begged him.

'I'll do whatever I want,' was his response.

Of course he would and I would let him. He already knew that. Carefully, he parted the lips of my vagina and ran his tongue along their shiny insides. He let the tip flicker over my clitoris, sending darts of electricity through me. Slowly, he moved his tongue from side to side. I pushed my pelvis up to meet his mouth, encouraging him to go faster, but he teased me horribly, keeping the pace slow. It was both agonising and completely wonderful.

At the same time as he licked me, letting the intensity build at such a leisurely pace, he put his finger inside me. I felt myself close around him, taking the finger greedily, only reluctantly letting it slide out again. I asked him to finger-fuck me again. He refused with a shake of his head.

Instead he quickened the movement of his tongue. I picked up a pillow and held it over my mouth, biting into it when the pleasure became almost too much for me. Round and round, his tongue traced the outline of my clitoris. With his fingers, he stretched my labia apart to better reach the tiny nub of pleasure that was already throbbing and hot.

I felt my stomach muscles tense. My toes pointed. My breath grew shallow and rapid. I knew I would not be able to hold on for very much longer.

I came, as I always did, in great crashing waves of ecstasy. My body bucked and twisted. I cried out in delight. I ended by laughing out loud.

Afterwards, I lay on the sheets, exhausted but very happy indeed. My masked lover climbed back onto the bed beside me. He ran a finger down the centre of my body, eliciting one last shiver of sheer joy. He slid up the sheets so that we were once again face to face. He kissed me on the lips. I felt the taste of my own skin on his tongue.

'That was delicious,' he said. 'But now it's my turn.'

6

I woke up feeling slightly less rested than I should have done, but all the same, I started work as soon as I'd had some breakfast. Greg Simon had given me quite a short deadline. There was no time to waste.

Fortunately for me, like my thesis subject Luciana Giordano, Augustine du Vert had kept a diary. More accurately, Augustine had written a memoir, about her life in Paris, beginning at the moment she went to work for Arlette Belrose. This Arlette was one of the most celebrated kept women of the age, a courtesan reputed at one time to have been the lover of Prince Napoleon. When she died, Augustine's memoir was found among Arlette's most precious treasures. No one knows whether Augustine had ever expected or hoped to see her story printed, but Arlette's enterprising grandson made a fortune from the tale, which he published early in the twentieth century.

It didn't take me long to track down the original manuscript of Augustine's book, which was kept in the Bibliothèque Nationale. Getting access to it was relatively easy; my credentials as an academic and a reference from Nick in Venice helped me in that respect.

Before I began my research, however, I decided I would try to get a more emotional feel for Augustine by visiting the two places in Paris where she still had some sort of real presence. One was the Musée d'Orsay, where her portrait hung in the permanent collection. The other was her grave in the famous Cimetière du Père-Lachaise, where other such great libertines as Oscar Wilde and Jim Morrison were also laid to rest.

I went to the cemetery first. The graveyard at Père-Lachaise was like a small city. I was astonished at the size of some of the tombs, which were almost as big as the last flat I had rented back in London. They were like proper houses for the dead, with doors and – in some cases – glazed windows. Some even had little tables inside. Vagabonds, who stashed their sleeping bags there among the long dried-out floral arrangements, had made some into real homes. Wandering aimlessly, I happened across the stunning Raspail family monument, with its enormous and mysterious veiled statue clinging onto one wall as though ready to fall down in grief. Later I found Oscar Wilde's fabulous Epstein tomb, with its stony sphinxes now behind a glass screen to prevent overenthusiastic visitors from kissing the white marble away. By comparison, Augustine had a modest gravestone, grey and plain, carved with only her names and the dates of her birth and death. I felt a wave of pity break over me as I realised she had not even made it to my age. Nowhere near. She had died in January 1847 at the age of twenty-four.

But she was obviously not forgotten. Her grave was not covered in graffiti expressions of love and small gifts like Jim Morrison's, but there was a small posy of peonies in the marble vase by the headstone. They were beautiful flowers, deep pink and almost obscenely vibrant in a place of such timeless solemnity. I wondered who had left them there. I wondered if, assuming the movie I was working on ever got made, Augustine's admirer would have more competition in the future as people came to love her screen reincarnation and so honoured her memory in this place where her old bones lay.

I took a few photographs of the grave to add to my notes and spent another hour or so wandering around the long alleys of the dead, spotting names I recognised from my A-level French literature class. Away from the celebrity graves and the crowds of morbid tourists, stray cats weaved their way in and out of the tombs. It was a scene that would have appealed enormously to my eighteen-year-old self with all her emo tendencies. It was those Gothic Romantic tendencies that made me choose to be a historian. I supposed they'd also made me susceptible to my great imaginary romance in Venice. I paused by the empty urn that had once contained the mortal remains of the great soprano Maria Callas. There was a woman who knew what it was like to be unlucky in love.

Far more cheering was Augustine's portrait in the Musée d'Orsay. She found herself there not because of her notoriety or even because of her beauty, but because of the fame of the portrait artist, one Remi Sauvageon.

Remi Sauvageon became famous for his work on the fringes of the Impressionist movement, but his portrait of Augustine was from an earlier period in his career and was striking in its realism. It might have been a photograph. You almost had to put your nose on the painting to see a brushstroke.

He had pictured Augustine standing next to a fireplace, leaning on the mantel with one elegant bare arm. She was wearing a long green dress that revealed her gently rounded porcelain-white shoulders. Her hair was pinned up with two plaits looped around her ears in a style that was fashionable at the time. She was covered in jewels and had three strings of pearls round her neck. I remembered reading somewhere that in the nineteenth century, before the process of culturing pearls was perfected, a string of almost identically sized pearls such as those Augustine sported would be worth way more than diamonds.

On the mantel behind Augustine the artist had painted a representation of another portrait, of a woman who looked strikingly similar to his subject. I wondered if that was because the portrait in the background was in fact a depiction of Augustine too. I wasn't yet aware of any such painting.

As I stood in front of her, Augustine seemed to be looking right at me but her expression was not as straightforwardly defiant as it had at first appeared. Her eyes were warm but they were also somehow sad and imploring. It was as though she was asking me to make sure this film did her justice.

'Don't worry,' I promised her silently. 'I think Angelina's too old for the part.'

I bought a postcard of Augustine's portrait in the museum gift shop and tucked it inside my notebook to help inspire me later on. Then I walked back to my new apartment, enjoying the warm evening air. All around me, Paris was at her most welcoming. Every bridge, every street corner played host to lovers. Two by two, hand in hand, was the only way to travel in the beautiful City of Light. Walking up the Rue de la Paix and seeing yet more lovers window-shopping at Cartier, I wondered how many people got engaged at the top of the Eiffel Tower in an average day.

Back in the apartment, I made myself some supper and sat down to read a book about courtesans that I had picked up from one of the book stalls that line the quays on the Left Bank. As I read, I decided it didn't sound like such a bad life. In fact, just like Ernesta Donato, the eighteenth-century Venetian courtesan and lover of Luciana Giordano, compared to their decently married contemporaries, the Parisian courtesans of the nineteenth century seemed to have had a great deal of freedom and power. One courtesan – a woman called 'La Paiva' – was born in a Moscow ghetto but by the time she was my age, she had amassed enough wealth to build a mansion on the Champs Elysées.

In his latest email Greg Simon had implied that the apartment I was staying in had once belonged to a woman who modelled herself on La Paiva. I smiled at the thought. It was a beautiful place. The high ceilings and parquet floors breathed quiet luxury. There was such space and light. Compared to any flat I'd stayed in before, it was as glamorous as a wing of the palace at Versailles. If I hadn't been staying in the apartment for free, I very much doubted I could have raised enough to make the rent by selling my body. Even if I tried selling my kidneys rather than my sexual favours.

That night, I thought about the portrait of Augustine as I drifted into dreams. There was a striking similarity, I thought, between Augustine's picture and the painting of Ernesta Donato that had hung in the library in Venice. If Marco and I had still been on emailing terms, I might have sent him the postcard, so that he could see the likeness for himself.

I missed that aspect of our relationship especially. Marco had always seemed very interested in my work. It was wonderful to be able to bounce ideas off him. He'd offered a new perspective that helped me to take my work deeper.

There would be none of that this time. I was on my own. If I'm honest, I was a little apprehensive. I knew how to research an academic project but what would a film producer want? Less attention to syntax and more to story, I supposed.

Could I imagine myself into Augustine Levert's shoes? Though I hadn't intended to, I had done something of the sort with Luciana Giordano. At first glance, the Venetian teenager and I could not have been more different but, in retrospect, reading about her sexual awakening had perhaps made me more willing to look for an awakening of my own. Young enough to be untroubled by the consequences of her nightly escapes to join her lover Casanova in the underbelly of Venetian society, Luciana had tried everything. She had opened herself up to love affairs with men and with women as her lover encouraged her to see her body as a vessel of pure pleasure.

One of the things my flirtation with Marco had done was help me make peace with some of my own body issues. Fresh from a break-up and suspecting that a younger and more classically beautiful girl had replaced me, I had been hiding away. My unhappiness was reflected in a wardrobe of baggy jumpers and a refusal to do so much as put a dab of concealer on a spot. Marco made me want to celebrate myself again.

That day in the library, when I had watched myself in a mirror while following Marco's prescription for ecstasy, I had seen myself through loving eyes. For just a little while I had not worried that I was carrying more weight than usual or my breasts looked less perky than before. I didn't wonder if my hair was too dry or my cheeks a bit too flushed. I had seen myself as a woman at the height of her seductive powers. However I looked, I looked perfect because Marco and I were connected via our minds.

How ironic then, if my suspicions were true and Marco was the man Bea met at the ball – the one with the disfigured hand – that I couldn't give Marco the same confidence in himself. I couldn't make him believe that what I loved about him was an awful lot more than skin deep.

7

Paris, 1838

How naive I had been to think that family riches supported Arlette's lavish lifestyle! Now that I thought about it, no truly noble family would ever let their daughters have so much freedom. Riding out in a carriage whenever she felt like it. Visiting the theatre on her own. And all the men who came and went! Why had I not before noticed what lengths Elaine would go to to ensure that none of the visitors so much as passed each other in the hall, though they would certainly have known each other from school or court or battlefield?

Arlette was a *prostitute.* The men who visited paid her for her favours. They simply paid more than the sailors who went to the brothels in the docks.

'I prefer to use the word "courtesan",' Arlette said to me when I finally admitted I knew the source of her wealth. 'Prostitute sounds so very downcast.'

'Why didn't you tell me?'

'I thought you knew! If not, you might have guessed by now. Any half-intelligent young woman would. Surely.'

Arlette smoothed my hair away from my face. 'Sweet Augustine, you really are as innocent as you look. It's rather funny.'

I didn't think it was funny at all. But neither was Arlette's story as to how she came to be in her position. I might have felt misled and somewhat misused as a result of my discovery, but when Arlette recounted the details of her early life, I could not help but admire her courage. If I thought I'd had some bad luck when it came to my childhood, then Arlette's story made me feel rather blessed. For my mistress, prostitution was a family business. Just as I had become a seamstress because my mother passed on her sewing skills to me as I sat on her knee in our kitchen in Brittany, Arlette had learned her own particular trade from her mama.

'My mother was uneducated but she was clever,' Arlette explained. 'She saw I had an unusual look of refinement and realised it would be my salvation. Though she could have sold my virginity a hundred times over from the moment I started growing tits, she insisted on holding out for a proper price – more than a year's wages to any of the idiots who lived on our street – and she invested the money from that first transaction in an education for me. She knew that's what she would have to do to make me more appealing to the upper classes. And it worked. Within a few months, I could pass as a real lady and I was soon out of the slums. She was a businesswoman, my mama. A sharp one.'

Arlette's mama sounded hateful to me, but it was clear that Arlette was fond of the shrewd city woman who had sold her to the owner of a factory when she was just twelve years old.

'What happened to your mother?' I asked.

'She was stabbed to death a couple of years ago,' Arlette said matter-of-factly. 'I did my best to help her after I got settled but she was proud, we had a fight, and she went back to working in Pigalle. And one night she met with a beast.' Arlette drew a finger across her throat.

I shuddered.

'Don't you ever worry about that happening to you?' I asked.

'Of course,' she said. 'There's always the possibility. Money doesn't necessarily equal manners. But far more women are murdered by their husbands than strangers.'

I think Arlette thought that might cheer me up. She squeezed my hand and gave me a wink. 'Come on, Miss Innocence. I need help with this bodice. The General will be back again soon.'

Though most of her clients, such as the general, liked to visit alone and in private, there were some people who Arlette allowed to visit as a gang. Charles, the poet who had almost disturbed the general the afternoon Elaine revealed the hole in the floor to me, was one of them. Charles ran with a pack of fascinating young men. At least, they liked to think they were fascinating. They called themselves poets, writers, painters and playwrights but they never seemed to do a stitch of work, creative or otherwise. Instead, they liked to spend their evenings in Arlette's house, drinking wine paid for by her wealthier lovers, while they discussed the pressing matters of the day. These pressing matters were sometimes political but they were more often simple gossip regarding their friends. Who was doing what to whom and who was having to take mercury as a result? I learned a great deal by listening in to their conversations and asking Elaine for explanations of the coarser points.

That said, though my mistress was a prostitute, she made certain her guests always treated me with the utmost respect. And they did. They never addressed a lewd remark towards me and often apologised for being uncouth in my company when I came to serve them tea. I quite enjoyed being around them.

I could tell that Arlette liked these young men best of all. She called them 'my boys'. Charles the poet in particular was very dear to her. I suspect that if he'd had any money of his own, she might have forsaken all her other lovers to be with him. While her other lovers turned up at the house in carriages laden with roses, Charles arrived always on foot and usually bearing some weed he had tugged out of the ground on his way through the Tuileries. But I knew when Arlette looked at those weeds they were as precious to her as any hothouse flower. She insisted on putting them in her best vases: scrubby little daisies in her best cut glass like they were as beautiful as roses.

'Love can perform alchemy,' she told me, confirming all.

I wondered if I would ever be in love as Arlette loved her young poet. I wondered also if anyone would ever be in love with me. When there were no visitors at the house, Arlette was happy for Elaine and me to wander in and out of her rooms like little sisters with a free run of the house. From time to time, she let me try on some of her clothes and did my hair in the latest fashion. When I looked at myself in the mirror then, dressed like the very chicest Parisienne on her way to the opera, I could almost imagine some gentleman calling for me. Arlette gave me one of her fans and showed me how to use the old Spanish semaphore to signal my readiness for flirtation. Or more.

'Open the fan and touch your cheek like this,' she said. 'That means you might be interested.'

As I posed in front of the mirror with Arlette's beautiful fan, I conversed with an imaginary lover. I held his gaze and smiled seductively. I flipped the fan open with one hand. I tapped it closed again. I covered my mouth with it in the way Arlette had explained, 'means you're sending him a secret kiss'.

What would he be like, the man I fell for? Would he be handsome? Would he be clever? Would he be rich? Would he be like my father, who though he had very little to his name, often told my mother he was the wealthiest man on God's earth because he had her love? That was what I really hoped for. A love such as I had seen in my childhood by the sea. It was no wonder my mother died of misery without the man she'd married.

Then, one day, my question was answered. It was a Friday evening. Arlette had been to the Comédie at the Salle Richelieu with the general, but dissuaded him from coming into the house by telling him that the soprano's screeching had left her with a terrible headache. Ever the gentleman, the general bid her goodnight on the doorstep. But no sooner had his carriage left the driveway than a new bunch of visitors arrived. It was the poet and his cohorts. Six of them had climbed into a carriage meant for two. When they tumbled out, it was clear they were already half drunk and ready to be rowdy. I expected my mistress to send them away but instead she insisted that they stay for dinner. Elaine and I flew into the kitchen at once.

I later learned that my mistress had decided to feign a headache upon seeing the poet and his young men on the other side of the theatre. Secret signals were passed by the flicking of my mistress's fan and a rendezvous was arranged. The poor general had no idea he was being set up for an evening alone.

Elaine and I set about making supper for the six. We knew five of them well but that evening they were joined by a new face.

'Who is this?' Arlette asked the question we all wanted to hear answered.

'Remi Sauvageon,' he announced himself. 'From Guerville.'

Introductions made, Remi Sauvageon told Arlette about himself. I must admit that I lurked about in order to listen. He was very handsome, this Remi. His face was noble and kind. His eyes were dark brown. His black hair had a wave to it. When he stood to warm himself by the fire, I took note of his fine legs, well-shaped and athletic in his fashionable grey trousers, which were cut very close. He held himself very straight, with an attractive confidence. When he looked directly at me, it made me blush.

In the contact of our eyes, I felt again that sensation which had come over me when I was watching Arlette and the general through the keyhole. My insides were all aflutter and I could hear my blood pounding in my head. I thought I might fall down at any moment, I hoped he hadn't noticed how distracted I became.

But when he spoke, the sensation only grew stronger. His voice was educated. It was manly but not rough in the least. He was the son of a wealthy family. He'd been educated at a very smart establishment with the intention that he would go into the family business. But the provincial life was not for Remi. He told us that he had come to Paris to be a painter. He wanted to meet Corot and several other famous artists, perhaps even get an apprenticeship. He felt he could learn from their work. Maybe they could learn from him too, he added with a touch of unexpected arrogance.

Arlette encouraged him. She said that she knew one artist he'd mentioned quite well and might be able to effect an introduction. She was very kind in that respect. She had recently introduced the poet to a publisher. The publisher said he thought the poet had no talent whatsoever, but for Arlette he would have published a laundry list, spelling mistakes and all.

Remi Sauvageon stayed until late that night. He praised Elaine's cooking and made Arlette glow with pride when he said she would be a good subject for a portrait. He seemed popular with his fellows; they all laughed at his jokes. Even Charles seemed happy for Remi to take centre stage, showing good humour when Remi teased him by intoning a scrappy poem in impersonation of the poet at some other high-society salon. When Remi turned his attention to me and praised my elegant method of pouring coffee, saying that he wished he could capture my style in a series of photographs, I slopped half a pot on the rug. Fortunately, Arlette found that hilarious.

'You like him, don't you?' said Arlette when we were alone in the kitchen later on.

'Who?' I feigned ignorance.

'Remi, the new boy, stupid.'

I looked at my hands. I was washing the pots. I felt too vulnerable to answer her.

'Don't worry,' said Arlette. 'I can tell he likes you too.'

'Really?' I clutched at her encouragement. 'How could you tell?'

'Every time you were in the room, he could not take his eyes off you. Every point he made for the amusement of his friends, he was really making just for you. He never failed to look in your direction to see what you had made of his jokes. He wanted to impress you.'

'Impress me? Why? I'm just a maid.'

'He doesn't see you that way. He sees a slim waist and an attractive bosom. He sees your soft skin and your lustrous hair. He sees the way your lips curve when you smile. He is besotted. Soon he'll be entirely in love.'

I hardly dared believe it, but I went to bed happy that night.

I got happier. Elaine, who was two years older than me but decades more worldly wise, had told me about a way to give myself pleasure. In fact she'd offered to show me but, horrified, I'd demurred. Later, however, in the privacy of my room, I had pondered Elaine's instructions and given them a try. What a revelation to discover that the part of me I had always considered most shameful was also capable of offering such joy.

With not enough light to read by in my dingy attic room, I soon grew quite expert at bringing myself to a climax. Sometimes, I thought of the goings-on I had seen in Arlette's room. This time, I thought of Remi. I'm ashamed to say that a few hours with my eye at the hole in the floor had given me a knowledge of sexual positions as wild and varied as the *Kama Sutra*. I knew about the *Kama Sutra* too; Arlette had several editions with illustrations so perplexing that I had to rotate some pages to be able to see what went where.

After his very first visit to Arlette's house, I imagined Remi in the general's habitual position: on his knees, on the floor, between mine. I had changed into my nightgown. It wasn't fancy, but it was soft through old age and I imagined it as a silken gown, a present from my ardent artist lover. I got under my blankets and pulled up the nightgown's skirt. I moistened my fingers in my mouth and then sought out my clitoris. Gently I began to rub.

All the time I played with myself, I imagined Remi's face between my legs as he ardently licked me towards ecstasy. How wonderful it would be. I could almost feel him sucking and tickling and probing me with his tongue.

As I got closer to the edge, I bit down on my pillow. I knew from the first couple of times I had played with myself that when I came, it would be with a little exclamation. Arlette was in her room downstairs and I suspected that she was as busy seeking after pleasure as I had been, but I did not want to risk drawing her attention to the ceiling and my spyhole with any unusual noise. Perhaps she already knew I watched her. I liked to think that she didn't though I'd heard some her tell some of her gentlemen friends she found the thought of being watched enticing.

So I came on my own and the pillow accepted my tremulous groans. When they were over, I lay like a beached starfish stretched right across my bed. I was more than ready to fall asleep. As I did, I tried to think of Remi in a more wholesome way. I remembered the way he had looked when he stood by the fireplace. I imagined him turning to me and falling onto his knees, begging me to be his wife.

I had the strangest feeling that it might just happen.

The following day, Remi came back again with Charles and the other fascinating young men. The moment I saw him, I blushed to the roots of my hair, as though he could have known what I had imagined the night before. I trembled as I passed him a cup and he caught hold of my hand to steady me. I had imagined Remi performing the most awful carnal acts on me, but just the brush of his fingertips in real life was enough to make me faint.

'Augustine!' Arlette cried out. 'That's two coffee pots in one week!'

8

I immediately related to Augustine Levert. Though the painting I had found in the museum showed her to be a goddess, her diary showed me the naive young girl, who had fallen on hard times and found kindness in the least likely of places. Reading about her falling for Remi, I couldn't help but be reminded of Luciana Giordano, falling for her teacher Casanova. How powerful first love can be.

But now, whenever I thought about my own first love, the memory was linked with someone else. With Marco Donato.

When I started researching Luciana Giordano in the Palazzo Donato library, Marco had asked me to keep him up to date with my progress. He said he had always been interested in the young woman's diaries but hadn't ever found the time to read them and doubted that he ever would. So, in return for permission to visit the library – which had been closed to visitors for years – whenever I liked, I gave him a synopsis of each diary extract as I read it. It was natural that we would enter into a sort of conversation about Luciana. And from that point, I suppose it was equally natural that we would start to share a few stories about ourselves.

As I've explained, we talked about our childhoods. We talked about our schooldays. Then, inevitably, we talked about first love. And first love led us on to talking – still via email – about losing our respective virginities. Mine was a fairly ordinary tale of two middle-class sixth-formers shagging to a soundtrack of New Order while their parents were away. Marco Donato, heir to a shipping fortune, had lost his virginity to his father's mistress; a voluptuous Sophia Loren lookalike called Chiara.

It was when I read Marco's description of that encounter that I first realised I might be developing my own feelings for him. I was unaccountably jealous when I thought of the Italian woman, at least fifteen years his senior, who had taken him to her bed. I wanted to know what Chiara had to make her so attractive. I wanted to know how I compared. I knew I couldn't look like a young Sophia Loren no matter how much make-up I wore.

After that intimate exchange, Marco and I started to correspond more regularly and on increasingly personal subjects. I told him almost everything about the end of my relationship with Steven. Marco was very kind in his response and his kindness went a long way towards restoring my confidence and making me believe that I could not have done anything differently.

With such a warm correspondence in progress, it seemed obvious that we would soon meet in person. I was nervous about that. I'd pored over pictures of Marco online since the first time I saw his name and it seemed he was always accessorised with a supermodel. Like Augustine, putting on Arlette's clothes and looking at herself in the mirror, I wasn't sure I could compete. Part of me had even worried when I urged Bea to wear the Dior dress to the ball that Marco would find her more beautiful than I could ever hope to be.

Talking of Bea, following Nick's revelation that Bea was going to meet her security-guard beau's mother, I had written to my old friend for more gossip. She had plenty, of course, but the most interesting part of her email to me was where she said that she had asked to be admitted to the Donato Library to see some of Casanova's correspondence there and had been told in no uncertain terms that the library was *never* open to the general public – never had been – despite the fact that she knew I had been allowed inside.

Bea was frustrated, of course, but my heart beat just a little faster when I read of her annoyance. So the Donato Library was closed again? Marco would admit no one, no matter the importance of his or her thesis? No one since me. That had to mean something, didn't it? Though quite what, I wasn't sure.

When I wasn't working, I spent time getting to know Paris. Over the course of a week, I tackled the Louvre room by room. I shuffled with the crowds to catch a glimpse of the *Mona Lisa*, though I have to admit that when I got close enough to see her, I wondered what all the fuss was about. Compared to Remi Sauvageon's portrait of Augustine Levert, the *Mona Lisa* seemed flat and plain. I couldn't understand why her expression had always been thought of as flirtatious or mysterious. To me, it seemed unlikely that she harboured any secret desire for the artist. There was none of the longing that was so obvious in Augustine's yearning look. Likewise, the *Venus de Milo* was disappointingly familiar. There was nothing new to be learned from seeing her in the flesh, or rather the marble.

I did find some gems, though. I especially loved the pensive dark-haired heroine of Corot's *La Femme à la Perle*, like the *Mona Lisa*'s more beautiful sister, inexplicably overlooked by so many. And I loved walking through the rooms that the average tourist didn't have time to take in. I had a room to myself for at least twenty minutes one afternoon. I wondered how many people had been lost in the museum after hours. I wondered how many had deliberately hidden themselves in a quiet corner to steal a kiss or even to make love, while centuries-old statues watched in mute amusement.

* * *

I had been to Paris before but I didn't get to know it at all back then. The first – and last – time I had visited the city had been four years earlier, when Steven and I came to France to celebrate his thirty-sixth birthday and my twenty-sixth, which was later the same week. Neither of us had much money but we found a small and strange hotel in Montmartre, called La Lumière, where we could afford the smallest room for three nights. We arrived on the Friday evening and barely left our bed before we caught the Eurostar back to London on the Monday morning. Steven said that could be my birthday present to him: a whole weekend of crazy passionate sex. I wouldn't have said it was crazy, but it was certainly passionate.

Back in Paris for a second time, glancing up on one of my rambles to catch a glimpse of the Sacré Coeur, I was reminded of that long-ago weekend. I wondered if the hotel was still open. When we had visited, the place was on its last legs; a refurbishment was long overdue. Using his best French on the receptionist, Steven discovered that it was one of the few places in the city that still rented rooms by the hour, which perhaps explained the exotic creatures that hung around reception, wearing nightclub clothes in the middle of the day. The receptionist continued to tell Steven that the owner of the hotel was keen to sell.

'If only I could make him an offer,' said Steven. He loved Paris and he especially loved the slightly seedy area in which we'd found ourselves.

Four years on I took a detour from my planned itinerary. I ventured up there and saw that the worst – as far as Steven was concerned – had happened. The hotel was indeed under new ownership. It had been refurbished and transformed. I paused by a board displaying pictures of the rooms inside. They were now as chic and bland as any hotel room in any city in the world. The tiny loft room with its peeling paint almost certainly had an en-suite bathroom by now. Would that make it more romantic? The room in the roof had been unbearably romantic to me. It had been unbearably hot as well.

'No reason to keep our clothes on,' as Steven had joked.

We had made our trip in high summer and, on our first night there, I had looked out to see swallows diving over the rooftops. It was such a beautiful view. Quintessentially Parisian. I wasn't to see very much of it.

'Come over here.'

I stripped off my clothes eagerly and joined Steven on the bed. He paid his usual respects to both my breasts, kissing one and then the other, as was his custom.

'Neither one must feel left out.'

I giggled and wrapped my arms round his head, forcing his face deep into my cleavage. Steven groaned with delight.

When I let him go, Steven kissed every inch of me, slowly, as though he were savouring the taste of my flesh. His warm lips left me tingling. Moving down to my thighs, he pushed them apart and nuzzled at my pubis. His chin was slightly stubbly. It scratched at my soft skin.

Carefully, Steven flickered his tongue across my clitoris. Then he pushed a finger into me, making me gasp in surprise. It was not painful though and I was soon wet enough to take another finger and another. Just the thought of having my lover inside me made me want to open up.

Meanwhile, I took his penis in my hand, enjoying the familiar weight of it. The skin of the shaft was soft and warm. It had a peach-skin texture. I wrapped my fingers round it and slowly began to move them up and down, establishing a rhythm and feeling pleased with myself as I felt it becoming harder still. Steven closed his eyes and let his head tip back. He let out a low moan that told me not to stop.

I did stop. With my hand at least. Instead, I slid down the bed so that my face was level with Steven's pelvis. Holding the root of his penis steady, I began to lick him. Long strokes to the side of the shaft, followed by a swirl around the top.

'I'm not an ice cream,' Steven protested.

'You're just as delicious,' I said. 'Though not so sweet.' I tasted the salty tang of pre-cum.

I moved so that I could take the whole tip of Steven's penis in my mouth. I sucked, gently and rhythmically. I felt his penis twitch against my tongue as it stiffened still further. Eventually Steven gently pushed me up and away from his crotch.

'Don't want to waste a good hard-on.'

He lay back on the bed and stroked himself lazily while I positioned myself over him. I climbed onto his lap and moved so that his penis was pointing straight upwards towards my pussy. Taking him by the hand, I guided him inside me.

When I was on top, I was in control. I could set the pace and to begin with, that day, the pace I wanted was slow. I oozed my way up and down Steven's cock, feeling every centimetre of his length as he slid into and out of me. Steven closed his eyes and sighed with pleasure at each stroke. He was helpless. He put his hands on my waist but I would not let him change the speed with which I moved on him. He was entirely at my mercy, just as I had been at his when he put his mouth against my clit.

I ignored Steven's protests that I was teasing him unkindly. I was enjoying myself as I dragged the moment out. Eventually, however, it was too much for me as well. I started to move more quickly. I put my hands on his chest to steady myself as I changed the pace from walk to canter.

And from canter to gallop. I rode him in triumph, while he bucked away beneath me, pushing up, up, up, as deep as he could go. When he came he begged me to stop. The sensation was too great, but I carried on until I had drained him and I started to come myself.

Back in Paris and on my own again, I stood outside the hotel where I'd had such an erotic weekend and tried to work out how I felt. Bea had once suggested that my virtual affair with Marco was a way of avoiding a proper mourning period with regard to Steven. Was she right? If she was, then now, without Marco as a buffer, I should feel the full force of my grief for the love Steven and I had shared and lost. A tear did spring to my eye, but I really couldn't be sure. Was it for Steven or was it for Marco?

9

Paris, 1839

Remi Sauvageon was soon a regular visitor at Arlette's house and we were always pleased to see him. While Charles the poet earned his keep in Arlette's heart with a series of ribald rhymes, Remi would draw cartoons for her amusement. He made caricatures of the other young men that were always piercingly truthful and yet somehow still kind. No one ever minded discovering how big his nose was if Remi had made the picture. He could make even a chinless weakling seem heroic.

He drew Arlette and Elaine too, but he always made certain to show them in their very best light. He drew Elaine from the side without the birthmark. He drew Arlette in such a way that you couldn't see that beneath her beautiful golden hair, she actually had rather large ears. He drew me too. I had been told too often about the sin of vanity to find myself beautiful, but to see myself through Remi's eyes was simply wonderful. He made me look like a princess, even if he pictured me washing the pots. I treasured those drawings and kept them under my pillow, as though the warmth of his hand was still upon them and it might somehow escape from the paper to caress my eager face.

* * *

Remi was fast improving as an artist. He explained to me that his father had cut him off when he decided to become a painter and so, having run through his small savings, he simply had to make a living from his craft. To please his landlady, he was painting a mural in her sitting room.

'She said she wanted it to be like Versailles. Well, I can't give her the extra space but I can give her peacocks prancing along her skirting boards.'

The landlady was thrilled with Remi's efforts and waived three whole months' rent.

At lunchtimes, Remi drew the patrons of our local bistro – Le Petit Ami. The restaurateur was delighted to offer his clientele such an unusual added extra: a caricature with your *menu prix fixe*? He gave Remi a daily free meal in exchange. And sometimes, if the clientele were especially pleased with their portraits, they tipped Remi a little more on the side.

'The patrons of Le Petit Ami are pretty wealthy,' Remi told me one afternoon, when he was drawing me in the kitchen. 'I am hoping that soon enough one of them will ask me to make a proper portrait in oils. I shall buy you a bonnet with the proceeds. Until then, I will keep making my sketches. Practice makes perfect. Sit still. You always fidget when I'm trying to preserve your beauty for all time.'

Now that really made me fidget. My beauty! I blushed to the roots of my hair.

'Oh, come on, Augustine. Don't be so coy! Everyone must tell you you're beautiful. There can't be a gentleman comes in here who doesn't wish he could be visiting you and not Arlette.'

I was shocked by his boldness and I protested that he was wrong. He put down his pencil and held my gaze.

'You don't think I keep coming here to see your mistress, do you?'

'Maybe not. But you come to keep company with your friends. You come for Charles. You come for a free meal in the evenings. You come for the wine.'

'Don't insult me or your own intelligence. You know I come here for something far more precious than the company of those buffoons who call themselves my friends or a plateful of Elaine's stringy horsemeat daube. I come here only for you.'

He got up from his easel and came towards me. He took up both my hands and fell to his knees in front of me.

'You are my goddess, Augustine. From the moment I first saw you, I could think of no one else. Say you feel the same way.'

'I did,' I stammered. 'I do.'

'Then let's stop dancing around each other. Let's show our feelings. Let's be in love – starting right now!'

He got to his feet again and pulled me up so I was on a level with him. He stared deep into my eyes for a delicious, stomach-flipping moment, then pressed his mouth hard against mine, taking me completely by surprise.

I had never been kissed before. I had imagined what it would be like, of course, and Elaine had demonstrated the technique on the back of my hand. In reality, that practice was worth nothing. I was suddenly rigid with fear.

'Let your mouth relax,' said Remi.

'I don't know how to.'

'What do you mean? You really have never done this before?'

'Never,' I confirmed.

'Then I will have to teach you. Be calm. It will happen naturally.'

How could I be calm? My heart was beating so hard I was sure he must be able to hear it. My ears were filled with the sound of rushing blood. When he finally released me, I had to sit straight down before I fell down on the spot.

'Augustine Levert,' Remi breathed. 'You are the most exquisite creature on God's earth. If I didn't have to be at the café in fifteen minutes I would stay here and kiss you all day.'

But he did have to be at the café. He was supposed to be drawing the owner's daughter as a gift for her fiancé. He gave me one more hard kiss and then he was gone, leaving me breathless and utterly, utterly transformed.

That afternoon, I had some time to myself so I met Remi at the café and we went for a walk along the river. He held my hand and we stopped every couple of minutes to practise kissing. I was so happy and so proud to be seen with him. A man had chosen me at last!

'He says that he loves me,' I told Elaine that night.

'Well well,' said Elaine. 'It must be true. I heard that before he saw you, he was well on his way to marrying a girl from his home town. That's the real reason his father has cut him off. It was less a marriage than a business merger.'

'What else did you hear?'

'That his family is very wealthy, so it's no small thing that he's fallen out of his father's favour. If he went back to Guerville, he would live a life of luxury. Instead, he's staying here to be with you, scraping a living from making sketches. He must really be besotted.'

'It's so romantic,' I said. 'I love him so madly. I don't care if he never has a penny.'

'Not now, you don't,' said Elaine. 'Give it time.'

Elaine was wrong. I was sure of that. How much a man was worth in crude monetary terms would never matter to me. In my parents, I had seen an example of true love at its finest. I don't believe my father could have loved my mother any more if she had been dressed always in the latest fashions and I don't believe she could have loved him harder and more enduringly if he had showered her with diamonds instead of the shells he sometimes brought back from the beach. Or the little painting that was my treasure. My father had put his heart into that painting.

I suppose it was not insignificant that Remi was an artist and in him I saw my father's dreams realised. I always held artists in the highest esteem.

'They're shiftless and unreliable,' was Elaine's view.

I did not listen to her. I had found my love.

At the same time, Arlette was embarking on a passionate tryst with Charles the poet. The general, who was Arlette's most frequent and most favoured visitor, had been called away on military business. There was more trouble in Algeria. Arlette told him she would miss him terribly and would remain cloistered like a nun until his return. As it was, she spent a couple of mornings with Girodin (politicians somehow never needed to visit the wars they started) and the rest of her time – every moment they could snatch – with Charles.

I watched them through the peephole. With Charles, Arlette was unlike I had ever seen her. She was not imperious and demanding, as she was with the general. She was not meek and silent, as she was with Girodin. With Charles, Arlette was at her most natural. Their lovemaking was accompanied always by the sound of laughter. They rolled over and over on the mattress like a pair of happy kittens. Sometimes he was on top. Sometimes she rode him as though he were a horse on a fairground carousel. Once, they pulled all the covers off the bed and slept on the floor. They curled around each other. Their bodies fitted together so perfectly, Charles' long brown limbs and Arlette's alabaster-white curves.

That was what Remi and I would look like, I decided. Matched like two pieces of the same puzzle. Once we came together, we would never be able to part.

IO

I'd been working on my research for a week and a half when it struck me that I had to know more about Remi Sauvageon. He would doubtless be an important character in the film – Greg had explained to me that it didn't matter if a movie was ostensibly about a woman, in Hollywood the male characters were invariably cast first – so I needed to get a better handle on the film's natural hero. Unfortunately for me, unlike his lover, Remi Sauvageon was not a man of letters. The only correspondence of his that I could find was a letter to his canvas supplier, asking for an extension of credit. There were, however, paintings and sketches by the artist all over Europe and far beyond.

To begin with I read his biographies. They concentrated largely on his career as it took off when he became associated with the Impressionists. There were hundreds of thousands of words on the men Remi associated with in the 1870s, but Augustine was hardly mentioned except as the supposed subject of the painting in the Musée d'Orsay, commissioned by the Duc de Rocambeau a good decade before Remi was famous. In one book she was not even given a name, just referred to in a single sentence: 'That year, Remi painted a notorious courtesan . . .' It seemed a cruel dismissal of the love affair that had meant so much to Augustine. History's footnote. Even the painting was dismissed as being relatively unimportant compared to his later works.

However, I now knew from Augustine's diaries that the portrait was not the first time Remi had captured Augustine's likeness, so I kept searching for more references in his archive. Then I found it.

A sketchbook of Remi's, from 1839, had been sold at auction in 2011. By rights, that sketchbook should contain at least some pictures of Augustine. I was delighted to see that it existed. I was absolutely flabbergasted, though, when I followed the auction house's paper trail to see where the sketchbook had ended up. The buyer: one Marco Donato of Venice.

I didn't know whether to laugh or cry. Of all the people in the world who might have bought that sketchbook, why did it have to be him? I wanted to see those pictures, but how could I? How could I ask Marco to let me see them when our correspondence had ended in such an embarrassing impasse?

In the end, it was too great a coincidence to resist. Much as I tried not to be swayed by superstition, I couldn't help but think I'd been sent a sign. This was the perfect excuse to get in touch with Marco and break the silence that had blossomed between us. After all, our correspondence hadn't exactly ended badly. Rather, it had ended *strangely* when Marco failed to appear at the ball, sending his excuses by email. Unconvincing excuses at that.

However, it had been a while since that last email. Perhaps I could pretend that there was nothing strange about it and I was just a friend sending a 'how are you'? I could only hope that he would be as pleased to hear from me as I was pleased at the prospect of being in touch with him again. I wrote:

Dear Marco,

I hope this finds you well and that business has been good and the troubles you were having in Hong Kong have

> long since been sorted out. I am sorry I have not written earlier. I'm sure you can imagine how busy I've been finishing my thesis on Luciana. I've attached a copy so you can see what all that time I spent in your library was really about. If you can bear to read such a dry academic text, that is.
>
> It's your library that brings me to write to you again. I've taken a job – a proper paying job this time – doing some speculative research for a Hollywood producer who is interested in making a biopic about Augustine du Vert, a nineteenth-century courtesan. I've been lucky enough to find copies of her diary in Paris, which is where I am staying for the meantime. But to have a real sense of her, it would be even more useful to have access to the pictures drawn by her lover Remi Sauvageon. I hope this is ringing a bell by now. Sauvageon worked on the fringes of the Impressionist movement, but when he first arrived in Paris, he ran with a crowd of young dilettantes who made a courtesan's house their meeting place. At the time, Augustine was a maid there. She and Remi fell in love.
>
> I tracked down one of his sketchbooks from that period to an auction at Bonham's and discovered that you were the highest bidder.
>
> Assuming you still have it, I hope you won't mind me asking if I might return to the library one more time to see the book. I know you have re-instigated your 'no visitors' policy but wonder if that rule pertains to friends, as I hope we were and still might be.

I struggled with that last paragraph in particular. We had been something more than friends, I hoped. Friends didn't generally share their sexual fantasies, after all. But friends was all we could possibly be now, after such an absence from each others' life. I signed off and pressed send.

For the next few hours I was on tenterhooks, just waiting for a reply. Finally, it came. I could not open the email quickly enough. Just the sight of his name in my in-box set my heart racing.

Dear Sarah,

By all means. Next time you are in Venice, the library will be at your disposal.

Sincerely,

Marco

That was it. Just two lines. Marco's email was as simple and cool as his very first email to me, all those months ago before he knew me. He didn't ask how I was. He didn't tell me what was going on with him. The email was bare bones. Utterly professional. The only way of telling that we knew each other at all was that he had addressed me as 'Sarah' and not 'Miss Thomson.'

I started to write back at once.

Dear Marco,

Thank you for responding so quickly. It will be enormously helpful for my research.

Are you well? Have you been having a good summer? Are you busy? Etc, etc.

I wrote a long email, telling him exactly what I had been doing since we saw each other last and how much I hoped we would be able to see each other if I came to Venice again. But I didn't send it. Instead, I kept my response to a simple expression of thanks. I'd let him know when I would next be in Italy.

I spent the rest of the day swinging between excitement and discouragement. The coolness of Marco's email suggested I should stay well away. How much could the book of sketches actually tell me, after all? I didn't really need to see them. But the speed with which he had responded to me was encouraging, wasn't it? My heart grasped at the flimsy excuse to try to deepen our correspondence.

When would I next be in Venice? That was the real question now, as far as my heart was concerned. I sent an email to Greg Simon telling him at length about my discovery and how it might help me to learn more about our movie's love interest. Then I took a walk to the cemetery at Père Lachaise. I bought a small posy of peonies from a flower stall outside the cemetery's gates. I wanted to say 'thank you' to Augustine for giving me this chance to be in touch with Marco again. Perhaps I wanted her to intervene on my behalf to make my wishes come true.

When I got to her grave, I found that someone had beaten me to it. There were already fresh flowers in the little marble vase. I arranged my flowers alongside them and muttered a quick prayer.

'Please don't let this be a mistake.'

Getting back to the apartment, I read Marco's email again, looking for a hidden meaning. A wisp of affection. Some sort of encouragement. But there were so few words that there really was nothing to parse. Instead, I looked back over older correspondence. Despite having felt at times pretty angry with Marco Donato, I had kept everything he ever wrote to me. Our direct-message conversations, I'd also saved. It felt important to have some kind of evidence of what had happened in the Palazzo library. But I had never until now plucked up the courage to read the words we had sent flying across the Internet to one another like a pair of teenagers passing secret notes in class. I hadn't dared. I thought it would hurt.

Perhaps now was the moment. I should read back through our emails with the benefit of time and distance. There, in black and white, would be the truth of the situation. Either I would find enough there to make it worth booking a trip, or I would see that we had nothing more than the kind of banter that popped up on dating websites every day.

It took me a while to read our correspondence. There was so much in it. That in itself seemed promising. And then I found the transcript of that day in the library when Marco sent Silvio on a spurious errand so we could be 'alone' at last.

11

Alone, though still not face to face. I could picture quite clearly the library that morning. It was a cold day, but the sky was clear and the library was illuminated with bright sunshine that made it feel warmer than it should.

I could see the desk that I'd made my own and remember the feel of the well-polished wooden handle as I pulled the drawer open. Then, inside the drawer, I saw the vibrator: as black and shiny as a piece of burnished coal. It was so incongruous, that sex toy in the drawer of a beautiful handmade antique desk. The desk had been in the Palazzo for generations. The vibrator was a piece from the future.

Marco began our cybersex session by asking me what I was wearing.

I told him. I was wearing a dress with a long skirt. Beneath it, stockings. They were hold-ups. A suspender belt just seemed like a cliché too far. I was wearing black silk knickers and a matching bra. Marco asked me not to take the knickers off but to push them aside so that I could attend to my clitoris. He instructed me to begin with the very lowest setting on the vibrator, which was barely more than the throb of a resting pulse.

Looking back now, the moment was tinged with all sorts of doubts and insecurities. Whenever I read about a saucy photograph or video that had been meant for just one set of eyes going viral, I remembered that day in the library and tortured myself wondering where the hidden cameras had been. Surely it was only a matter of time before the girl in the video clip was me?

It seems crazy that I trusted Marco enough to make myself so vulnerable, but I did. I think I thought that it was going to be the day we met. I'd persuaded myself that once I had passed this test he would reveal himself to me.

I'm convinced that he was in the house that day. Perhaps even in the next room. Of course he would never admit it.

I had a vibrator with me in Paris. It nestled in the corner of my washbag, which had seemed the best place for it given that I was crossing a border. As I stood in the queue to pass through security at the Eurostar terminal, I had a vision of being taken to one side and asked to unpack. That didn't happen. The vibrator had not moved from its hiding spot. Now, alone in my apartment, I took it out.

It was very different from the vibrator that Marco had chosen for me. He had picked one so cleverly designed and so subtle you might have mistaken it for a fancy remote control for an iPod dock. It was the size of a chicken's egg but flattened like a pebble. It was finished in shiny black.

My own vibrator was a more colourful affair. I had bought it at a sex-toy party, if you can believe that. One of my fellow academics back in London had thrown the bash, like a subversive Tupperware party. It was excruciating. A game saleswoman tried to encourage us all to try on French-maid outfits and showed us how to hold the cock-shaped toys to the tips of our noses to feel the strength of the vibration.

I bought the vibrator because I felt sorry for my friend. No one else seemed to be buying. I told her I was going to give it to another friend as a gift on her hen night. In reality, it was always just for me.

I had never owned a sex toy before. I didn't feel I'd ever needed one. Before I met Steven, my love life had been so pedestrian I hadn't even considered the possibility I could be orgasmic. With Steven, I had no need for anything but his hands, his mouth and his cock. Or so I thought. While Steven was at the rugby the following Saturday afternoon, I got out my new vibrator and made myself come eight times in a row. I felt daring and naughty and ridiculously alive. When Steven came back from the rugby, I jumped on him the moment he walked through the door.

Now I used my vibrator to relive that moment in the library in Venice. Reading the transcript of Marco's instructions, I recreated the situation as closely as I could. I took the laptop through to the salon, where I had my desk. With the laptop set up, I started to follow Marco's commands, not turning the vibrator on full blast from the beginning as I would ordinarily have done, but increasing the power slowly, taking care to properly savour each tiny increase in intensity. As Marco had suggested, I didn't concentrate all the energy on my clitoris either. I moved the vibrator all over my pussy and with my free hand I pinched my own nipples, until they stood to attention, throbbing and begging for more.

That morning in the library, Marco had led me through several peaks of sensation and I let the same thing happen again now. I pressed the vibrator against my clitoris and fondled my own breasts. Just when I thought I would be able to hold on no longer, I followed Marco's command to turn the vibrator down a notch again. Then I let him take me through another crescendo and another and another, building in power until I felt like I was plugged into the mains. Eventually, it wouldn't have mattered if I had turned the vibrator off altogether; I'd reached a point of no return.

Every muscle in my body was tense for just a second. Then that melting feeling overcame me. That rolling sensation as though a speedboat had just ripped across a tranquil pond and I was rocking in its wake.

Staggering to the bedroom, I fell onto the pillows and let the vibrator drop to the floor, where it buzzed like an indignant beetle flipped over onto its back, until I gathered myself enough to retrieve it and turn it back off.

Getting up again, I went and looked at my laptop screen, as though there was a chance that in the brief time I'd had my eyes shut, another message might have come through. There was nothing new apart from the two lines he had sent that day. The last message from Marco before that still bore the same date and time it always had. It was almost five months old.

12

Paris, 1839

My musings with regard to what love would look like had been answered in the most wonderful way. Love looked like Remi Sauvageon. It had his height, his bearing, his kind brown eyes and his soft pink lips. It had the shadow on his jawline when it was time for him to shave. It had his voice. It had his way of walking. It had the way he brushed his floppy hair back from his face. It had the way he took my face in both his hands and kissed me as though I were his angel.

I could not imagine that any moment in my life would ever match the moment when he declared his affection to me, but after that declaration, our love grew ever more wondrous. Every chance we could, we snatched the opportunity to be together. Arlette merely smiled when Remi said that he would help me peel potatoes.

'If your love means that supper is on the table more quickly, then I very much approve,' she said.

If she had not approved, of course I would have run away to see him in an instant.

How happy I was. It was almost impossible to believe that two years earlier I had been that wretch in the Bois de Boulogne, with no parents, no money and no hope whatsoever of getting out of Paris alive. Now I didn't want to leave Paris for a second. The dirty old city was transformed when seen through loving eyes. Suddenly the river seemed fragrant. The scrappy flowers in the parks seemed magnificent. Even the filthy pigeons were as beautiful as turtledoves to me now.

But it wasn't all hearts and flowers. Remi had awakened something else in me. I was sixteen. Almost seventeen. Girls my age were married. Some had babies. Through the hole in the floor of my bedroom, I'd had more of an education in sex than most of them, I was sure, but I was still a virtual innocent. For months Remi and I only kissed. He ran his hands over my body, of course, but always and only over the top of my clothes.

It wasn't that I didn't have desire for him – I wanted him very much indeed – it's just that sex had somehow become linked in my mind to Arlette's endless visitors. I wanted my first time to be very special indeed. I wanted to make love to just one man in the whole of my life, as my mother had done. I needed to know that I would not be throwing my most precious gift away on a man who did not deserve it.

Remi said he understood but that if I were waiting for a proposal, I would have to wait a good deal longer. He had not a penny to his name. If he could have afforded to take a wife, he would have been on his knees in an instant but for now he could offer me nothing more than his highest esteem. One day, he promised, he would have all the wealth that he needed.

Of course, I insisted to Remi that he would need a great deal less than he imagined to keep me.

'My love,' he said. 'Your insistence moves me, but I will not be persuaded. You have no father to give you away, so the costs of the wedding fall quite squarely on my shoulders and I want you to have a proper wedding. You must have a fine dress and flowers and there will be a feast.'

He said that the waiting was agony for him. It was agony for me also. After we had snatched a moment together, and kissed and cuddled ourselves into a frenzy, it was not in the least bit easy to pull ourselves apart. When Remi left, I would often go back to my bed and lie there, imagining his hands upon me. My fingers would stray between my legs. If Arlette had a visitor, I would roll back the carpet and touch myself, watching her avidly and imagining everything that happened to her was happening to me with Remi. I was insane with longing and so was he.

Then, one day, Remi brought me a ring. He said he had found it in the street. It was not much of a ring – Elaine said it would probably make my finger go green – but it was the first piece of jewellery I'd ever been offered.

'This is a promise,' he told me. 'One day I will replace this with a ring of solid gold.'

He got down on one knee right in the middle of the kitchen and asked if I would be his. When, of course, I told him 'yes', he jumped to his feet and we concluded our very own wedding ceremony with Elaine as our only witness.

'Under the sight of God,' said Remi, 'We promise ourselves to one another. For ever and ever, amen.'

'Amen!' I shouted.

'Poor foolish girl,' said Elaine.

So, there was no legal ceremony, but to my mind, we were very much married. Certainly, I knew that no other man would ever lay claim to my heart.

We went back upstairs and to our kissing, after which Remi asked me tentatively, 'I know it was not proper and it wouldn't be recognised in a court, but I have given you my promise. You know that whatever happens, I will look after you. That being the case, I wonder if we . . .

Remi was not a virgin. I suppose I should not have expected it, given the sophisticated crowd he ran with. I knew that Charles the poet, while he nursed an undying passion for my mistress, had availed himself freely of the prostitutes he could actually afford. In fact, those encounters formed the inspiration of his first terrible collection of poems. Another of Remi's friends had actually published a book like a catalogue, describing the best Parisian whores and where to find them. When he neglected to include Arlette, she said she didn't know whether to be relieved or offended. I thought I would have been relieved.

So I was not surprised when Remi admitted to me that our first time together would not be his first time overall. Or even the tenth, he later added with a boyish little smile. But he hoped I would be glad that he would be able to show me exactly what to do. He promised me also that he had learned much that would make him the ideal husband. He would show me pleasure I had hitherto only dreamed of. Still I hesitated.

I wished I could have spoken to Arlette about it. Elaine, I knew, would only encourage me. She'd already told me that she'd lost her virginity when she was eleven, to the family's landlord. Her parents had been more than happy for the situation to continue if it meant they didn't have to pay the rent but Elaine hated the landlord and ran away as soon as she could. The circumstances of her defloration made me feel sad for her indeed. It should be a moment of mutual discovery. Of pure joy.

I wished I might have been Remi's first, but since that was not going to be possible, it would have to be good enough for me that I would be the last, as he had promised me from the bottom of his heart. In our eyes we were married in the sight of God, since Remi had convinced me that the Almighty is everywhere and not just in church.

'And if God did not mean for us to love each other, why did he make the act so delicious?'

'Dear husband,' I said. 'I quite agree. You have my consent.'

So, we went to bed. I was dressed in white. It wasn't deliberate. My white nightgown – a cast-off from Arlette – was the one that was clean and it was the only one that wasn't patched and darned like a beggar's coat. It was voluminous and a little unfashionable but Remi told me that it was the perfect attire for our 'wedding night'.

Of course, he had touched me before and I had touched myself, far more intimately than the nuns at my first school would have recommended. I was not an entirely innocent girl who would be shocked by the sight of a penis. I had felt Remi's erect member through his trousers. But to be properly naked with each other at last was something different.

Remi undressed me slowly and reverently. He gazed at my body with such awe and desire that I felt I must really be beautiful. When he was undressed too, we stood side by side in front of my small, scratched-up mirror. We matched one another. His lines and my curves.

'We make a perfect picture,' he said.

Remi lifted me and placed me gently on the middle of the bed. He lay down beside me and we started to kiss. His hands moved tentatively over my body. I echoed his movements and wrapped my legs round his, as I had seen Arlette doing with Charles.

Gradually, Remi worked his way down to my most secret part. He rubbed at my clitoris and then he tried to push a finger inside.

I was immediately tense. I had never before let anything inside me.

'You have to trust me, my darling,' he said. 'You have to believe that this will be a wonderful sensation for you or you will never let me in.'

Remi moistened a finger in his mouth and tried again to massage me into a state of more openness. It did not seem at first to be working.

'Perhaps we should wait,' he said.

'No, no!' I begged him. Not when we had already gone so far. I had a notion in my head that once Remi had my virginity, we would be properly married. Our vows would have been consummated. Until then we were not as firmly wedded as I wanted to be.

'If you're sure,' he said. 'We'll try just one more time.'

After he got his finger inside me just a little, he moved on top of me and tried to replace finger with penis. He could gain no purchase.

'Perhaps if I were a little bit harder.'

'I think I know what to do,' I told him.

I thought of Arlette with Girodin, the politician with the penis that would never stand to attention. I remembered how she took him into her mouth in order to encourage him into hardness. I told Remi to sit on the edge of the mattress while I got to my knees on the old Persian rug.

'Gosh,' said Remi, when I took him between my lips. 'You're . . . you're quite expert at this!'

'Oh no,' I broke off to assure him. 'I've never done it before.'

'Well, you have a natural talent in that case.'

I was glad to hear that. I wanted to give Remi all the pleasure he deserved. I took him between my lips again and sucked for all I was worth.

Remi soon told me that he felt his penis was as hard as the cock on Michelangelo's *David.* At the same time, a strange thing had happened. While I had been sucking Remi's cock, I myself had become aroused. When he put his finger into me again, I was more ready to receive him. I was wet.

'This is perfect,' he said. 'I think at last you may be ready for me. Are you?'

I nodded. I lay back down again and let him climb between my legs. He put his hand down between us and gently parted the lips of my vulva to let the tip of his penis between them.

Carefully, he pushed forward. All the while, he looked into my eyes, making it clear to me that we were becoming connected not only in body but in mind and in spirit too. When he pushed a little harder, I screwed my eyes tightly shut. When I opened them, he was regarding me with such concern and such softness.

'I must stop,' he said again.

'No. Go on,' I told him. 'Please go on.'

I wanted this moment to happen. I desperately wanted to feel Remi deep inside me.

'Please,' I repeated. He pushed a little more. I was still tight but little by little I was becoming more welcoming. Each time Remi withdrew and pushed forward again, he went a little further. Each time it hurt a little less and I felt a little better.

'Lift yourself up to me,' Remi instructed.

He slipped his hands beneath my buttocks to tilt my pelvis more.

I rocked against him as I had seen Arlette rocking with Girodin and the general. I wrapped my legs around his back and he was suddenly so deep inside me I cried out.

'I am hurting you!'

'No. No.'

I smoothed my hand across his hair, comforting us both at the same time. I started to move again and he picked up the rhythm. Within moments we were in perfect unison. He kissed me passionately. We were so perfectly connected. It was as though the blood from his veins was pumping through my heart.

'Oh!' Remi came in as calm and gentlemanly a manner as I would have expected.

'I'm sorry,' he said. 'That did not take long. I'm afraid I have been in a state of complete agitation since the moment I first met you, Augustine Levert.'

I assured him that I did not mind.

'There will be plenty of time for us to practise,' I said. 'We will practise every day!'

I could feel Remi softening inside me. Eventually, he had to withdraw. He rolled off me onto the mattress and pulled me close.

'I love you,' he told me. 'You are my darling girl.'

All that night, Remi held me in his arms and rocked me as though I were a precious china doll. He told me that I would always be his and he would always be mine. In giving him my virginity, I had proved the depth of my love.

I could not have loved him more.

Our first time together had been lovely enough but the more we were together, the more delightful our love-making became. Thanks to Arlette, I suppose, I was not under the impression, as I might otherwise have been, that there was only one way to make love and so Remi and I soon had a repertoire of different positions. There were some that made me sigh and some that made me laugh. Remi liked to take me from behind. I liked to go on top of him and thus control how fast and deep he went.

When we weren't making love, Remi continued to use me as a model for his practice sketches. Now that he had seen every part of me, of course I did not mind when he asked if he might draw me nude. Still he promised me that the sketches would never be seen by anyone but we two lovebirds. Likewise, he said that when he got round to making an oil painting of the sketches, it would be for our pleasure only.

'I will hang it on the back of our bedroom door,' he joked. 'To remind me of what you were like when you were young and lovely.'

I threw a small cushion at his head.

'But you will always be young and lovely to me,' he assured me, putting down his sketchbook and pencil and pinning me to the bed.

I felt like the luckiest girl in the world.

'You should paint me,' Arlette suggested, one Sunday afternoon when Remi and his friends were lounging by the fire with her. 'You say you want to be a portrait artist but all you have as your calling card is a few charcoal sketches. Paint me and then you will have something to show anyone who expresses an interest. It can hang here in the salon and perhaps one of my lovers will buy it. Perhaps they'll commission matching portraits of their wives.'

Remi could not refuse Arlette's offer. She even said that she would pay for the canvas and the paint.

Elaine was amused by the whole idea.

'She's making it sound like a favour to him, but you know how much she's wanted a picture of herself? It drives her mad that none of her lovers has ever suggested it. She'll hang that picture in the salon and have them all going crazy guessing which of the others stumped up the cash to pay for it. It's quite a clever ruse.'

I didn't care why Arlette wanted her painting. I was just glad that Remi would have the chance to exercise his talent properly.

Remi began work right away. Arlette chose a blue dress for the first sitting. It was a dress that we all thought suited her particularly well, but for the second sitting she changed her mind and decided that she would wear a green dress instead, green being suddenly more fashionable. And then she decided that the cut of the green dress was all wrong. It did not show off her shoulders to best effect. She pulled out a red frock, but what was the point of being immortalised in only your third favourite dress? She changed back into the blue. Remi tried to remain patient.

Remi was not in a hurry. He stayed in the house now. When his friends went home, he remained. He came upstairs to my *chambre de bonne* and we lay down together on my narrow little bed. It did not seem to matter that the bed was so small because we fitted together so well. It was as though we had been made from the same piece of clay and thus we moulded ourselves around each other easily.

I lived for the touch of his lips upon me. In the daytime, whenever I passed him in the house, he would reach out to grab my hand or – if no one else was around – grab me by the waist and pull me to him for a kiss so deep it made me swoon. At night-time, we continued our explorations of each other.

Remi assured me that though I thought him a man of the world, he was, in fact, almost as naive as I was when it came to matters carnal. I didn't tell him about the things I had seen through the hole in the floor. Instead, I feigned the utmost surprise when he brought a book up to my room one evening. He had borrowed it from the poet. It was called *The Lover's Lessons* and it recalled the experiences of a young girl in Venice, from the night she lost her virginity until such time as she met a courtesan and embarked upon a Sapphic adventure.

'We could re-enact this book,' suggested Remi. 'For your courtesan, you have Arlette.'

'Oh, I couldn't,' I told Remi, though of course I had thought about it. Who could help but think about it when they had been as close to Arlette as I had been? I had touched her soft skin as I dressed her and smelled her scented hair as I brushed it loose at night. I knew what attracted the men who beat a path to her door. I had seen her in the throes of love and I knew they made her even more beautiful. But would she ever have felt the same about me? I doubted it. I let Remi have his fantasy though.

'I could paint you both,' he said. 'Entangled in each other's arms. What a sensation that would be!'

'You would be drummed out of Paris for indecency.'

'People would queue round the block to take a look.'

I laughed along but I wanted Remi to be content with me and only me. I was glad when he put the book away. I didn't want to follow in the footsteps of some long-dead girl from Venice. I wanted to make my own story.

Remi was gazing at me but had that faraway look in his eyes again, as though he were looking but not seeing. I might have been a vase of flowers.

'Kiss me,' I begged him.

His eyes changed. He smiled at me, engaged once more.

I wrapped my arms round his neck and pulled him down towards me so that the tips of our noses touched. I grinned widely. In that little room, in that narrow bed, with Remi in my arms, I was as happy as any princess.

In the room down below, we heard Arlette's exultant shriek of ecstasy.

'Must be the general,' I said.

13

I didn't expect Greg Simon to fall for my line that going to Italy to see a book of sketches would greatly inform my characterisation of Remi Sauvageon – especially since he was already paying me so much and I was living rent-free in Paris – but next thing I knew, Greg had paid for me to make a round trip. Business class. He had also had his assistant make my hotel reservation. I had been prepared to stay with Nick or Bea – a sofa would have been fine – but Greg's assistant booked me a room at the Hotel Bauer. In fact, it was a suite. I could not have been more thrilled. I was going back to Venice.

It felt as though I was being paid to go on holiday. I was being paid to try to rekindle my silly affair. I felt slightly guilty when I thought of it that way.

But the week could not pass quickly enough. I spent the mornings working directly from Augustine's manuscript in the Bibliothèque Nationale. In the afternoons, I embarked on something of a makeover. I sat in cafes and watched the endless parade of effortlessly elegant Parisiennes who turned the pavements into a catwalk. I tried to work out what it was that made them look so chic, then I visited every little boutique in the sixth and seventh arrondissements in an attempt to recreate that stylishness and pull together the perfect wardrobe for a weekend in Venice.

I also booked myself into the beauty salon I passed every morning on my way to the library and spent an extremely indulgent afternoon undertaking all those grooming rituals I had not bothered with since I flew home from Venice to London back in February. While the beautician painted my fingernails a dark, bloodstain red, I mused on how ridiculous it was, all this artifice. Especially since Marco said he had fallen for me while looking at a photo in which, by my own admission, I looked as though I had just come in from picking the potato crop.

But the preparation gave me confidence. That was the important thing about it. As I left the salon, freshly waxed and primped and varnished, I felt at last that I could hold my own against any of the uber-chic women who frequented the Rue du Faubourg St-Honoré or hung out in Harry's Bar in Venice. I needed that extra boost.

One of the things that had bothered me most about Marco Donato was the thought of the women who had populated his past. He'd been so wealthy and handsome. He was always photographed with beautiful women – women who spent their time in spas rather than university libraries. And as much as we say that beauty comes from within, it can be hard not to envy those who have so much beauty without, too. The great heroines are rarely plain. What if *Beauty and the Beast* had been reversed and the young girl was the one who looked like a monster? Would a male beauty have bothered to try to see what lay beneath?

The night before I was due to fly to Venice, I sat down with my notes on Augustine's life so far and read them through again. But I was distracted.

I posed in front of the mirror in the bedroom, looking at my new haircut. The hairdresser had persuaded me that losing a couple of inches in length would make my hair infinitely more chic. I liked it. Would Marco? I ran my hand through the new choppy layers, remembering what Marco had said about my hair back in February, when he told me what he thought of my photograph on the university website.

> I admit upon first inspection you were not what I might call 'my type'. Your hair. Why did you wear it at such an unflattering length? But your best efforts with that knife-cut fringe could not hide your beautiful cheekbones. Michelangelo might have carved your generous mouth and your perfectly straight nose. Your chin is feminine yet determined. You have the face of a mythical heroine. A goddess. No amount of bad lighting and ill-chosen costume could conceal your beautiful bones.
>
> Or your eyes . . . There is mischief in those perfect blue irises. Blue like a pair of old Levi's. That is a great compliment, I hope you know . . .

I hugged the memory of that compliment to me now and smiled at my reflection as I imagined Marco smiling back at me. In less than twenty-four hours I might be in his arms.

14

Paris, 1839

Life was very happy in the *chambre de bonne* at 76, Rue de la Ville L' Evêque, but alas, unbeknownst to me, trouble was brewing in the salon downstairs. Remi had been working on his portrait of Arlette for weeks now and Arlette was growing impatient. It was Remi's belief that the subject should not see the painting until it was finished, lest they be disappointed with the work in progress. Remi had warned Arlette of this, explaining that he worked in a very particular way and for quite some time it might look as though he was making no progress at all, when in fact he was making those tiny adjustments that would add up to perfection.

Arlette took Remi at his word and promised she would not try to take a peek at her portrait until Remi gave his permission. I believe she stuck by her promise because several times she complained to me that she was growing impatient and begged me to tell her what I had seen. Was Remi making her beautiful? Should she have worn the green dress after all?

I could tell her truthfully that I did not know. Arlette was not the only person forbidden to see Remi's work until such time as he deemed it ready. I could only tell her I thought he seemed happy and that was a good sign. I was sure I would have some inkling if he was dissatisfied.

Finally, six weeks after he started the portrait, Remi told Arlette he would not need her for another sitting. He had only to put the finishing touches to the background and then it would be complete. Arlette was beside herself with excitement. She had one of the men take down the old painting above the mantelpiece in preparation. She told all her friends about the portrait's imminent unveiling.

Elaine and I were with her when Remi said he was finally ready.

Arlette had put on her blue dress for the occasion, so that we could properly marvel at the likeness. The portrait was covered with the paint-spattered cloth that Remi draped over it every night. Remi stood to the side of it, smiling proudly. I was already pleased with whatever he had painted. I knew it would be wonderful.

Arlette stood in front of the painting. Elaine and I hung back a little, though we were no less excited than she. Remi reached up to grab the cloth and pulled it off with a showman's flourish. You could almost hear the blast of horns.

'What?'

Arlette's face had changed. Her smile had disappeared. 'But it doesn't look anything like me.'

'It looks exactly like you,' said Remi. 'It's like you're looking in a mirror.'

'But my ears . . . They're not that big. And you've made my face all lumpy. I look like a . . . I look like a potato!'

Elaine sniggered into her hand and tried to disguise it as a sneeze, which only made things worse. I dropped my eyes to the floor. It was true that the portrait was not quite what I would have expected from Remi, who was ordinarily so careful to flatter, but it was also true that it was a very good likeness.

'I promise you,' said Remi. 'I painted exactly what I saw. This, dear Arlette, is exactly what you look like.'

'Like a peasant!' Arlette exclaimed.

By this time, Elaine could not control herself at all. She had to run from the room. I could hear her gasping for air in the corridor. I stared at the carpet, determined not to suffer the same outbreak. Remi was not so wise. He heard Elaine laughing in the corridor outside and let her hilarity infect him. His mouth began to twitch into a smile.

'Is that what you think I am? A peasant?'

Arlette fixed Remi with the hard look that made sure no one ever took advantage of her unless she wanted them to.

'Arlette, please be reasonable. I painted what I saw.'

'Perhaps you should get some eyeglasses.'

'Perhaps you should get a looking-glass. This is what you look like. Tell her, Augustine. Tell her this is exactly what she looks like.'

I could feel Arlette's eyes upon me.

'It is a good likeness,' I said in an attempt to be diplomatic. 'And I think it's rather lovely.'

'Oh, shut up,' said Arlette. She turned back to Remi. 'If you think I'm going to pay for this rubbish . . .'

'If you think you're not going to pay . . . After all the effort I've made.'

'What? While you've been living under my roof, eating my food, sleeping with my maid . . .?'

She made it sound so seedy.

'The way I see it, you owe me money. Perhaps if you hadn't been so fixated on Augustine, you would have taken better care over my portrait.'

'The only thing that's wrong here is your self-perception. You have an inflated idea of your beauty, Madame. As though *that* is what your gentleman callers flock to your door for. If you were really beautiful, one of them might have married you.'

I could see now that Remi had taken a step too far. Arlette's face grew red with fury.

'Leave my house at once,' Arlette shouted. 'Leave and never come back. And take that horrible painting with you.'

'With pleasure,' said Remi.

'You've no more talent than a child. I hope you don't think you're ever going to make a living from such pathetic daubs.'

'I'm sure when I start to attract better models, my talent will improve immeasurably.'

'You're no gentleman,' said Arlette.

'Well, it goes without saying that you're no lady.'

'Oh!' Arlette dealt him an open-handed slap to the face.

I tried to intervene, but Arlette pushed me out of the way. Remi bade me stand behind him. I knew he would not return Arlette's latest insult in kind, but I did not think she had finished with him and I wanted him to leave before she scratched out his eyes. She would calm down. Perhaps she would even come to see that the portrait was lovely. But not if Remi continued to trade insults with her.

'Remi,' I begged him. 'You must leave. Go to the bistro. I'll come and find you later.'

'No, you won't,' said Arlette. This time she was talking to me. 'Augustine Levert, you are a member of my household and already I have turned a blind eye to your goings-on these past few weeks. You have been distracted from your work by this ignorant ruffian. I know you have been feeding him from my kitchen and doubtless he has been drinking from my wine cellar too. He has taken advantage of you and you in turn have taken advantage of me. Now it is time for you to choose. Are you loyal to me or to him?'

'Arlette, please don't make me choose between you. I love you both. You are my family. No one has ever shown me such kindness . . .'

'And how little gratitude you show for it. Me or him?'

Remi was already covering up the portrait, ready to take it away.

'Come on, Augustine,' he said. 'If she can't appreciate great art when she sees it, then it's highly unlikely she appreciates you properly either. Come on. You've worked like a slave here. You don't owe her anything.'

At one time, I had felt I owed Arlette everything. But right then she seemed childish and surly, insisting that I choose between her and my true love all because she didn't like the way he'd painted her. I decided I would go with Remi. I never thought for a moment that I might not have the chance to come back to Arlette's household later.

* * *

That night, I stayed with Remi in a little hotel in Saint Germain. He told the man on the desk that we were married but I had lost my wedding ring when we encountered robbers on our first day in the city. They'd taken our papers at the same time. The hotelier did not look convinced but neither did he seem to particularly care about our marital status. He handed Remi a key and wished us a good night with a horrible wink.

'This is much better than the *chambre de bonne*,' said Remi. 'At last a bed we can stretch out in.'

I agreed, though the *chambre de bonne* had been dry and warm and this hotel room smelled distinctly of mildew. It was a smell that took me back to the room I had shared with my mother. How I had longed to be able to take her to a better place, so that she might be cured of the consumption. The memory made me tearful. Remi misinterpreted my weeping.

'Arlette is a silly woman. She is vain and stupid. To think she believes anyone could have painted a better portrait! Of course, I could have made the picture more flattering but I am a true artist. I don't just paint what I see. I paint my subject's inner life as well.'

Remi was completely absorbed in his own justifications. I didn't dare tell him that I had liked it better when his pictures were less realistic but kind. Instead, I snuggled close to him and let him talk until he decided he wanted to make love to me.

Then I let him undress me and touch every inch of my body.

'Here,' he said, 'is a vision worth wasting paint to capture.'

Perhaps realising that I was as upset by the evening's events as he had been angered, Remi showed extra-special attention to my happiness for once. He had me lie back on the bed and think of nothing but pleasure as he got to his knees between my legs and buried his face in my mound. I relaxed just a little as I felt his tongue on my clitoris, but the thought of Arlette's angry tears soon distracted me again and Remi grew impatient for my climax.

Not wanting to disappoint him, I gave a reasonable impression of a woman satisfied. Then he climbed on top of me to take his own pleasure. I sighed as he pushed into me and wrapped my arms round him, holding his face against my neck so that he would not see my own wet eyes.

For a moment, while he was inside me, I forgot about my worries and focused instead on the good that had come from the argument. I was spending a night away from home in a big bed. A proper marital bed. At least I would not wake up with a crick in my neck. And we did not have to worry about keeping anyone awake.

However, in the morning, while Remi went to Le Petit Ami to see if he could find a tourist willing to sit for one of his sketches, I went straight back to Arlette's house. It was wash day on the Rue de la Ville L'Evêque. I was certain that Arlette would be happy to have me back to help out with the laundry and perhaps might even have changed her mind about the painting. But she would not see me. She told Elaine to let me know that since my betrayal she considered me as good as dead. I had shown where my loyalties really lay.

'She says you cut her to the quick.'

'I can't believe it!' I said. 'She knows I would never deliberately hurt her.'

Elaine squeezed my hand. 'She'll get over it, I'm sure. It's just her vanity that's smarting. Between you and me, that painting was an incredible likeness. Couldn't have told the portrait and the model apart. Though I'd never dare say it to her face.'

Elaine and I were in agreement about that.

'But you'll have to tell Remi that no woman really wants to be painted as she is. Flattery is what we're after. Don't matter how confident she appears on the outside, Arlette has never believed she's beautiful enough.'

I agreed. And then I went back to Remi to tell him I was still out of a job.

'It doesn't matter,' he said. 'I have some savings. I heard there are places to rent on the Rue de Seine. We can take a flat there.'

'We?'

'Of course,' he said. 'You're my responsibility now.'

Unromantic as his words were, I didn't think I had ever heard anything quite so lovely. I was Remi Sauvageon's responsibility. It was almost as good as being his wife.

15

The flight from Paris to Venice was entirely uneventful. Still, it was strange touching down in Venice for a second time. On the first occasion I arrived there, it was January. The weather was bright but cold and I was full of sadness at what I'd left behind in London. This time, the weather was sultry and I was both excited and nervous at the thought of rediscovering what I'd left behind at the Palazzo Donato.

I had a water-taxi take me straight to my hotel – Greg Simon was paying after all – and spent just a couple of minutes in my room there, dumping my luggage and straightening up my appearance, before I headed straight back out again. I had sent an email to Marco telling him I would be at the library at two o'clock that afternoon if he was interested. It was already ten minutes to. I didn't want to be late and not only because I wanted to appear professional. If Marco was waiting for me, I didn't want to waste a single second of time that could be spent in his company.

When another water-taxi brought me to the pontoon outside the Palazzo Donato, I was so eager to disembark that I almost fell backwards into the water. What a disaster that would have been. Soaking wet and covered in slime was not the look I hoped to achieve.

I knocked on the heavy door. Just as on my very first day at the house, Silvio was there to let me inside. There was no effusive acknowledgment. He merely nodded as though I had been away for a couple of days rather than for almost five months.

'You know the way,' he said, once I was inside the house.

My heart sat in my mouth and I struggled to control my anxious nausea as I pushed open the door that led into the interior courtyard, where two sparrows had once played in the broken fountain. That day at the very edge of spring, nothing had been in bloom but a single rose. Now, in full summer, the secret garden was bursting with life and with colour. The lemon trees were heavy with little green fruit, foretelling a bumper harvest. The white rose bush was covered with extravagant blooms. I stroked one affectionately, remembering the white rose still pressed between the pages of my notebook, thin as the paper itself.

Before I pushed open the door into the far corridor, I could not help looking up at the gallery to see if anyone was looking down. But I saw no one and, if I was honest with myself, when I monitored that inner sense we all have of when we're being watched, I felt nothing. Perhaps there really was no one there.

Or perhaps he would be waiting for me in the library . . . With my hand on the door handle, I paused again. I took a deep breath and tucked my hair behind my ear. I plastered on a smile and knocked.

No answer.

I pushed open the door.

The library was empty. Nothing to see except books.

I walked inside. The library was exactly as I remembered it: a double-height room stuffed with books on every subject you can imagine. Two antique desks, polished by a thousand scholars' elbows. Two armchairs on either side of the fireplace. Above the mantel hung the portrait of Ernesta Donato, the notorious courtesan and canny businesswoman who had made the family fortune. She was still smiling, though now I thought her smile seemed slightly sad. Dust eddied in the sunlight. The room was not so scrupulously clean as it had been before. It was as though someone had told Silvio not to bother with the library now that it was no longer in use.

Though the fire was not lit, the summer sunshine made the room feel much warmer than it had ever done and I soon took off my jacket. I draped it over the back of one of the armchairs before I sat down at the desk. As I did so, I noticed that the mirror was still in its place too, reflecting the desk, reflecting me.

Silvio had laid out Remi Sauvageon's sketchbook on the desk where I had sat for hours, reading Luciana Giordano's diaries. It was also the desk where I had been sitting when Marco Donato and I made a strange sort of love.

Of course I couldn't help remembering that morning again when it had been cold outside while Marco had me burning with desire for him.

I ran my fingers along the edge of the desk. I could not control my curiosity. I went to open the drawer where once upon a time I had found a vibrator. It was not locked. It opened easily but there was absolutely nothing inside apart from some incongruously chintzy floral-patterned lining paper, brittle and faded with age. I didn't remember that. I opened the other drawers. They were similarly empty. I sighed.

I opened up my laptop. Perhaps . . . The modem automatically began to search for Wi-Fi connections. What if the Palazzo Donato network was active and he was waiting for me to log on? The modem found nothing but a nearby free Wi-Fi spot. There was no sign of the closed network through which Marco had sent me instructions to undress and bring myself to an orgasm. Clearly he had no intention of restarting our relationship where we had left off.

I got up again and walked the perimeter of the room, looking first for a hidden camera but also for a hidden door. After

Bea's unfortunate encounter in the library, she had run away down the corridor. I'd returned to the library to confront the stranger myself but found no one there, though I'd seen no one come out. There had to be a hidden door, but I couldn't find it. Perhaps I'd simply missed seeing the stranger slip away while I was distracted by Bea.

Giving up, I decided I had better turn my attention to the official reason for my visit. Remi Sauvageon's sketches.

Like Luciana Giordano's diaries, the ancient sketchbook was protected from dust and sunlight by being kept inside a marbled paper box. I opened the box carefully and lifted the sketchbook out. It was nowhere near as old as Luciana's diaries but it was similarly fragile.

I laid the book on the blotter and, with reverent fingers, opened it to the first page.

I recognised Augustine at once, though she was obviously younger in the sketches here than in the painting I had seen at the Musée d'Orsay. The first quick drawing showed her sitting at a table, working on a piece of sewing. A second showed her up to her elbows in some sort of tub. Must have been wash day. She was turning to look at the artist over her shoulder. Her expression was one of mock annoyance. This sketch was the nineteenth-century equivalent of a snap taken when you're not ready.

In this one book, Remi had made hundreds of drawings of Augustine. He captured her in all her moods. Here she was wistful. Here she was laughing. Here she looked angry enough to spit. I especially liked a depiction of her in an armchair by the fire. She had another piece of sewing on her lap, but she had her eyes closed, having dozed off.

The portrait that hung in the museum in Paris was a grand affair. This sketchbook was more of a family album. Here was their real life together. Remi and Augustine. There was a definite charm in that. Remi's sketches spoke of his great affection for Augustine and she looked like somebody who was easy to love.

Marco Donato had once said something similar about me, as I recalled, when I asked him why he had admitted me to the library when he had turned down so many previous requests. He said it was because I had kind eyes. I thought about that exchange. So intimate and affectionate. The absence of that intimacy made me feel suddenly cold.

I stayed at the library for an hour that morning. It was long enough to get a sense of what the sketchbook might tell me. I could have stayed longer but I was disappointed to find myself alone there. I was hungry too. The thought of a bowl of pasta pulled me towards the door.

I saw Silvio on the way out.

Once upon a time, I had pussy-footed around Silvio, keen to ensure he did not recommend to Marco that I not be allowed back, but now I felt that our acquaintance was such I could be straight with him.

'I was hoping to see Signor Donato today,' I said in Italian. 'Is he in Venice right now?'

I thought Silvio hesitated for a moment before he replied. 'He is on business.'

'Right,' I pushed on. 'Business in Italy or business overseas? I'm in the city for a few days and if it's at all possible, I'd like to see him before I go. I'd like to thank him personally for having allowed me to come back to the library.'

'I will pass on your thanks.'

'Please tell him that I would far rather thank him in person. I will be staying at the Hotel Bauer.'

Silvio nodded.

'Please,' I reiterated. 'Please promise you'll pass that news on.'

'Of course.'

Silvio turned away to indicate that the exchange was over.

That night, for old time's sake, I joined Nick and Bea at the little bar where we had shared a great many wonderful evenings. When the bar got too busy for easy conversation, they were keen to come back with me to the Bauer, where we ordered cocktails on Greg Simon's tab. He had, after all, told me to make sure I had a good time.

Later, alone in my hotel room, my mind drifted to the little flat near the Campo Santa Margherita where I had stayed during my research trip. Nick had told me that the current occupant of the flat was a marine biologist with a big hairy beard and dubious hygiene. Bea chipped in, 'Even I don't fancy him.'

It was strange to think of a big, hairy man in the four-poster bed where Luciana Giordano had lost her virginity and I had spent many turbulent nights, dreaming of an unknown lover. I wondered if the bed would have the same effect on the biologist. Or was it Marco who made me dream?

I sat in a chair by the window, remembering the early extracts of Luciana's diaries, when she had sat by the window night after night waiting for a glimpse of the man who would become first her teacher and then her lover. Venice certainly was a romantic city. I watched as a gondola rocked silently by, a young couple kissing passionately in the seat. The gondolier looked up at me and touched the brim of his hat with his fingers. I slipped back into the room.

This suite I was in, at the Bauer, must have seen plenty of romance. Proposals, honeymoons, passionate affairs. Auspicious beginnings and happy endings and all shades of emotion in between. It was – as Bea had told me – a terrible shame to be there all alone.

It was so hot that I lay on top of the sheets. The window let in a gentle breeze and the sound of the water traffic passing by. During those odd moments when no vaporetto was revving its engine, I could imagine Venice as it had always been.

I dreamed about Marco again.

I was standing at the window. Mist swirled up the canal, hiding everything more than a few feet away and softening every sound, like a ghostly veil. Like Luciana, I was watching for someone and eventually he came. A sleek black gondola. The gondolier did not look up at me as he paused beneath my balcony, but the passenger in the *felce* leaned forward and beckoned me with a white-cuffed hand.

I climbed down from my balcony, crawled into the *felce* and joined my lover there. Without a word, the gondolier pushed off into the canal.

I lay down on the cushions alongside the man in the mask. He stroked my face with his cool hand. A smile played on his lips as he let his finger trace the curve of my jaw. He planted a gentle kiss upon my mouth. I held his head and kissed him again when he tried to pull away all too quickly.

As my tongue searched his mouth, he put his hand inside my nightgown and squeezed my longing breasts. Reluctantly taking my lips from his, I raised my arms above my head and let him take the nightgown off. His fingers followed the lines of my body from my shoulder to my hip.

Naked at last, I could keep no secrets from his hands and his tongue. I could only offer my body up to him and let him have his way. But I wanted him to take me. I wanted him to do whatever he liked because I knew it would be wonderful. His touch and his kiss were intoxicating to me. I felt myself falling into a trance. My whole body was vibrating with pleasure.

There wasn't much room in the *felce* and at one point I kicked the curtain out of the way. As I did so, I caught the eye of the gondolier, who was looking down towards us. Thinking of his eyes on my nakedness should have been embarrassing but instead I found I wanted him to stare. But my lover closed the curtain behind us again and once more it was too dark to do anything other than feel him making love to me. He held my hands above my head and sucked on each of my nipples in turn.

Then at last he was inside me. His humping pushed me back into the cushions. I lifted my pelvis to meet his. Faster and faster. Harder and harder. He came with a triumphant cry, thrusting hard against me as though to wring every last drop from his orgasm. I felt my body respond accordingly. I contracted around him, massaging him to a shuddering climax.

When we came apart, my lover laid his cloak over me to cover my nakedness. He opened up the curtains of the *felce* so that we could see the world outside.

The ghostly gondolier continued to row us silently through the lagoon. Venice was far behind us. There was just a sliver of new moon to guide us. I could not see what was ahead.

16

Paris, 1839

I could not go back to Arlette. Even a month later, she had not changed her mind or mellowed in her opinion in the least. Remi was a beast and I had betrayed her. 'She's says you've made your bed,' Elaine told me, on my fifth visit to beg for work.

So, Remi found us a place to live in Saint Germain. I had some small savings. We could afford it for a couple of months. It was tiny, just one room. But I was used to the *chambre de bonne,* which was half this room's size, and thus it seemed like a palace to me. Besides, it contained everything I needed. A double bed and Remi.

Having Remi to love, I thought that I had it all. I couldn't imagine needing anything else to survive. And for those first few months, I didn't need anything much. I took in sewing and Remi sold sketches to tourists on the quays. In the evenings, he worked on a painting of me. He used the canvas on which he had painted Arlette, blotting her out with a layer of grey paint before he started again. He had me pose naked on the bed. He told me to imagine I was the Queen of Sheba. I should be proud and unembarrassed of my triumphant nakedness, he said. I was the most beautiful woman on earth. I was the best loved.

But that winter in Paris, everything was to change. Now that I was not living in Arlette's house, with its eternally glowing fireplaces, I would come to know the true meaning of cold.

The winter was a harsh one. Beginning in December, right before Christmas, the wind blew from the northeast for two months straight, bringing with it more snow than I had ever seen. At first it seemed jolly and festive. The pristine white snow covered the litter and the horse-shit for a start and the thought of a new year made everyone happy. But after a week or so, we all wanted the snow gone again. Anything. Endless drizzle would have been better than the biting cold and the wind that seemed to want to rip your coat from your back every time you stepped outside the door.

I bundled up and carried on as best I could. I wrapped rags round my hands to stop my fingers from turning blue and wore every pair of stockings I had at one time, though it made my tight boots pinch. I would not be defeated. Remi, however, seemed to be taking the weather especially personally. Each morning when he got up and looked out of the window, he cursed to see that another layer of white had dusted away his footprints of the day before. Sometimes he would sit for hours at that window, while I stitched the shirts I had taken in to repair. He only looked up when I handed him a hot drink to warm his fingers, and then only briefly. It was as though he was grieving the summer as a husband grieves a wife lost in childbirth. He stopped drawing.

Once he told me that the whiteness of the snow was blocking his imagination. He needed colour to paint, he said. He was briefly animated as he explained to me, making huge sweeping gestures as though putting shades on our walls. But then he collapsed back onto the bed as though the fight had gone out of him. He couldn't paint in endless tones of icy nothingness and if he couldn't paint then what reason was there left to go on?

'Because the winter will be over before you know it,' I reminded him. It was already the end of January.

I tried all the time to cheer him up and sometimes I succeeded. We would usually make love and I would wrap myself round him, forcing my heat into him. When I kissed him I imagined myself infusing him with my passion. I did everything I could to remind him what a joy it was to be living. When he didn't want to make love to me, I took his manhood in my mouth and sucked and caressed him with my tongue until even the snow could not keep him from exploding in ecstasy. All the same, he got a small cold and convinced himself that he was dying.

'It's this weather,' he told me. 'It's going to be the end of me. I won't last the winter in this house.'

I stuffed every crack in the floorboards with rags. I made a sausage of fabric to stop the draught at the door. I took every job I could find to pay for fuel for our fire, but no matter what I did to keep him warm, Remi sank still deeper. The winter carried on. It was Remi or the weather and the snow seemed to be winning.

'It's no good,' he said. 'We need more logs and we need more to eat. We've got to get some more money from somewhere. I need to sell a painting.'

'You've only got one painting,' I pointed out.

'And it's the best thing I've ever done.'

We both looked at it. Me as the Queen of Sheba. Remi had painted an imaginary bower filled with silken cushions in place of our modest home. I was in agreement with him. It was his most accomplished work, for sure.

'I'm sorry, my love, but now its duty is to keep us warm. I either sell it or I burn it on the fire to give us just a moment of heat.'

'You can't sell it! I'd rather it burned. But you can't burn it either. You can't!'

I was distraught. I did not know which was worse: my naked image on the fire or in a stranger's home? But Remi was right that it was the only item of any value we had left to sell.

'If no one likes the painting,' he continued, 'then at least the frame might fetch the price of some bread.'

'Oh Remi.' I battled the urge to cry.

He seemed determined and I knew better than to try to stop him. He had been distressed by the fact that I'd taken on so much work to raise money for our rent while he had been unable to do anything since the snow came down and he couldn't draw cartoons on the quays any more.

I consoled myself with the thought that at least desperation had made Remi animated again. He dressed up in every jacket he owned, wrapped my portrait in a sheet to protect it and set out into the wintry weather. I did not know what I hoped would happen out there. A big part of me wanted him to return with the picture unsold, but I was human too and I was hungry. Yes, I would swap my chance at eternal beauty for a piece of bread and chicken.

When Remi returned three hours later, he did not have the painting.

'Who took it?' I asked.

He named a furniture dealer I particularly disliked. I put my hands over my eyes to stop the tears as I imagined what a poor return Remi would have got for the painting that had taken so much of his talent, his time and his affection for me.

'How much did he give you?' I dared to ask at last.

It was only enough to feed us for two days. Especially since Remi had no idea how to get a good price for anything in the market and had paid almost twice as much as I would have done for a loaf of bread and some mouldy cheese. He'd also spent a good chunk of the money on wine, I noticed with some distress. After the few provisions we had were gone, we were in the same position as before. A worse position, because now we did not even have the portrait to remind us of warmer and happier times. Still, I let Remi drink all the wine. It made him amorous. I was glad to give myself to him and to see that familiar smile on his face. With his arms around me, feeling his manhood pressing to enter me as ardently as ever, I felt momentarily protected. Something would happen to make everything better.

With the food almost finished, Remi announced that he would have to make an even more drastic sacrifice than selling the painting. He would have to throw himself on the mercy of his father. To Remi, who had not spoken to his father since the day he announced he wanted to go to Paris to become a painter, it would be the equivalent of selling his soul.

'He will be happy to see me grovel. And I will be happy to grovel for you, my little love.'

I tried to tell him he should not go to Guerville. We would manage. I would find a way. I could sell one of my dresses, I suggested. I could go and beg Arlette to take me back again. But Remi would not hear of it. He told me that my efforts to keep us fed so far had unmanned him. If he couldn't provide for me then what kind of a man was he? He was not the kind of man he thought would be worthy of my love.

He would not hear any disagreement so I had to let him go, though if I was honest I would have said I did not see how going to his father could be thought of as being especially manly. It was clear that Remi thought he was making an extraordinary gesture for my love. With the snow still falling, he dressed in all his jackets again and I bid him a good journey out of the city. Little did I know that I would not see him again for quite some time.

17

In truth, I did not need to go back to the palazzo a second time. There was no real writing to be translated in Remi Sauvageon's sketchbook, apart from the odd title. *Augustine in the kitchen* or *Augustine sewing*. But something dragged me back there. You know what it was. When Silvio opened the door again he didn't seem in the least bit surprised to see me.

The sketchbook was still on the desk. Silvio must have known I would come back. I took off my jacket and arranged myself again, opening up my laptop to make notes.

I don't know why I tried again. Foolish optimism, I suppose. Still, I was surprised to find that the Palazzo Donato network was active that morning. I was even more surprised to find that the password Marco had given me all those months ago – Ernesta1973 – still allowed me access.

But what use was it to have that access now? I didn't want to spend my precious time in the Donato library surfing the *Daily Mail* online. Keeping the Wi-Fi connected could be a dangerous distraction, though truthfully, that's exactly what I was hoping for. A dangerous distraction. And my hope did not go unrewarded. After ten minutes or so spent staring at the empty instant-message window, I got back to my work. I was soon absorbed in Augustine's account of life in Paris. I matched the events she talked about to the little scenes in Remi's sketchbook. It was easy to imagine the garret on the Rue de Seine and the bustle in the streets below his window.

Remi had drawn many of the local characters and so my mind's eye had very little work to do to recreate a street full of faces, some friendly, some not.

I was so absorbed in my work that I forgot to keep checking my laptop. The screen went into rest mode – completely blank. Until, that is, I wanted to make a note in my calendar to remind me that I should call my aunt later that day. It was her birthday and I was in danger of forgetting. I inputted my password, which was, since I felt superstitious about changing it, 'Venezia', and the screen came back to life. It was not, however, as I had left it. There was a message in the instant-message box from 'Marco D'.

I felt a little sick at the sight of his name, not because it repulsed me but because the idea that he had reached out to me filled me with nerves. It might be spam, I told myself. Several of my friends had had their DM accounts hacked so that they sent out endless exhortations to try new diet pills. But it was really Marco.

How are you?

was all the message said.

'Fine,' I responded. 'I'm in your library.'

'I know. Silvio told me. How is the research progressing?'

'Well. Thank you for letting me come back.'

'Least I could do.'

'I really do appreciate it.

'What exactly is it you're hoping to find?' Marco asked.

Oh Marco, I thought. There's a question. I replied, 'I'm not sure. I suppose I was hoping that seeing Remi Sauvageon's sketches would give some colour to my account of Augustine's life. It's the closest thing I can get to photos.'

'They're great sketches,' Marco wrote. 'The work of a master.'

'Which is why you bought them.'

'I didn't just buy them because they were drawn by Sauvageon. I think I would have wanted them regardless. They're not just cartoons. They have a life of their own. A vibrancy. I suppose that comes from the artist being in love with his muse.'

'Yes,' I replied. 'I agree his feelings seem to shine through.'

'I've spent quite a bit of time looking at them in the past,' Marco continued. 'I was fascinated by the thought of the relationship the pictures represent. I tried to find out more about his early life and the woman he so clearly adored. I did get to see some letters. From her to him and to her employer at the time.'

This was so strange. Marco and I had not corresponded properly in months and now it was as though that last week in Venice had never happened. Just like old times. I took a chance.

'I wish you could take me through your findings. I'm staying at the Bauer. I'll be there until the end of the week. Why don't you come and join me for dinner? You can tell me all about it then.'

'Not this week,' he responded. 'I'm away.'

'On business,' I finished the sentence for him.

'Took the words right out of my mouth.'

'You're very busy for an international playboy.'

'I haven't been a playboy for a very long time.'

'But your work does seem to rather dominate your life. I mean, it must have been quite some crisis in Hong Kong that made you abandon such a big party back in February.'

'It was.'

'Tell me about it.'

'I don't want to bore you.'

'You could never bore me.'

'I don't want to take the chance. But if you're really interested, I had to fly to Hong Kong to visit one of the cruise line's offices. A senior manager quit under a cloud. I had to support the other staff and try to avert a scandal. The timing was terrible, I admit. Believe me, I had been looking forward to that party as much as anyone. I was especially looking forward to seeing you in that dress. Did it fit?'

'It did. Though quite how you got my measurements . . .'

'I had Silvio make a wild guess. He's quite good at that sort of thing. Takes much more of an interest in women than you'd suppose. Did you like it?'

Of course, if Marco was telling the truth about having been away on business, he wouldn't have known that I didn't actually wear the dress. Then why did I have the sense that this throwaway comment was intended to put me off the scent? Was it a clever double bluff?

'I imagine you were the belle of the ball.'

'I don't know about that,' I wrote. 'Everyone looked so wonderful. You have some very beautiful friends.'

'It's easy to be beautiful in a mask.'

'I saw a man I thought might be you,' I continued. 'Right height. Right hair. And he was in the library. I had this idea that you might wait for me there, since it was the scene of so much of our virtual friendship. Would have been the perfect place to meet for the first time, don't you think?'

'Yes,' said Marco. 'If I had been there, I probably would have tried to lure you to the library.'

'Scene of the crime,' I interjected.

'Ha! You could say that. I suppose I'm lucky that guy who was in the library that night didn't choose to impersonate me, in that case.'

Marco was sticking to his story. Was there any point in my trying to call his bluff?

'He might have been in the library with the intention of making off with Luciana's papers. I suppose I should have introduced myself. Let him know I had my eye on him.'

'Perhaps you should have.'

Was that another carefully planned response to lead me away from the truth?

'The really weird thing was, he was there one minute but when I looked in on the library again just a few moments later, he was gone, without having walked past me on the way out. I don't know how he did that, unless he climbed through a window. Or is there a secret door?'

'Ha. No. Maybe he did jump out of the window.'

'It's a long fall.'

'Our friend Luciana made a bigger jump every night. Look, I really am sorry that I didn't make it to the ball. It was supposed to be a grand romantic gesture and it backfired because I had to put work first. But that's my life, Sarah. Back when you and I first started writing to one another, I was having a quiet spell, but right now I have got so much going on I barely have time to sleep. I certainly don't have time to be writing to you like this. It's why I haven't been in a relationship for so long. It isn't fair. When you're in a relationship, you have to make time for the other person. I can't make time for anything but spreadsheets and AGMs right now.'

'I understand,' I wrote.

'And I'm sure you've got work to do too. I'm glad I could help out by letting you loose in the library again.'

'Thanks. I really appreciate it.'

I was in the middle of typing some more, about feeling especially honoured given that he'd refused access to Bea, to keep him online for a little longer, but he had already logged off.

'Goodbye.'

'Goodbye,' I typed to the empty air.

I sat back and reread our conversation. Was it friendly? Was it perfunctory? Was it back to square one? Two strangers talking about history? I tried to take comfort from the fact that, though he'd logged off in a hurry, he was the one who had initiated the conversation. And I had that peculiar feeling again, the prickling of my skin that told me he was nearby.

About an hour later, I left the library again.

On my way out of the house, I stopped in the courtyard garden and sat down on the stone bench between the two statues, which I now knew to be Orpheus and Eurydice, saying goodbye for the last time. I pretended to be absorbed in a message on my phone, but really I was waiting to see if Marco would be tempted to reveal himself. I waited for several minutes. No sign of him. I waited until Silvio came out into the courtyard and expressed his surprise that I was still there.

'I thought you had gone,' he said.

I waggled my phone at him.

'Stopped to return a text.'

'Ah. Everyone is always on their phone these days,' he said. 'Living in a virtual world. I don't understand it. People live whole lives without ever seeing the people they love any more.'

'It isn't healthy,' I agreed.

'It isn't natural,' Silvio echoed. 'And it isn't any substitute for hearing a loved one's voice and seeing her beautiful smile.'

He shook his head and wandered off. It was the closest thing Silvio and I had had to a conversation.

18

I went straight from the Palazzo Donato to meet Bea for lunch. She looked remarkably demure. She had always been a big fan of miniskirts and cleavage – believing as she did that you should maximise your assets – but that day she was wearing a pretty tea dress. It was clear that her new boyfriend was having quite the effect on her. I hoped her personality wasn't becoming similarly subdued.

'So how are you finding Paris?' she asked.

'It's OK,' I said. 'Though it's been harder for me to find my feet than it was here, not having the automatic social life associated with turning up at a university.'

'Don't you know anyone out there?' Bea asked.

'I know *one* person in Paris. At least, I think he's still there. My ex-boyfriend Steven,' I reminded her. When Steven had written to me, asking if there was any possibility we could rekindle our relationship, I had told Bea all about it. Almost all. I hadn't told her exactly why we'd broken up and neither had I told her about the conditions Steven had suggested before we could effect any reconciliation. That is, he wanted me to consider how we would avoid slipping back into a 'vanilla kind of life'. Specifically with regard to sex, of course.

'Ah. The ex-boyfriend,' said Bea, a smile creeping across her lips. 'You know, I googled him. He's really very good-looking. Are you telling me it's not worth looking him up for old time's sake?'

'Please,' I sighed.

Bea was the kind of girl who stayed in touch with all her ex-boyfriends. That way she was never short of a date in an emergency. I knew what she would do in my situation. But I didn't think I could ever go back to Steven, even as a friend. Though, as the months had passed, it was getting easier to remember the good times as well as the ugly ending, I didn't think we could ever rebuild the trust which was important for a solid relationship, sexual or otherwise. I couldn't see how it was possible that we weren't irrevocably broken.

'You should drop him a line. At the very least, you need to have someone in Paris you can contact in an emergency,' Bea continued.

'The concierge in my building is very nice,' I responded.

'You know what I mean,' said Bea.

I did my best to change the subject and convince Bea that I wasn't bothered about my ex and certainly didn't need to be in touch with him, but I thought about Steven still. Of course I did. You can't spend seven years with someone and expect to forget about them in as many months. But lately I wondered if I had ever felt as connected to him as I did to Marco. In his emails to me, Marco had occasionally been goofy and vulnerable. I didn't feel that Steven ever really let his guard down in the same way. He was always the cool guy. The funny guy. I was the one who got teased. We got along just fine so long as he was feeling confident. When Steven wasn't feeling good, he would shut down and become a different person. He wouldn't express his vulnerability and if I tried to help him through some rough patch or other, he would eventually act as though I had caused it.

Marco and I had an email conversation about it once.

I'd asked him, 'Isn't intimacy about showing our vulnerabilities and knowing that they won't be held against us?'

Marco's reply surprised me. Or perhaps it didn't. He wrote, 'We men more often find it hard to forgive our loved ones for uncovering those vulnerabilities in the first place. We don't want to know it's safe to be weak in your arms. We want to be the strong ones. We want to be perfect for you.'

Steven would never have admitted such a thing. But had I eventually pushed for too much intimacy from Marco too?

Thankfully, Bea changed the subject.

'I just can't believe you've got a suite at the Palazzo Bauer and no one to share it with! That's such a waste.'

'Well, how about you stay there with your security guard? I'll stay in your apartment tonight.'

'I don't need a fabulous setting to get romantic with Ugo. How about you find yourself a man and make the most of it?' A sly smile spread across Bea's face. 'You could call Nick. He's still single. Still utterly besotted. I can't tell you how excited he was to hear that you were coming to town. He's been moping since you left.'

I batted away Bea's teasing. Inside I was thinking, it's always the way: there's always the lover and the loved. Nick was besotted with me, while I saw him as nothing more than a friend. At the same time, it seemed I was in love with a man I'd never met. We were all miserable as a result.

That afternoon, I indulged myself by taking a wander around some of my favourite spots in the city. The weather was glorious. I jumped on a vaporetto and criss-crossed the Grand Canal until I got to the Peggy Guggenheim museum. What an amazing woman she must have been. I wondered if Marco had ever met her. His parents must have known her, as they vied to throw the best parties in Venice every Carnevale.

The museum was busy. Tourist season was in full flow. Still, I found my favourite exhibit almost totally ignored in favour of the larger, flashier pieces. It was a stool, a simple stone stool, carved with the words SAVOR KINDNESS FOR

CRUELTY IS ALWAYS POSSIBLE LATER. How very true, I thought. I took a photograph of it on my mobile phone and set it as my screensaver. It was a sober message but a useful one. It was an exhortation to make the most of what we had. I was in Venice on a beautiful summer's day. I was staying at a hotel I could never have afforded on my own. With that in mind, I wasted no time in taking myself for a gelato at Grom on the Campo San Barnaba. I chose Bacio, my favourite flavour. It means 'kiss'.

In the evening I met up with Nick, Bea and Ugo the brooding security guard. We visited just about the only restaurant in Venice that doesn't serve fish. There was a long queue to get in and we had to hang around in the square, drinking spritz for almost an hour, before we got a table. We talked in stuttering Italian for the sake of the guard, who did not speak any English. Not that he seemed especially interested in the conversation anyway. He was only interested in watching Bea's lips move.

Nick remembered the Martedì Grasso ball at the Palazzo Donato. He told Ugo about how Bea and I had switched costumes to fool my mysterious billionaire boyfriend. He managed not to make it sound completely ridiculous.

'They had wigs too, so you really couldn't tell them apart. Two peas in a pod. They're exactly the same size. Have you noticed, Ugo? Same height, same . . .'

Nick had had a couple of drinks. More than a couple. He mimed a pair of voluptuous breasts. Ugo frowned as though he thought Nick might be making an especially off-colour comment about poor Bea.

'Nick,' I warned. 'I really don't think your Italian is up to it.'

Bea, thankfully, changed the subject to a party that she and Ugo would be attending later that week. It was to celebrate Ugo's cousin's wedding. I could tell that this was a huge deal for Bea. She was being introduced to yet more of Ugo's family. That had to be a good sign.

After dinner, all three of them walked me back to the Hotel Bauer. They left me in the lobby, with much nudging about the honeymoon suite.

As I undressed, I thought about the evening. It was always fun to be with Nick and Bea. The conversation ranged wide and was always peppered with plenty of laughter, but that evening what stuck with me was Nick's telling of the anecdote about the ball.

Did Bea and I really look so alike? Was it possible that the wig and the change of outfit really had fooled Marco? Though the courtyard of the Palazzo Donato had been illuminated with what seemed like hundreds of flaming torches for the ball, the corridor on which the library had been situated was dimly lit. Likewise the library itself, where the only light had come from a reading lamp on the desk I habitually used and the glow from the fireplace. In such a dimly lit room, perhaps Bea and I were easily mistaken for one another.

I remembered watching Bea through the crack in the door. She was flirting, talking in Italian. But then, Marco knew that I could speak Italian. As far as he was concerned, my accent might be as good as Bea's. And he had never seen my face except in that online photograph, with its harsh lighting that was so unflattering.

If he had been genuinely confused and still thought that I was the one who had shrieked upon touching his hand in the library, then no wonder he was being so distant. Though I had gone into the library after the incident and called to let Marco know I was there, perhaps he hadn't heard me. Perhaps he had already left the house.

Should I tell him about the incident in the library? I decided that I would.

* * *

I climbed into the honeymooners' bed and listened to the sounds on the canal outside. There was a snatch of 'O Sole Mio'. You heard that all the time in Venice. Those old Cornetto ads had a great deal to answer for. More music. A gondolier singing one of the old traditional tunes. Tinkling laughter. The chug-chug-chug of an idling vaporetto. A shout. An echoing whisper. All the noises of Venice were distorted by the water. They seemed to be coming from somewhere far away. Not just in distance but in time. Rome may be called the Eternal City but there is something timeless about Venice, too.

I rolled onto my side and pulled the sheet up over my shoulder. First thing in the morning, I would go to the Palazzo Donato, I would explain about the dress swap and I would ask Marco to tell me the truth in return.

19

Paris, 1840

The snow stopped the very next morning. It was as though the bitter weather had been hanging around with the sole purpose of tormenting Remi, my beloved. Now that he had gone from Paris, the sun came out. The ice melted. It wasn't exactly warm but the very tips of my fingers started to grow pink again. I did not need to wrap my hands in rags and put on all my stockings before I could even venture out of the house.

And venture out I had to, because there was not a thing left in the cupboard. I had wrapped the very last of the bread and cheese for Remi since he was facing a horrible journey. I could take a little hunger for the greater good. But after two days, it was too much. I took a couple of strings of beads to the pawn shop and bought enough wormy old vegetables to make some nasty soup. So much for '*la vie bohémienne*' that inspired Remi's old friends, the 'fascinating young men'. Without Remi to share that soup, there was nothing romantic about it.

Remi had told me it would take him at least a day to walk to the town where he had been born. The snow would have made the journey more difficult than usual. He'd said that when he got to his father's house, he would know at once whether he would be there for a minute or a day. I imagined his father opening the door to him. Remi had not seen Monsieur Pierre Sauvageon in a year. Surely he would not send his son away without inviting him in to warm himself by the fire. And if he had arrived in the afternoon, it would be cruelty itself to send him away again before morning. Remi's father would insist that he stayed the night. And if he stayed the night, he would have to give him breakfast. And lunch too. Any parent would want to make sure that Remi was strong enough to make the return journey – and they'd have more to catch up on than could be talked of over breakfast alone.

I spent the long days making calculations. The earliest he could possibly be back was Tuesday evening. Tuesday evening came and went. I sat by the window. No sign of Remi. But that was a good thing, I told myself. It meant that his family had properly welcomed him. I would not allow myself to think of the other prospect: that he had frozen to death on the walk and never made it to his family's home at all.

Wednesday passed without sign of him too. I had hoped I would receive a letter at least, to tell me how matters were progressing. Nothing. Thursday, the same. Friday. Still nothing at all. I took my best dress and sold it to buy enough to eat over the weekend. I told everyone I met I was looking for work. Anything would do. I would clean. I would sew. I would look after babies. They asked about Remi. I told them he had gone in search of a job too.

Sunday. I listened to the church bells that had once serenaded our lovemaking in the garret. Where was he?

Where was my man? Now I really began to worry. Guerville was not so very far. A letter could have reached me within a day. Why hadn't he written, if he was going to stay away so long? He was dead. He must be. The baker explained to me that the snow was still deep outside the city. It was the city's filth that kept it warm.

Monday. Remi had been gone for a whole week. Though we had never properly married, I was ready to consider myself a widow. I walked through the market like a ghost, not acknowledging my friends, until Jeanne-Marie pulled me into her kitchen and insisted on giving me supper. She warmed my hands between her own.

'We will find your love,' she told me. 'When my husband next goes out, I will tell him to scour the ditches between here and Guerville. If Remi has fallen into one, I promise you, you'll soon know.'

And if he had? He must be dead. I was in agony and misery. I wanted to throw myself into a ditch after him. Until the post arrived . . .

Jeanne-Marie made me a hot drink while I opened the letter with trembling fingers. It was in Remi's hand. That, I said to Jeanne-Marie, was a good thing. He was alive enough to write. I pulled open the seal. Some sort of promissory note fell out. I put that to one side as I read the letter. The more I read, the less it made sense.

> My love for you is putting you in danger of your life. As an artist, I cannot keep you. I cannot put food on the table. I cannot put wood in the fire. How can I love you properly when I am lacking in so many ways?
>
> 'I have made peace with my father and agreed to let him find me employment in the family business.

In return, he will pay off my debts and put a roof over my head. His one condition is that I do not ask you to join me here in Guerville. I told him I have never loved a woman more ardently and he says he understands, but your former mistress's reputation has reached this sleepy town and my father says that to allow you to live under his roof would be to sully the whole family with Arlette Belrose's debauchery. He would be a subject of gossip. My sisters would be unmarriageable. Everyone would suffer. And so I must try to limit the suffering to my own heart.

'I am sorry, Augustine. I send you the enclosed promissory note to bide you over until you are able to find employment again as I am sure you will. Remember me fondly, dear heart.

Ever yours in affection, your Remi.

Limit the suffering to his own heart! What about mine? When I finished reading the letter I collapsed in misery. Jeanne-Marie and her husband carried me upstairs and laid me in their own bed to keep safe while I recovered. When I came back downstairs, I found Jeanne-Marie with the letter in her hand. She and her husband gave me their sympathy.

'I always knew he was a worm,' said Cyril. 'He was playing at being a pauper to inform his bloody art.'

'He loved me,' I tried to say, but the letter certainly suggested otherwise. 'He loves me still. He must.'

'He loves no one but himself,' Cyril told me. 'He loves having a full belly and fancy clothes. He loves the idea of painting a poor person's life. He doesn't want to have to live it.'

'But what should I do?'

'Take the money,' said Jeanne-Marie.

'I couldn't possibly.'

'Take it. There's only enough to keep you for a week, anyway. You deserve a million times more. Get the cash and start looking for a job. Forget all about him. If I see him again, I will not even waste the energy it would take to spit on him.'

'I'll spit on him,' said Cyril. 'I'll black both his little eyes too.'

I burst into tears. I let Jeanne-Marie fold me in her arms. Though the snow had gone completely and spring was on the breath of the wind, I had never felt so cold.

20

I was back in the library for a third day. This time I did not hesitate to log in to the Palazzo Donato's network and send a message to let Marco know I was there. I got no response. I tried to busy myself as usual by looking at the sketches, but they didn't hold my attention for long. Perhaps it's just that I don't know how to appreciate art properly, but after three days of studying the drawings, I wasn't sure what else I could get from them. But I was loath to leave the library in a hurry while the message on the screen was still unanswered.

I got up from the desk and made a tour of the room. There were enough books in the Palazzo Donato library to keep a person reading for a hundred years and, though I had spent many hours there, I didn't really have that clear a view of what the library contained.

I browsed a few of the shelves, picking out books and opening them at random. As a teenager, studying for my A-levels, I had often broken up the monotony of revision by playing a game with myself, whereby I picked up a book, closed my eyes, opened the covers and picked out a line. I later discovered that the game is called stichomancy and it's a well-known way of telling fortunes. I told myself that the line I chose would have a message for me, though of course, I just kept on opening books until I got the exact message I wanted.

That's what I was doing again in Marco's library: pulling out books as if they might give me a sign.

And perhaps they did. While I was absorbed by my little project at the shelves, I became aware of something moving behind me. I spun round, only to realise that I'd been distracted by my own reflection in the mirror where I had once watched myself undress. It was then that it came to me. If there was a secret door in this library, it was perhaps not behind the mirror, but opposite it.

Standing right opposite the mirror, I looked at the shelves again. I ran my fingers along their expertly smooth edges to find a join that might indicate the edge of a door, but it was more difficult than finding the end on a new roll of sticky tape. I couldn't see anything obvious. But then I saw the book. It was *Beauty and the Beast.* My favourite story in an old edition, well-thumbed and well-read. Well-loved. I picked it up and – like a scene in a Hollywood movie – I heard the sound of something shifting. Where the book had been sitting was the tiniest wooden button. The weight of the book must have been holding a lock in place. I pressed the shelf in front of me and it started to move away from me. I had indeed found a door.

As the door shifted, it released a little cloud of dust like a puff of genie's smoke. I was triumphant and at the same time filled with trepidation. My suspicions had been confirmed. I'd found the door and I'd opened it. What now? I found myself looking into a short corridor that I would have to duck to get into. And what was beyond that?

It was dark. It smelled musty. I tentatively put my foot inside, to see if I'd revealed a straightforward hallway or a staircase that I might go tumbling down. There was a floor. It seemed solid.

I stood there for just a few seconds before I decided I would go for it. I would see what was on the other side. If Silvio caught me? So what? I had seen Remi Sauvageon's sketches. I didn't think I could get anything more from staring at them for another day. And if I found Marco sitting on the other side like some modern-day wizard of Oz? At least I would have seen him in the flesh. A mystery would have been solved. And maybe, just maybe, he would be pleased to see me.

So I stepped into the corridor. The first thing I wanted to do was satisfy my suspicion about something. I closed the door slightly again and examined the back of it. Yes. There it was. A little spyhole. I put my eye to it, just as Augustine had put her eye to the hole in her bedroom floor and watched Arlette with her clients. As I had also suspected it might, the spyhole made perfect sense of the positioning of the mirror. Though it was difficult to see anything close up, I could see the reflection of my desk and chair quite easily.

Turning back into the corridor, I could see another door just a couple of feet ahead of me. Another door with another spyhole. I put my eye to this one too.

I'm not sure what I expected. A dungeon, perhaps? A red room of pain? Thankfully there was none of that. Beyond the second door was a room that appeared to be an office. It was a small room but it had a high ceiling and was beautifully lit by a large, long window, as though it had once been part of the library. Right in front of me as I looked, was a desk. On the desk, a computer. In front of the desk, a modern office chair, ergonomically designed to prevent backache. There didn't appear to be anyone in there.

I felt like Bluebeard's wife as I pushed open that other door to this room that I was obviously not meant to know about, let alone enter. But I was somewhat emboldened by my discovery of the spyhole that led into the library. If I was confronted, I now had plenty of ammunition with which to turn my trespassing into a righteous search to find out what exactly went on at the Palazzo Donato. I still hoped that I would not find a camera.

I propped both doors open using my shoes. The last thing I needed was to go into this secret room and find myself trapped inside it. What if Silvio didn't know about the secret passage either?

So there I was in the secret lair. It was an ordinary sort of room, insofar as a room in a Venetian palazzo can ever be ordinary. But what I mean to say is that there was nothing in the room that was immediately shocking, or even surprising. I could see no camera, either for stills or otherwise. That made me very relieved.

Had someone been here very recently? I wondered. A jacket hung over the back of the ergonomic chair as though its owner had just stepped outside for a cigarette and wanted to keep his place. I lifted one of the sleeves and put my nose to it. The grey woollen fabric was soft and expensive. The label proclaimed it to be Italian cashmere, of course. A faint scent clung to it. A smell of sandalwood and musk, fresh soap. It was a good smell, one that I wouldn't have minded inhaling as I buried my face in the jacket owner's neck. And surely the owner had to be Marco.

Next I picked up a wooden sculpture of Buddha, which was holding some papers in place. It was worn smooth by years of worrying by someone's fingers. Marco's fingers. Had to be. The thought of touching something he had held gave the cheap wooden knick-knack a quality of pricelessness. I wondered when he had picked it up. Was it a souvenir from his travels or a gift?

There was another Buddha on an occasional table by the window, but this one was made of marble and looked heavy and precious. It was almost certainly a genuine antique rather than a reproduction. I touched its face and wondered about the significance of these two symbols of tranquillity.

Apart from the two Buddhas, there were no other works of art that I could see. At least, there were no paintings and no photographs. I found the lack of photos in particular a little strange, but then perhaps people don't bother so much with printing out photographs these days, preferring instead to keep everything digital.

The computer on the desk might hold the secret, I thought. It was a fairly new Mac. It was in rest mode, so I moved the mouse to see if I could bring it to life. The screen glowed, but asked for a password before it would show me anything more. I tried the password Marco had given me for the Palazzo Donato's network. Nothing. I tried my own name. That didn't work either. I tried 'Chiara'. Still no joy. The screen remained blank and impassive. But it must be Marco's computer, I decided. Why did he need to lock it when it lived in a secret room?

Thinking I heard the sound of footsteps somewhere behind me, I stepped back to the doorway for a moment and listened to see if there was anyone in the library. Nothing. It was safe to keep looking.

I turned my attention to the pile of papers beneath the wooden Buddha. Mostly bills. City rates. Maintenance. A place like the Palazzo Donato must require plenty of that. But there were also invoices from auction houses. And Marco had been on something of a spending spree with an online antique book dealer based in London. I read the titles in a list of recently acquired volumes with interest. There were several which I'd read myself when I was studying for my MA. They were books that I had mentioned to Marco, when explaining how I came to be interested in Luciana Giordano. I remembered that. I found it quite flattering that he had sought the books out. My heart swelled when I saw how recently he'd ordered them. He'd bought the books *since* the ball but before I emailed him about Sauvageon's sketchbook. I allowed myself to believe he had been thinking of me, despite the fact that he hadn't been in touch.

Buoyed by that thought, I continued to sift through the papers like a detective, taking great care to replace them exactly as I found them.

Then I found the first drawing.

It was at the very bottom of the pile of papers on Marco's desk. A thick sheet of cartridge paper, ragged at the edges as though it had been torn from a sketchbook. I lifted it up to the light of the window to see it better. I wondered at first if this was a loose sheet from Remi Sauvageon's sketchbook. I had noticed while I was studying his drawings that some sheets had been pulled out. The style of the drawing was familiar. The confident pencil strokes could have been by Remi's hand. But the subject . . . well, it definitely wasn't Augustine.

It was me. There was no doubt about it. I had found a sketch of *me* sitting at the desk in the library. It must have been made back in January, judging by the clothes I was wearing. I was dressed in my favourite jumper: the one that Bea said was just a little too much like the one the detective in *The Killing* wore for weeks on end. It was a good likeness. You couldn't see my face, but the shape of my head and the way my hair fell down my back was definitely me. As was the hunch of my shoulders. I cringed a little at that. My secondary-school PE teacher had always nagged at me to work on my posture. She warned me that a life spent at a desk could land me with a dowager's hump. I was certainly hunching over my books in this sketch.

But though I wasn't entirely flattered by the artist's accuracy, I could see that the sketch had been drawn with affection, just as Remi had drawn Augustine with a tenderness that made her domestic chores as beautiful as ballet. That the sketch had been drawn without my knowledge, however, was another thing.

This drawing must have been by Marco's hand, which meant I had confirmation, beyond a shadow of a doubt, that he had been in the house while I was there. At least once. He had watched me for long enough to make a sketch, for goodness' sake!

I wondered if there were any more.

I went back to the door and listened for any hint of movement in the library beyond. When again I heard nothing, I returned to my fingertip search of the secret office. Not that I cared so much if I was found out now. I would just flourish the drawing in Marco's face.

'Try and deny you were here all the time!'

And indeed, I found another sketch. In this one, I was wearing a pair of trousers that Bea had picked out for me. I had kicked off my shoes beneath the desk. I was chewing on the end of a biro. My face was turned slightly towards the artist now and he had captured me very well. He'd got my good side, in fact. Whenever I had a chance to pose for a photograph, I would always try to turn slightly to the right and that was how he had me posed.

I looked at my feet in the sketch. He'd captured them beautifully too. I was rubbing them together, trying to keep them warm while my socks dried next to the fire.

I was desperate to see more. I flicked through a pile of papers on a shelf to the side of the desk, looking for the telltale thickness of the cartridge paper. I quickly found two more drawings. In one I was standing, with my head slightly to one side, looking at the portrait of Ernesta Donato that hung above the mantelpiece. Not only had Marco made a beautiful likeness of me, he had drawn the antique portrait too, finding the essence of Ernesta with just a few patches of shading.

Marco was a wonderful artist. I tried to recall if he'd ever mentioned a love of drawing. I didn't think so, but this must be why he was drawn to Remi Sauvageon. He'd found a kindred spirit.

Then I found the drawing that took my breath away. It was me, at the desk, with the skirt of my dress hitched up to my thighs and my hands between my legs.

There was no way that he could have imagined this pose. I knew he had drawn it from life and I knew exactly when he had done it. I stared at the picture. My head was tipped back. My mouth was slightly open. My eyes were tight shut. I was in a state of utter abandon.

This was all I needed to see. I was tempted to fold it up and put it in my pocket. Instead, because I still did not know quite how I was going to play this latest development, I put the sketch back where I had found it. And because now I really could hear noise nearby, I decided it was high time I left. I picked up my shoes and closed the doors behind me. When I met Silvio in the courtyard minutes later, I was the picture of innocence. The very opposite of the last sketch I had found in Marco's secret room.

'How is your research coming along?' Silvio asked.

'Very well,' I said. 'I think something about the Venetian air must inspire me.'

'Even in the summer, when everything smells of rotting fish?'

'It's not that bad,' I said.

Silvio shrugged.

'I will be leaving to visit my sister soon. I need to close the house up.'

'Of course,' I said. 'I think I've done enough for the day.'

I'd certainly seen enough.

I left the house in a buoyant mood. I had uncovered some of the Palazzo Donato's secrets and confirmed for myself what I'd always suspected. Marco Donato may once have been a globetrotting playboy but on several occasions earlier that year, when he claimed to be away on business, he must have been very much at home.

I held the secret of those drawings close to me as I wandered back through the twisting streets to my hotel.

Apart from anything else, it was an enormous relief to discover I had not been entirely deluded to think that Marco had feelings for me. Those drawings – just like Remi Sauvageon's drawings of Augustine – showed me as my best self. They showed me through the eyes of someone who liked, maybe even loved, the person he was looking at. They gave me the courage to keep trying to break through.

That night, I sent Marco another email.

'I had a very productive day in the library,' I wrote. 'Very productive indeed. In fact I think I may have made a sort of breakthrough which has enabled me to see Remi Sauvageon's sketches in a totally different light.'

I hoped that sentence would pique Marco's interest. Tantalise him. Worry him, even.

'I'd love to tell you all about it,' I continued. 'I'm still at the Bauer. You can call me here. Perhaps you'd like to meet for dinner. Short notice would be fine.'

I pressed send and felt the familiar flutter of anticipation and anxiety.

But of course, I heard nothing. There was no reply. I spent the rest of the evening writing up my notes about Remi and adding my own observations and thoughts on his relationship to his sitter. Remi had obviously been greatly in love with Augustine. His pictures were the evidence of that. They corroborated Augustine's memoirs. Afterwards, I picked up Augustine's book again, hoping to read that Remi had found a way to persuade his father to accept the prostitute's housemaid as his daughter-in-law and that the young lovers were safely back together again. I was in a state of mind where I thought that love could conquer everything. I was to be disappointed. On Augustine's behalf, at least.

21

Paris, 1840

A couple of days after I received the news that Remi would not be coming back to Paris, I took the promissory note he had sent me – I noticed with disgust that it was drawn against his father's account – and exchanged it for some money. It was enough to pay for our room for another two weeks. However, I was determined not to let that be the end of it. I used some of the money to send a letter back to him, writing on the unused side of his own letter because I could not waste a sou on a clean sheet of paper. I begged him to reconsider. I told him, which was true, that I had persuaded three people to let me mend their clothes in the space of an afternoon. With determined effort, I could build up a proper clientele. I might find some people who wanted me to make clothes as well as mend them. Start an atelier. He could paint there. We would easily have enough to live on once he got a few commissions. Things would turn around.

The winter would soon be over. Come the summer, our little garret on the Rue de Seine would be Heaven again. 'Remember how happy we were last summer,' I pleaded. 'When we ended every day naked in one another's arms? Remember what it felt like to make love as the daylight faded.'

Knowing that this might be my last chance to persuade Remi to come back, I decided I would not hold back. I described the first time we made love in our little room.

> Do you recall how very happy we were that evening? You told me we were beginning our new life and that we should take a moment to savour the day in all its glory so that when we were old, and living in a château on the profits of your painting, we could tell our children how it all started, when we were young and had nothing but our love and this little room?
>
> And then you said that we should try out the bed, to make sure that the landlord had not given us a lumpy mattress. You picked me up and threw me down onto it, so that I landed in a heap of skirts and giggles. You had me naked within a minute, underneath the scratchy blanket. You promised that the very next day you would sell ten sketches to buy me some silk sheets. I didn't care. I would have slept on a sack so long as you were beside me. In any case, I soon forgot about the scratchy blankets when I felt your hands upon me, smoothing away any trepidation and cares. In your hands, I always felt most safe and alive.
>
> We can have all this again, dear Remi. Next year will be easier, I know it.

But Remi was not to be persuaded. He did send me a response but he told me that it wasn't just a matter of practicality. He told me he had been trying to spare my feelings by suggesting as much. Long conversation with his father had convinced him that he had taken a wrong turning in life. He loved me deeply but we were two people who should never have met in normal circumstances, let alone considered making a life together. He had responsibilities to the people who raised him. I would find the life of a middle-class wife stifling and dull.

If only he would let me find that out.

'We're from different stock,' he wrote.

'Not that different!' I exclaimed to myself. We may have met in a kept woman's house but I came from an honest family. My parents were good people who taught me right from wrong.

'To continue on this path will only bring misery to us both. It is for the best,' he finished his letter.

'Those words should harden your heart,' my friends told me.

My heart would never do as it was told. I could not give up on my love.

22

Augustine's was not the only heart that would not do as it was told.

I had no reply to my email, but the following day, I was still buoyed by the thought that Marco had been in the house while I was there and that he was interested enough in me to sketch me with such delicacy. I thought about the things he had said about Sauvageon's sketches and wondered if he was actually projecting his own thoughts: that to produce such a beautiful drawing takes a special degree of feeling between the artist and his subject.

Back in the library, I sat down at the desk. I opened my laptop and logged on to the Palazzo's network. I sent a message of greeting.

This time I got a reply.

'Did you get my email?' I asked.

'I did. I'm sorry. I was busy. I should at least have responded in the negative.'

'That's OK,' I said. 'Marco, I have been meaning to make a confession to you.'

'Really?'

'Yes. That beautiful dress you bought for me, the one I was supposed to wear to the ball. I didn't wear it. My friend Bea did.'

Marco did not respond.

'I had an idea that it would fun to double-bluff you on the disguise front. I guessed that you had sent me the dress so that you would be able to pick me out easily in the crowd of masked revellers. I thought you'd make a beeline for the dress you'd picked out so I persuaded Bea to wear it so that I could observe you from afar. You see, wearing the dress would put me at something of a disadvantage, given that I assumed you would be wearing the same as every other man at the party. I'd never be able to pick you out until you revealed yourself to me. I wanted to see you from a distance. Just for a little while.'

'I see.'

'But, of course, you weren't even there.'

'No.'

'You were in Hong Kong.'

'I was.'

He still wasn't going to change his tune on that front.

Of course, having seen the whole scene, I knew for sure he couldn't have mistaken Bea for me. Now, I was just trying to draw him out.

'I hope you're not offended,' I pressed on. 'I realise that the dress must have cost you a fortune. Perhaps it was an ungrateful thing to do – pass your gift on to a woman you don't even know – but I was also feeling very vulnerable about our first meeting in person. After that morning in the library, I was left with the sense that you suddenly knew me rather better than I knew you.'

'What makes you say that?'

'I would have thought it was obvious. You called all the shots. I was the one who stripped off. There might have been a camera.'

'There was no camera.'

'I believe that now.'

'You do? Why?'

'You'd have put the footage on YouTube, surely.'

'I'm really not that kind of man.'

I let the screen stay still for a moment, giving him a chance to take the conversation forward. He didn't and so I asked.

'Marco, do you ever think about that morning?'

Ten seconds, twenty seconds, thirty seconds passed.

'Yes,' his answer appeared.

'But what do you think about when you remember that day? Just the words on the screen? I at least got some physical enjoyment.'

'I got plenty of enjoyment thinking about you following my instructions.'

'Wouldn't it have been better to be able to see me at the same time?'

'We agreed, no cameras. I didn't want to betray your trust. It was enough for me just to think that I was having some influence over you from afar and to receive your confirmation.'

'It was quite an experience for me,' I said. 'To let you give me those instructions.'

I waited for a moment again.

'I've often thought about repeating the experience.'

As I typed those words, it was difficult not to glance in the direction of the shelves which I now knew for certain concealed the door to Marco's very private office. I forced myself to keep my eyes on the screen and a smile off my lips, but it was thrilling, thinking that he was almost certainly just a few metres away from me, sitting at the desk I had explored in the room where I had discovered so much about him. And about his feelings for me. After a minute, his reply came.

'Me too.'

'We could do it again right now, if you like. I'm waiting for you to tell me where to start.'

'There's nothing in the drawer,' wrote Marco.

'I know,' I wrote back. 'I've already checked. It doesn't matter. I can use my fingers.'

A pause.

'It's not the right time. Silvio is in the house and—'

'Silvio won't come in,' I typed. 'He hasn't disturbed me in the library since the first couple of days I was here. I can't think of a better time. You've already got me thinking about that morning back in February. Are you really going to let me go back to my hotel in a state of frustration?'

I looked at the words I'd just typed. They seemed slightly out of character, a little too forward. 'Frustration'? I wondered if I'd made a mistake and pushed too far too quickly. But then I thought of Marco on the other side of the wall, hiding in his little office. What a coward. He deserved a bit of a prod.

'OK,' he wrote at last. 'If it's what you want.'

'Is it what *you* want?' I asked him in reply.

'Of course. I always want to think of you in the library, turned on by the thought of me.'

'Turned on *by* you. Following your instructions. Talk to me, Marco. Tell me what to do.'

'What are you wearing?' he began.

23

What am I wearing? You *know*, I wanted to tell him. Because you're looking right at me now.

Instead, I played the game. 'It's hot outside today so I am wearing a summer dress. I've had it for years. The fabric is linen. It's been washed countless times and it's very soft and worn. The dress is blue like faded denim. It has a fitted bodice with short cap sleeves and a big skirt. It's a shirt dress, with buttons all the way down the front. I've undone the top two buttons so you can almost see the top of my bra.'

'What's that like?' Marco asked.

'It's cotton,' I said. 'Because of the heat. It's a pale pink colour, with lace round the edge of the cups. It isn't underwired but it fits me perfectly and holds me in place very well. The main fabric is quite thin. You can see the outline of my nipples clearly.'

'And knickers?'

'They match, of course. They are bikini style, but quite scanty. They cover my pubic hair but you can see the shadow through the thinness of the cotton.'

'On your feet?'

'Sandals. But now . . .' I kicked them off. 'Nothing.'

I thought of Marco's sketch of me sitting at the desk with no shoes on. It must have been made the day I got soaked on my way to the library and had to take my shoes and socks off because they were so wet. I'd draped the socks over the bench in front of the fire to let them dry. Now I had no socks on because it was so hot.

'I've painted my toenails,' I told him. 'It's a deep sparkling red called "I'm not really a waitress".'

'Sounds sexy,' he wrote.

'It is.'

I stretched one foot out in front of me and admired my own handiwork. I was putting on a far better show than I had the last time we did this, now that I knew Marco could see me if he wanted to, yet I was still careful not to give my secret knowledge away. Was he at the spyhole already, sending his messages using a laptop or a tablet? I had to assume that he was. Had he moved his chair into that tiny dark corridor? Did he have his sketchbook open on his lap, ready to capture me for posterity with his expert pencil strokes? Was that all he did? Did he merely set down the scene with a pencil or was he touching himself as I touched myself?

'What are *you* wearing?' I ventured to ask.

'This isn't about me,' came his reply.

'OK. Tell me what you want me to do next.'

'Undo some more buttons on your dress. Undo them all, so that it falls open and your underwear is exposed.'

'OK.'

Slowly and very deliberately, I began to undo the buttons. The dress was old and the buttons came undone easily, so I hesitated between each one, prolonging the moment when the dress would fall open completely.

'Stand up. Push the dress off your shoulders. Let it fall to the floor.'

I stood up. It was different this time. I did not feel as vulnerable as before. Not now that I had knowledge of Marco's little secret. I was playing him. I was in control. This moment was going to be a game-changer. I decided I would force Marco into a situation where he had to reveal himself. I would be so wild and wonderful that he simply could not resist.

I moved my chair so that it no longer faced the desk directly but instead faced the mirror. Knowing that the mirror had been placed to enable Marco the best possible view, I played up to his ingenuity and made sure that he got my whole reflection. I moved my chair a little closer to the mirror too.

I let my hand stray to the front of my knickers. I pulled the fabric to one side, exposing just a glimpse of my pubic hair.

'Are you touching yourself?' Marco asked me.

I typed with one hand. 'You know I am.'

'Good,' he wrote. 'Do what you usually do to turn yourself on.'

'Tell me what that should be?'

'I don't know,' Marco's words appeared. That was odd. It was almost nervous. I couldn't stop myself – I glanced in the direction of the hidden door. 'Stroke yourself?'

'OK.'

I began to play with my clitoris. Moistening my finger between my lips, I started to circle the little pink nub. I held my labia apart so that it was more exposed. I kept glancing to the screen to see how Marco responded.

'How does that feel? Is it good? I want you to think of my hands upon you. I want you to think of me standing behind you and holding your breasts while you continue to play with yourself.'

I let my head loll back, consciously emulating the pose in Marco's drawing. I let my mouth fall slightly open as I began to breathe more heavily. I wasn't faking my excitement.

I opened my eyes again for Marco's next instruction.

'I want you to imagine that I am between your legs now. I am standing in front of you with my cock in my hand. I want you to open yourself up to me. Make yourself wet so that I can slip into you. I want to be inside you.'

He had not suggested such a thing before. The thought of it made me more excited than ever. Continuing to touch myself, I looked steadily in the direction of the place where I knew the spyhole to be. I imagined his eye to that hole. I was looking straight into it. I kept my gaze right on him as I started to come.

The 'ping' of a message notification broke through the moment.

'I think that's enough,' Marco wrote.

I stood up abruptly.

'What?' I said out loud. 'What's the matter?'

But of course, Marco couldn't answer that. Not when he wasn't supposed to be able to hear me. I typed my frustration for his benefit.

'We shouldn't be doing this,' he responded.

'But we are,' I wrote. 'And I was enjoying it. Weren't you?'

'That's beside the point. This isn't right. I shouldn't have got involved in this. You should leave as soon as you can after you've got all the information you need regarding that sketchbook.'

'I didn't come to Venice for the sketchbook,' I confessed then.

'Then I don't know why you did come here,' wrote Marco.

'Are you crazy?'

'I'm just not sure I understand what you're getting at.'

'The sketches were an excuse. Though they seemed like a Heaven-sent one. Like a sign.'

'A coincidence.'

'A coincidence that you could have stopped from developing any further. When I asked to see them, you wrote straight back to me. Why would you have done that if you didn't want to see me too?'

'I wrote back out of politeness. I always respond to email.'

'Not true,' I pointed out. 'And in any case, you don't seem to find it so hard to tell people they can't come to the Palazzo.

You told Bea that the library was no longer open to members of the general public only a couple of weeks ago.'

'What does that have to do with anything?'

'You could have said the same to me. But you didn't, because you wanted me to come here again. You wanted to see me as much as I wanted to see you.'

'But we haven't seen each other.'

Ah. It was so tempting then to tell him that I knew that wasn't entirely the case.

'We could see each other right this minute. Marco, I know you are in this house. I know you've been watching me.'

'That's not true.'

'Why should I believe you?'

'Sarah, this isn't a conversation we need to have. I shouldn't have disturbed you. Please, carry on with your work.'

I sat down at the desk and typed a diatribe at high speed.

'Why do you try to act as though nothing ever happened between us? We may never have been in the same room at the same time, but with your encouragement, I did things I would never have considered without you. Does that really mean so little to you? I'm sure it will come as no surprise to you to hear that I worried you'd set up a webcam in the library but I pushed that to the back of my mind because I trusted you. When you announced that you were throwing a ball in my honour, I started to think that you were the honest person you claimed to be, but then you disappeared.'

'Sarah, I did not mean to lead you on in any way and I am sorry if I did. I thought that you and I were just having a bit of fun: killing time while we both had to be at our desks. I am sorry you're disappointed at the way things have worked out – or rather not worked out – between us. I've explained my reasons. I'm too busy to have a relationship.'

'That's the lamest excuse I've ever heard. No one is too busy to have a relationship.'

'I didn't ask you to come back to Venice. I let you back into my library because I know how important it is to you that you be thorough in your research. Had I known that you would see the existence of Remi Sauvageon's sketches in my collection as some kind of "sign" that you and I were meant to continue our silly online romance, then I would have had Silvio package them up and send them to Paris instead.'

'You said that you missed me.'

'And I did miss you, in the way that I miss lots of my friends when I'm working too hard, but you have to let go of the idea that we can ever be more than friends.'

'We're hardly even that, having never actually met.'

'Then perhaps we should just leave this conversation where it is and get back to our respective lives. You are, of course, welcome to stay in the library until you've finished everything you wanted to get done. Goodbye.'

Is that it?

I sent another message into the void.

That was it. Marco Donato had nothing more to say to me.

I glared at the wall that held the secret door, willing it to open, willing him to step out from his cave and tell me to my face that I should give up on him. If he was watching me still, he did not respond to my challenge. I had to give up. I picked up my dress from the floor and pulled it on. I buttoned it quickly, suddenly wanting to hide myself away.

If the book in front of me hadn't been a priceless original sketchbook by one of the world's greatest Impressionist painters, I would have swept it off the desk and onto the floor. I was so angry. Marco Donato was such an asshole! He had let me try to seduce him, then talked to me as though I were some stupid schoolgirl with an inappropriate crush.

I put Remi Sauvageon's book back into its protective

covering, shut down my laptop and loaded it into my bag. Forget staying in the library until I'd finished everything I wanted to get done. I just wanted to get out of there. I felt stupid and humiliated. If Marco wanted to obliterate every shred of friendship we'd built up over the past few months then he had done a damn good job.

I would leave Venice as soon as I could. Not that night, because Nick and Bea were expecting to see me, but first thing the following morning. Never mind that I had one of the best rooms at the Palazzo Bauer and I didn't have to pay for it. I just wanted to be a long way away from anything that reminded me of Marco Donato. I didn't need to stay in a city where even one person considered me unwelcome.

24

I met Nick and Bea again that evening. It was a Friday and they didn't need much encouragement to embark upon a truly epic night, fuelled by innumerable spritzes and three bottles of prosecco.

It was so nice to be in their company, though frustrating too. I was longing to tell someone about my latest experience in the library but of course I couldn't tell anyone. I mean, how would the conversation have gone? 'Hey? Guess what? I took off all my clothes in the library again and brought myself to a climax while a man I've never met sent instructions via laptop from his secret room.'

What kind of response would I get to a story like that? Instead, I regaled my friends with stories about the lives of the great courtesans of Paris. I stuck to history. That was what I did best and, of course, I had a willing audience in my fellow historians.

We sat outside the bar, as usual. It was a tiny place and, even on the coldest nights, the clientele spilled out onto the bridge opposite. While Nick was inside, getting the last bottle of prosecco, Bea raised the subject I had thought I would avoid.

'So?' she said. 'Did you see him?'

'Who?' I bluffed.

'Who! The mysterious billionaire. Marco Donato.'

'Of course not.'

'Has he emailed you since you've been here?'

I thought about lying but instead I nodded. 'He has.'

'And was it the same as before?'

'No. It wasn't.'

'Good. It was all a bit strange, him emailing a hundred times a day but refusing to meet up. You don't need strange,' said Bea. 'I don't understand why it ever attracted you.'

I couldn't claim to understand myself, though I tried to elaborate for Bea.

'I felt like I knew him,' I said. 'We wrote to each other so often. He seemed to be so open and vulnerable. He was in my head all the time.'

'It was just a way of distracting yourself over Steven,' Bea suggested. 'And now you're properly over Steven – or so you say – you don't need that crutch any more.'

And then Nick was back and the conversation was over as quickly as it had begun. He poured out three glasses. We toasted each other. We toasted Venice. We toasted each other again. Then Nick toasted me.

'Sarah. We're so happy to have you back.'

Bea gave me a sly look.

Later, I invited Nick into the hotel for a drink. After all, I wouldn't be paying.

We'd drunk an awful lot that night. I don't think anyone would be surprised by what happened next.

The bar at the Bauer was closed by the time we got back there, so we went up to my suite and opened the minibar. It was still so balmy outside there was no question that we would sit on the balcony. I had noticed that when the days were so hot, the citizens of Venice became nocturnal. The canal was still busy with people making the most of the slight drop in temperature before the sun came back up and it was too hot to be out again.

Nick and I positioned ourselves on two chairs, looking out over the scene. The moon was almost full. It cast a silvery sheen over the inky blue water. There was a sense of magic taking place, as there always was in Venice at night. It was as though we had fallen through a tear in the fabric of time and might be anywhere in the continuum from three hundred years past to three hundred years into the future. I made the observation to Nick.

'Being in Venice is like being in a loop in reality,' he agreed. 'It's quite humbling to think that this place hasn't changed in so long and isn't likely to change much for generations to come either. But it's quite liberating too, to realise that it doesn't really matter what we do. The city will outlive us. The world will outlive us. We're unlikely even to be a footnote in its history.'

That much was true. I thought about Luciana. If she hadn't left her diary, who would know anything about her at all? And Augustine. How many of their contemporaries had been completely forgotten?

'So what you're saying is, we should eat, drink and behave as badly as we like because no one will remember?'

'Pretty much. I certainly don't think I'll remember a great deal tomorrow morning,' said Nick, as he examined the label on the bottle we had barely begun.

'Me neither.'

'In that case . . .'

Nick got up from his chair and walked over to mine. He pulled me to my feet. And then he kissed me.

Nick's kiss was so gentle. It was full of meaning and yet there was no real sense of expectation. I had held him at arm's length for so long. But this time was different. When Nick pulled away from me, I took hold of his collar and pulled him close again. This time, I was the one planting my lips on his. Nick was clearly startled. He froze, with his hands fanned out stiffly at his sides, as though I had slapped him on either side of the face with a kipper instead of a kiss.

'Sarah,' he began.

'Don't talk,' I said. 'Just kiss me again.'

Nick didn't need to be asked twice. Right there on the balcony, we embraced as ardently as any of the city's lovers that night. I needed to be held. I needed to feel attractive. I was so frustrated by that morning's events in the library that I was ready to do anything. I let my hands roam all over Nick's back, feeling his muscles beneath the fabric of the shirt. I felt his hands begin their own tentative exploration. Why shouldn't we do this, I thought.

Then, from the corner of my eye, I saw a gondola. It seemed to pause in the middle of the canal, as though waiting for something. Watching. The *felce* might have been empty, but I had the distinct feeling that it wasn't and, furthermore, that it contained someone I knew.

'Shall we—?' Nick asked.

'I—' I was momentarily lost for words. 'I can't. I'm sorry. I can't.'

Once again, I left him hanging.

Nick shrugged and picked up his jacket.

I cringed when I considered what I had done to poor Nick. I had needed a boost to my ego and he had been kind enough to provide one. If I hadn't seen that gondola, would I have carried on? Why did it stop me, anyway? Was it because it reminded me of Luciana's lover? And, by extension, of Marco? It wouldn't have been him. It couldn't.

Splashing water on my face, I chastised myself for having taken advantage of Nick. It was a good job it had not gone further. I mean, it was bad enough as it was but at least I wasn't going to have to wake up beside him. Thank goodness I would be gone first thing in the morning.

I bustled around the room, throwing my clothes back into my suitcase in preparation for my early start.

What was the matter with me? Why did I persist in banging my head against a brick wall? If Marco wanted to keep me at arm's length or keep himself hidden away in that little secret office, then all I could do was leave him to his hermit-like misery. It didn't matter that he had drawn those beautiful pictures of me and that I was certain he had fallen in love just as I had. I had to forget those drawings. It was too complicated. Too difficult. I didn't need a tortured and tortuous sort of love. I had to move on. Just like Augustine.

The following morning, I had the hotel concierge order a water-taxi to take me to the airport. I learned, alas, that there really was no other way to get out to the Lido except by going onto the Grand Canal and past the Palazzo Donato. But this time, as I passed the house, I did not strain for one last glimpse of a beloved face at a window. Instead, I kept my eyes firmly fixed on the houses on the opposite side of the canal. Marco Donato no longer existed for me.

25

Paris, 1840

Remi was lost to me. I was entirely on my own again, just as I had been when my mother died. But that felt like a hundred lifetimes ago. Back then, newly orphaned in the attic room at Monsieur Griff's house, I was naive and thought that everything would work out for the best if only I prayed hard enough. Now I had a less hopeful view of the world. People were not as they first appeared. You could not rely on their kindness.

That said, my neighbours in the Rue de Seine helped me whenever they could, but in truth they had as little to their names as I did. I could not continue to rely on their charity. I had to look further afield. I had experience as a lady's maid, of course, but who would want to take me on when the only position I had ever held was in the house of a courtesan? And the way my employment there had ended! If even a courtesan would not give me a good letter of recommendation, why should any decent woman take a risk?

But then, about two weeks after Remi left my arms, I saw Elaine in the market. I had expected her to ignore me as she'd told me Arlette commanded after my last visit, but instead she grabbed my hands and kissed me as though I were a long lost sister.

'You poor thing!' she said. 'I heard what that posh bastard did to you.'

'How?' I asked.

'You stayed with Jeanne-Marie.' Elaine rolled her eyes. 'How could I not hear? She's the biggest gossip in the whole of Paris. But what are you doing now?'

I told her my predicament. No lover, no job and rapidly running out of favours.

'Come with me,' she said. 'Arlette has dismissed three maids since Remi spirited you off. Now that he's off the scene, she will be delighted to have you back.'

It was more than I could have hoped for. Like Elaine, Arlette greeted me as though I were family. She clucked as I told her about Remi.

'What use is such a cowardly heart to any woman?' she sighed.

'But he's my true love!'

'He's just a man.'

Within an hour I was back in her household. I was back in my *chambre de bonne*, small but warm and comforting and entirely my own for as long as I needed it. I even looked forward to the arrival of my mistress's guests. I felt I had come home.

For the next six months, I worked hard to show Arlette how much I appreciated her renewed trust in me. It soon felt as though I had never been away. The only difference now was that I no longer rolled back the carpet in my little room to watch Arlette and her lovers through the hole in the floor. I could not bear the feelings or the memories it aroused in me to see Arlette in the throes of love. Thank goodness she had broken with the poet. I did not want to hear anything of Remi Sauvageon.

'Not even that he's dying of syphilis?' asked Elaine. She had a dark sense of humour.

'Especially not that,' I confirmed.

I just wanted to forget I had ever met him and live out the rest of my days in a sort of cloistered existence: cooking, cleaning and repairing clothes. I would never allow love to touch me again.

But I was not to remain Arlette's maid for very long. About seven months after I had moved back to her house, she had a visit from an old friend. Clemence Babineaux was one of the wealthiest kept women in Paris. She'd had more lovers than there were days in the year and had amassed a finer collection of jewels than a tsarina. At that moment, she was the mistress of a Prussian count, a Reichsgraf, who had bought her a château and a diamond that was said to be the second largest in the world.

Arlette was in awe of Clemence Babineaux. She hung on the older woman's every word, looking to her for the best advice in fashion, art and etiquette.

'Hard to believe that Clemence was born in a Marseilles slum,' Elaine whispered to me.

It wasn't so hard to believe that Clemence was born in a slum when you watched her closely. She may have looked as elegant and delicate as any high-born lady, but beneath her delicacy was the shrewdness that could turn three sous into an empire. Like Arlette's mother, Clemence had seen how beauty could be turned into riches with just a little effort. Clemence was about to work that alchemy on me.

* * *

When I went into the salon to serve Arlette and her esteemed friend some tea, Clemence tipped her head on one side and regarded me with interest.

'And who is this?' she asked.

'Oh, this is my beloved Augustine,' said Arlette. 'She's an orphan from Brittany. I found her in the Bois de Boulogne.'

'What? Living there?'

I explained the actual circumstances, to Clemence's great amusement.

'Well, you're wasted as a housemaid. Arlette, you must bring this girl to the Opéra. I can think of a great many people who would like to make her acquaintance.' Then Clemence leaned in close to Arlette and whispered something I couldn't quite hear. In response, Arlette looked at me and smiled broadly.

'Yes. Yes!' she said. 'You are exactly right. And Augustine loves music. We will see you at the Opéra on Thursday.'

26

So I went back to Paris. My hopes for my trip to Venice had come to nothing but I still had a job to do. Greg Simon was anxious to see some of my work. He told me that a handful of very hot young Hollywood stars were interested in the roles of Augustine and Remi and he wanted to give their agents something to look at. In fact, Greg emailed later, it was urgent. I was beginning to understand how the Hollywood system worked. Greg explained that the sooner we had some stars 'attached' to the project, the easier it would be to raise more funds.

I duly promised him that I would distil Augustine and Remi's great love story into 2,000 words by the following weekend. That would be much easier to do in Paris, a city that had no associations with Marco. I could put him to the back of my mind and simply get on with my work.

Or so I hoped, but no matter how hard I tried not to think about him, Marco kept creeping back into the corners of my mind. It didn't help that I was reading about Augustine's own efforts to put Remi out of her own thoughts. I knew exactly how she felt when she wrote about those horrible hours in the middle of the night, when you wake up alone and know that your lover is lost to you for ever. Worse still, you can't stop going over and over the last time you were in contact, wondering what you did, what you said, to make them run. It doesn't even help when your friends tell you – as Bea did – that you're not the one to blame.

I wasn't the one who was hiding in a secret room and watching through a peephole. Despite acting like a nut over Marco, my behaviour was still within the realms of normal. I clung to that idea.

Soon I had been in the apartment for three days straight, not venturing outside the front door at all, just reading and writing and editing for hours on end. It was ridiculous. It wasn't just that I was running out of provisions and was living on biscuits. I was in Paris, a city that people crossed oceans to visit, having saved for years to be able to afford the trip. What's more, I was there all expenses paid, staying in a beautiful apartment in one of the chicest parts of town. It was rude not to take advantage of the opportunity that lay before me. Besides, I told myself, taking a walk around the city might rejuvenate my creative spirit and help me get those 2,000 words finished in time.

Closing my laptop for the first time in seventy-two hours, I set out.

It was a beautiful day. Warm and bright. Not a cloud in the sky. The streets were crowded with tourists enjoying the sunshine. I hadn't been walking for long when I started to feel so hot that I had to unwind the scarf that had been the chic touch I hoped would mark me out from the daytrippers. I wrapped it round the handle of my bag.

I decided to head for the Rue de Seine, where Augustine and Remi had their little love-nest that ill-fated winter. I wasn't sure the building where they had lived would still exist, but I hoped at least to be able to soak up some of the atmosphere. I crossed the wooden Pont des Arts, with its criss-cross metal fences weighed down by thousands of love locks. A group of teenagers had set up camp in the middle and were singing along to a Nirvana song written long before they were born. Meanwhile, an artist sketched passing tourists for a couple of euros, just as Remi Sauvageon had sketched the clients in his local café.

Playing a game with myself, I decided that any lock that drew my eye would have a special message for me. I spotted a red one, heart-shaped and professionally engraved. The couple who attached this lock to the bridge must have planned their visit. I walked across and lifted it so that I could read the engraving.

SARAH AND STEVE, it said.

I dropped the lock as though it were red hot. Really? Sarah and Steve? If that was a message from the other side, it must have been from a malevolent spirit. Steve, Steven, my wicked ex. I looked at the locks to either side of the heart-shaped one for a more useful sign. PAULA AND RYAN. ANGIE AND DEV. LEYLA AND STEVE. I smiled at that one. Steve was a very common name. It was just a coincidence. And then I found a lock left by SARAH AND CLARE, which confirmed that my superstitious game was nonsense.

I carried on across the bridge and ducked through the archway at the side of the Bibliothèque Mazarine. Rue de Seine wriggled up from there. Here on the Left Bank it was very different from my part of town, with its carefully planned streets, courtesy of Haussmann's grand vision. This part of Paris was like a set for *La Bohème*. I found myself constantly having to jump into the road. The narrow pavements were too small even for a single Parisian dowager and her miniature handbag dog – her *sac-a-main chien*. The shops, which once must have been the bakers and grocers Augustine wrote of in her memoir, were now chichi galleries and expensive restaurants. I chose one for lunch. It was called 'Fish' and it occupied the space where once had been a real fishmonger. I sat down at the bar and was just reading the menu when I felt a tap on my shoulder. Slowly, I turned round.

'Of all the gin joints . . .'

I couldn't believe it. The evil spirit of the bridge must have been on to something after all. Steven Jones, the man who had occupied my thoughts almost constantly until I met Marco Donato, was standing right next to me, large as life and twice as ugly. Though of course he wasn't in the least bit ugly – and he knew it. He was wearing a blue linen shirt that flattered his tanned skin and brought out the colour of his eyes. He was wearing his hair a little longer than usual and it suited him horribly well. He held out his hands in a 'look at you!' gesture that made me feel light-headed and weak.

'Sarah, what are you doing here?'

'What are *you* doing here?' I countered.

'I'm working at the Sorbonne. I sent you an email, remember? You didn't reply. Did you get it?'

'I got it but . . . I didn't know what to say.'

'Fair enough.'

'But thanks for writing it.'

'No need to say more. Mind if I sit next to you?' He started to pull out a stool. 'Oh, God. How stupid of me. You're here on a romantic weekend, right? And you're waiting for your fiancé to arrive?'

'No romantic weekend. No fiancé,' I admitted.

'Then . . .?'

'I'm working here too.'

'On your thesis?'

'Research for a film.'

Steven looked interested. 'You'll have to tell me more.' He sat down. 'But why did you come to Paris without telling me? You knew how to find me.'

'I guess I forgot you were here.'

'*Forgot*?'

It did sound as though I was making a point. I felt a little embarrassed.

'Well, I've found you now.' He gave me a playful nudge. 'What are you drinking? Assuming you don't mind shooting the breeze with your old boyfriend for a little while.' My heart was still throwing itself against my ribcage. I wasn't sure if I minded or not. I decided to tell him I didn't mind at all.

This time last year, Steven and I had been together but on the point of collapse. We had been a couple for seven years, but in the final eighteen months of our relationship we had drifted apart so that we were living like flatmates rather than lovers. Ironically, it was my attempt to change all that with a dramatic shift in our sex life that eventually caused us to fall apart for good. I hadn't seen him since the morning after that heady night and now we were exchanging small talk at a restaurant bar in Paris.

'Where are you staying?' he asked me now.

I told Steven about the flat that came free with my new research job.

'Sounds great. Nice neighbourhood.'

'Seems like it. It's quiet and safe.'

'On the surface. You know one of Paris's most famous sex clubs is just around the corner.'

Once upon a time, Steven would have been able to throw that into the conversation and neither one of us would have flinched, but things were different between us now. Thinking about another sex club, back in London, we both looked deep into our glasses. I wondered if our memories were similarly fraught.

'Not that I've been there,' Steven added.

But apart from that moment, it was surprisingly easy to talk to Steven again. One of the things I had enjoyed most about our long relationship was the banter we'd always shared. Conversation flowed like wine. It flowed even better when there was wine, as there was that day in Fish. I had always found Steven interesting and amusing. I hoped he'd felt the same way about me. He certainly seemed to be interested that afternoon. Two hours passed in the blink of an eye. All the other customers ate up and left. The barman dried glasses and feigned disinterest in our chat.

'Listen, I've had a really nice time talking to you today. I know you didn't intend to see me here in Paris. *Forgot!*' He made a face to indicate that he didn't believe that for a second. 'But perhaps we could get together again? I can show you some of my favourite places – though you managed to find my very favourite place on your own.' He indicated the bar we were sitting in. 'Let me give you my French number.'

He picked up my phone and tapped in his digits. He commented on my screensaver. It was a photograph of the Grand Canal. The Palazzo Donato could be seen in the distance, though I hadn't known that at the time I took the picture.

'Venice,' said Steven. 'Always so beautiful. You haven't really told me how you got on out there.'

I wasn't about to go into it then.

'I had a nice time,' I assured him. 'Got lots of work done.'

'Perhaps I could read your thesis,' he said then. 'You know I'd like to.'

'And I'd quite like for you to read it,' I said. Truthfully. Before we were estranged, before we were lovers, Steven had been my teacher. That was how we met. I still respected his academic opinion.

'Email it to me and we'll have lunch to talk about it. How about that?'

'OK,' I said. 'But I'll buy lunch.'

'If you insist.'

He hugged me close and kissed me on both cheeks. It was the strangest thing, to be kissed on the cheeks by a man who had once known every inch of my body as well as he knew his own. It was stranger still to breathe in his oh so familiar aftershave, Chanel's Egoiste. Long after we parted that afternoon, I could still smell that Chanel and it made me confused. It awakened part of me that I thought I had long since put to sleep.

Steven always wore too much aftershave, I thought to myself as I got ready for bed that evening and found that his scent was even then still lingering in my hair. It was remarkable that such a brief contact had left such a lasting impression. Annoying, even. But later I found myself pressing my hair against my face to intensify the memory. Proust was not wrong. The slightest whiff of a familiar odour can take us back in time more effectively than a face or a song.

When I lay down in bed, I was still thinking about Steven. He had been pleased to see me. He must have been, or he wouldn't have insisted on joining me for a drink. And he said he wanted to see me again, but was I ready to make the transition from estranged ex-lover to friend? On the one hand, I should have been glad. It was the grown-up thing to do. On the other hand, I couldn't help but wish he'd seemed more troubled after the way things ended between us.

I suppose it was inevitable that I dreamed about Steven. He was at the forefront of my mind and his distinctive aftershave enveloped me as I drifted to sleep.

27

Steven's body was so beautiful to me. It had always been enough for me just to be naked with him. To make love in the most ordinary way. Face-to-face. With affection and respect. Kissing. Sharing eye contact. But the passage of the years had eroded our passion for one another and then the night in the sex club had changed everything in an irrevocable way.

It was my fault. It was my idea. I don't think he would have suggested it first. I'd wanted to give our relationship the equivalent of an electric shock. A little surprise to reset us, back to the way we were. I thought we would just go and watch.

I was shocked when Steven bought me a set of underwear that looked like the kind of thing a hooker would put on for a night with an oligarch. A bra without cups and a pair of panties with a string of pearls that was intended to drive me wild by rubbing against my clitoris when I walked. And when we got to the club, I couldn't help noticing what caught his attention. Women dressed in little more than leather straps, which cut into their skin. A girl in an actual dog collar.

It was an uncomfortable realisation to think that Steven might be more turned on by my body in this get-up than he was by my naked flesh. Bondage was not something I had ever thought about in great detail. I was not entirely naive – I had seen the pictures and understood that a black leather basque and a pair of pointed stilettoes were shorthand for sexy in many a language – but there was something demeaning about it that I thought I would never find sexually appealing. Yet, that night in the club, part of me had definitely enjoyed submitting to Steven's fantasy. We'd gone to a party before the club and while I'd worried that the other guests might guess what I was wearing beneath my demure black dress, it was a moment that I'd returned to several times since in idle moments. Remembered and embellished.

I dreamed about that moment now. I was walking into a room full of people, dressed in my black dress with the high collar. It wasn't a short dress; it reached almost to my knees, but it was close-fitting and left little to the imagination with regard to my curves. The fabric was thin – too thin – a fine knit that demanded I choose my underwear carefully. It required something seamless to keep it from crossing the line from stylish to sluttish. That night, I was breaking all the rules.

In my dream, the party host, politely attentive, asked if he could take my coat. I let it slip from my shoulders and handed it to him, watching him try and fail to conceal his delighted surprise when he saw what his courtesy had revealed. I glanced down and saw that my nipples were erect and clearly outlined by the flimsy fabric. Lower still, the beads that rubbed against my crotch were visible too.

The host caught my eye. I regarded him steadily. He blushed and hurried away to put my coat in a bedroom.

I circulated around the party. I took a glass of champagne from a fellow historian. He was a man I did not much like in real life. In my subconscious fantasy, however, he was an object of desire. He licked his lips as I looked at him, in such a way that made it clear he would like to lick something more. I felt my nipples pucker at the thought.

Responding to his subtle signals, I followed him into the bedroom. He closed the door behind us. He didn't bother with any preamble. There was no kissing and no caressing. A jumble of coats was piled high on the bed. He stripped me of my dress as though it were a burning rag, then lifted me and half-threw me so that I landed on the soft coat mountain.

He stepped towards me and started to rub the beads on my G-string against my clit.

'You like it like this,' he said.

I didn't disagree. I let him press the beads harder and even moved my pelvis up towards him to increase the pressure still further.

With his free hand, he undid his trousers and loosened his cock. He rubbed at it frantically until it was hard. He didn't bother to try to make me wet before he entered me. He pushed the string to one side and I could feel the beads digging into me every time our bodies came together in a thrust. I looked up at him – this person I didn't really like – and found the revulsion turned me on even more. The more he grunted and gurned, the more I wanted him. I felt myself growing wetter. He pinched my nipples until I winced. My discomfort inspired him. It inspired me too.

He came with an animal groan.

While I could still feel his cum seeping from me, someone else walked into the room. It was the party host. Another man I wouldn't have said I found attractive in a million years. He was skinny and balding. His face was mean and fox-like. His eyes were darting and furtive. He saw me on the pile of coats and rubbed his hands together in glee.

I did not try to cover myself from his scrutiny. I let him position himself between my legs just as his colleague had done. He dropped his trousers and unleashed an angry-looking cock. I closed my eyes and offered myself to him. He slipped into me easily. His colleague's cum made me wet, I suppose. And by now I was definitely aroused. Embarrassingly so.

He fucked me almost angrily. He came quickly, throwing himself against me.

Then came another. And another. The fourth man turned me over and fucked me from behind, not caring that my face was stuffed into someone's leather jacket. A popper left an imprint on my cheek. I got another imprint on the backside from my thoughtless lover's hand.

Hands came from everywhere. I let them roam wherever they liked. I felt fingers all over me. Fingers inside me. A stranger poked his tongue into my mouth. Moments later, another stranger was licking at my clitoris, making me squirm with uncontrollable desire. I didn't try to stop them. I didn't want to.

The men – most of them strangers – took it in turns to come inside me. They laughed and encouraged each other. The guy who had fucked me first recovered enough to have another go. He lifted my legs and draped them over his shoulders so he could go into me harder and deeper.

I let myself go with the flow. I was no longer Sarah. I was an object. I was merely a conduit for the desire of these men I hardly knew. They could do whatever they liked.

It never took me long to climax when I remembered the sex club and the staid academic party beforehand. Afterwards, however, I couldn't help but think of myself with a slight sense of shame. It wasn't right, was it, to fantasise about being fucked by so many men at one time? When I woke up in Paris, having orgasmed myself into wakefulness, I felt extraordinarily exposed. Though I was entirely alone, I couldn't shake the sense that I had a secret audience.

Which was the real me? The part that kicked against the idea of wearing such uncomfortable things to please a man, or the part that revelled in the thought that Steven got hard just seeing me in the scraps he'd bought? The woman who thought she wanted a 'vanilla' sort of sex life or the one who indulged in cybersex with Marco Donato? Or how about the woman who'd let a girl she'd never met before make love to her in a London sex club?

I'd blamed Steven for that. That night in the sex club, when I thought we would just watch, I'd ended up doing so much more. I'd let a girl dressed in a cat mask, calling herself Kitty, undress me and bring me to orgasm. Afterwards, when I discovered that Steven already knew my sexy stranger – that he'd actually suggested this particular club because she'd told him about it – I'd flown into a rage. Though I was the one who'd ended up with her, I felt betrayed and couldn't see any way to deal with the situation but to break off my relationship with Steven. But she still seeped into my fantasies. Had I got it wrong? Was I suppressing a set of darker impulses that might actually bring me greater freedom and happiness than I hoped?

The following morning, I sent Steven an email, attaching a copy of my thesis on Luciana Giordano. I told myself that all I wanted was his opinion as a fellow academic but, of course, I felt a guilty frisson of pleasure when he wrote back to me almost immediately, saying that he had been worried I would not remember my promise to send the thesis over. Better than that, he ended his email with an invitation. Since I was researching a woman from the nineteenth century, how would I like to go to the opera that weekend and have a Saturday night out courtesan-style?

I responded that I would be delighted.

28

Paris, 1840

Arlette was true to her word. On Thursday evening, she took me to meet Clemence and her friends at the Opéra Comique. Of course, I couldn't go in my maid's clothes, so in the afternoon she called me into her dressing room and decked me out in a pink dress I had once admired. She told me it looked far more striking with my glossy dark hair than with her own fairer locks. I was worried that people would know it was a cast-off but she assured me, 'No one will remember it's my dress. They will be mesmerised by the woman inside it.'

I could not comprehend at the time why Arlette was being so kind to me, but later on, as my naivety fell away, I would understand how she could only benefit from my rise. She must have known all along how her generosity for us poor orphaned girls might pay dividends if we eventually followed her into her profession. Especially if we hooked someone wealthy.

Unknown to me that afternoon as I twirled in front of Arlette's mirror, I was being groomed for greatness. Clemence Babineaux was well-known for making introductions between members of high society and the low professions and she had told Arlette of a man who was looking for someone just like me. He would be at the Opéra that evening. Arlette didn't hesitate to take her up on the plan. Clemence was a queenmaker and I was the most promising princess she'd encountered in years.

So, when we went to the opera that evening, Arlette and I were almost equals. I was no longer her maid. If anyone asked, I was her young cousin from Brittany and she was keen to show me the very best the city had to offer. She even suggested that I change my name from 'Levert' to 'du Vert' to give me an extra touch of class. I said I would think about it.

Along with her dress, Arlette gave me an Indian silk shawl so gossamer-fine it could be threaded through the eye of a darning needle. It was a present from the general. She had also offered me the choice of her jewels. I chose a modest string of pearls. Arlette pronounced them perfect for the tableau of blushing innocence I was to create. And, of course, she let me borrow one of her fans.

'In case you need a moment of anonymity,' she explained.

Clemence Babineaux agreed that I looked just perfect.

Clemence had her own box at the Opéra, paid for by her lover the Prussian count. Arlette and I joined her there. The count was not in attendance but several other men were. Clemence introduced me to them all and they greeted me as though I was a true lady. I almost felt myself become one as a result of their polite attentions. But the man Clemence thought might like to meet me was on the other side of the theatre. She pointed him out to Arlette. He was the Vicomte de Chanteduc. He was at least four times my age and he looked like a tortoise.

Clemence nodded a greeting in his direction. Arlette smiled broadly. Then both women gestured towards me as though I was a pig they'd brought to market.

'Didn't I tell you?' said Clemence to Arlette. 'She's absolutely what he's looking for.'

I affected not to know what they were talking about.

Arlette and Clemence kept up a running commentary throughout the opera. I tried to concentrate on the stage – I had never been in a theatre before – but for my friends the much more interesting performance was taking place in the audience.

'The Vicomte's mind is not on the opera at all. He cannot take his eyes off you, dear Augustine. Every time I look at him, he's got his opera glasses trained right on you. Give him a show. Sit up straight,' said Clemence.

There was no other way to sit on the hard gilded seats. Who would have thought the opera would be so uncomfortable?

'Let your shawl fall from your shoulders,' said Arlette.

'But I'm cold,' I complained.

'For goodness' sake.'

Arlette tugged the Indian shawl down for me.

'There. Don't hide your assets, silly girl,' Clemence tutted. 'You have to make small sacrifices. A little chill here in the theatre in exchange for a blanket of spun gold later on.'

Arlette focused her opera glasses on the Vicomte's box again.

'It's working. The Vicomte is utterly enraptured. Oh, this is so exciting! Who would have thought my little Breton housemaid could pull off such a coup? He is one of the wealthiest men in all Europe. You cannot fail to make your fortune if you just indulge him, Augustine.'

'Amuse him,' Clemence added. 'Pretend to be interested in him, though he talks about nothing but horses and war, and you could be his lover before the week is out. I know it.'

I turned to Arlette, my mouth dropping open in shock. 'But . . .'

She understood at once my objection.

'Remi Sauvageon? Forget Remi, my dear. He has long since forgotten you.'

Arlette's words stung. They brought tears to my eyes.

'The Vicomte is a thousand times richer than Remi. He'll never leave you in the cold to go back to his papa like some milksop.'

Arlette was right to remind me that Remi had let me down most terribly and yet, as I sat there and failed to concentrate on the scenes playing out on the stage, I was not ready to love anyone but my beloved, cowardly artist. I only wanted him back. As the opera drew to a close, I resolved to tell Arlette and Clemence that I could not be their protégée. I would thank Clemence for offering me the opportunity to see an opera but there was no way I could ever lie down with the Vicomte. He was old enough to be my *grandpère*! I would beg to keep my job as a maid. I would work for Arlette until I was an old crone, but I could never love another man. Especially not one who looked so close to death.

Then the opera reached its finale. The singers tried to break our hearts with their soaring voices. My heart was broken far more easily when I looked down into the stalls and saw Remi among his friends.

It was the first time I had seen him since he kissed me goodbye on the doorstep in the Rue de Seine and stepped out into the snow wearing every scrap of clothing in his possession.

Why had I not noticed him before? He must have crept in while the theatre was in darkness. Despite everything that had happened, my heart leapt at the sight of him. I prayed he would look up at me. I scoured his demeanour for news that he was as unhappy as I had been. But the truth was that Remi looked far from unhappy. In those few months at his father's house, he had recovered his health. He looked well, he looked energetic, and he looked pleased with himself. And then he turned to the woman at his side and I was suddenly sure I could tell from his eager expression that he was trying to make her love him, just as he had captured me. My heart cracked in two. I turned my face away before he saw me and put up Arlette's fan as a shield.

Arlette, who had been following my gaze, reached for my hand and squeezed it tightly.

'Love has such thorns,' she whispered. 'Hold steady, dear girl. Keep your dignity.'

I sucked in a quavering breath.

'Will we meet the Vicomte now?' asked Clemence.

Arlette nodded. 'I think Augustine is ready.'

'I knew you would come to your senses,' Clemence told me. 'I have already sent a note to invite him for supper. I feel sure he will accept.'

The Vicomte did accept. That night Elaine had to eat supper alone back at Arlette's house while I was seated alongside the Vicomte de Chanteduc in pride of place at Clemence Babineaux's dining table. Ordinarily, I would have been delighted by the rich food Clemence's servants laid before me, but I could not concentrate. Not while the elderly Vicomte stared at me as though he were a starving dog and I was a sausage. He praised my eyes, my hair, my lips and my cheeks until I felt them burning.

'I would like to see you again,' he said. 'Alone.'

Dread crept up my neck like icy fingers.

'Alone?' I whispered.

'Yes, indeed.'

Arlette interrupted. 'I will talk to my young cousin in private and ascertain her wishes,' she said. 'But for now I can tell she is getting tired. I must take her home.'

The Vicomte nodded. 'I understand. Well, thank you, dear ladies, for allowing me the pleasure of your company tonight.'

Once Arlette and I were back at home, Elaine joined us by the fire and we discussed the evening at length. Arlette told me I had done her proud. I was as poised and beautiful as any of the women in the theatre that evening. There wasn't a lady of noble birth who could have outshone me in my pink dress and pearls.

'The Vicomte is all but yours,' she said. 'Clemence is absolutely sure of it.'

'But what if I don't want him?' I protested.

'My dear, do you think anyone ever did? That face!'

'Exactly,' I said. 'He is a hideous old man.'

'But generous to a fault,' said Arlette.

Elaine was already spending his money.

'He'll have to set you up with a place of your own. And you'll need a companion,' she told me. 'I'd be very happy to come with you. Any time. Just give me the word.'

'Elaine!' Arlette exclaimed. 'Where's your loyalty?'

'Perhaps the Vicomte will give her a house big enough for the three of us,' said Elaine to mollify her. 'You've seen the monstrosity that funny prince from Portugal is building for Madame Delaflotte on the Champs Elysées. He'll want to compete with that. I hear it has nineteen bedrooms.'

'Oh yes,' said Arlette. 'Our little Augustine will have twenty rooms, an orangery and fountains. She will have a beautiful carriage and her own horses. She will make a fortune with her looks, just as I predicted when I pulled her out of the dirt in the Bois de Boulogne.'

Arlette brushed my cheek as though she were brushing that dirt away. 'My clever little girl. You're on your way to becoming a very wealthy woman.'

'No. I cannot lie down with that man. I cannot!'

'And neither will you have to,' said Arlette. 'At least, not if you get a better offer.'

Arlette and Elaine were happy. I tried to be happy too. I tried to remind myself that this new way of living would be better than starving. And if Remi no longer loved me, then in any case the rest of my life would be nothing but a long wait for death.

But I could not believe that he didn't love me. That night, when I went to bed, I tried to communicate with Remi across the distance between us. I told myself that if I thought about him hard enough, he would feel my wishes across the whole of Paris. Silently, I tried to push my love towards him.

How I missed the feeling of his warm body next to mine. Without Remi, the *chambre de bonne* was once again just a tiny room full of shadows and spiders. The draught blowing in through the badly fitted window was twice as cold as I remembered it. I pulled the covers up to my chin and tried to warm myself with a happier memory. I went back to a day when Remi and I were in this room together. The day when he gave me the tin ring that I kept in a matchbox beneath my pillow still.

I had been so happy and so had he. We'd made love so tenderly. How many girls could claim to have enjoyed the moment of their deflowering so well?

That kind of love didn't just disappear. As much as I missed Remi, I was certain that he was missing me too. That girl in the opera might have been anyone. She might even have been one of the sisters upon whom he claimed to dote. Yes, that was the real story. I hugged it to me. Remi was with his sister. He did not seek me out at the opera because there was no reason on earth why I might be there. I was a lady's maid. Maids did not generally go to the opera.

But he was back in Paris. I wondered then why he had not gone back to our old neighbourhood and asked about my progress. Much as my friend Jeanne-Marie had insisted she would turn him away and spit on him as he went, I was sure that if he had asked about me, she would have told him I'd gone back to Arlette. He might have guessed that and come straight to the Rue de la Ville L'Evêque anyway. The thought of his last encounter with my mistress wouldn't have put him off. Surely not.

A little voice deep inside me urged me to face the truth. I could continue to mourn Remi and face the inevitable threat of destitution should I ever fall out with Arlette, or I could earn some security for myself. I could embrace my fate. And the Vicomte.

29

On Saturday evening, Steven arranged to pick me up at my flat. I'd considered meeting him at the opera, so he would not be able to get a look at my new private space, but then decided that was just petty. If Steven and I were going to be friends – and only friends – why shouldn't he pick me up from my door? All the same, I spent time tidying up in a way I would not have done for any ordinary pal. I flung open the windows to let in the air and decorated the stark white sitting room with an arrangement of red camellias, bought from the expensive florist down the street. I knew that Steven would appreciate the contrast. He had an eye for interior design. He had an eye for beauty.

I needn't have bought flowers for myself. When Steven arrived, the bouquet he was carrying dwarfed him. More camellias. Though his were white.

'Must be the season. Plus,' he added. 'I thought they would be apt. Given your new project.'

He was referring to one of the most famous Parisian courtesans of all. Marie Duplessis, the younger Dumas's tragic *Dame aux Camélias*, who was never seen in public without the flowers and used them to signal her availability. White for yes, red for no.

'They're beautiful,' I said, arranging them in yet another white vase.

'So is this place,' said Steven. 'And you say you're staying here for nothing while you do the research?'

I nodded. 'Greg Simon, the producer, said his company took this place on a long lease when they were filming in Paris last year. It was just standing empty.'

'They must have money to burn,' Steven observed. 'Lucky you. I've never heard of accommodation this luxurious going with the job before. Not unless the job is Président de la République.'

'Well, I'm making the most of it,' I said. 'Shall we go?'

Steven nodded. 'You look amazing, by the way,' he said. I was wearing a dress I'd bought just that afternoon. As with tidying the apartment, I'd told myself that I shouldn't make an extra-special effort on Steven's behalf, but when it came down to it, I had just one dress suitable for the opera in my wardrobe and it was the dress I'd worn to L'Infer, the sex club where we finally pulled ourselves apart. I couldn't wear that. So I had to hit Galeries Lafayette and buy the dress I was now wearing.

It was a simple little black number but what made it special was the quality of the fabric and the cut, which subtly clung to my contours and gave me curves in all the right places. It was sleeveless. I knew I looked good in it. Even the sales assistants, who were ordinarily so disdainful of anyone less than a supermodel, were grudgingly complimentary when they saw me step out of the dressing room. When a man passing by gave me a nod of approval I knew I had found the perfect LBD.

'You've changed your style,' said Steven.

'Paris makes you feel like you ought to make an effort, don't you think?'

'I like it. It's very sophisticated.'

Steven helped me into my jacket.

It was a warm night and it wasn't far from my apartment to the Opéra, so we walked. I was wearing heels, forgetting that the pavements of Paris are notoriously tricky, so when Steven offered me his arm I took it gratefully. It was strange to be hanging on to him like that. Once again I was close enough to get a deep lungful of his delicious aftershave – my own equivalent of Proust's madeleine.

I wondered what he had been doing in Paris. When he wasn't at work, that is. At the same time I didn't really want to know. There were bound to have been other women; a man like Steven never wanted for female attention. I wasn't certain I was ready to hear about it. We kept our conversation to uncontroversial subjects. He told me he had already dipped into my thesis and was finding it very interesting.

'She was quite a girl, your Luciana.'

'Yes, she was.'

'Funny, isn't it, how every generation thinks they've invented sex, but here's a seventeen-year-old in the eighteenth century getting more action than I ever could have dreamed of at that age. And you say you think you ended up living in an apartment in the house where she used to visit Casanova?'

'I think so. It all seemed to add up. The route she took to the house and then the bed. It was like something out of a horror movie. All covered in carved monkeys, which were the emblem of Ernesta Donato, who actually owned the house. There can't be more than one.'

'I'd like to see it. Maybe you could show me one day. The bed.'

That comment sent a strange frisson through me. I looked at Steven. I could tell that he was watching my reaction carefully.

'It's not exactly available to the general public,' I said. 'There's someone else in the flat now.'

'Of course.'

He smiled at me in a way that was heartbreakingly familiar.

* * *

The Opéra Garnier was everything I had expected. From the outside the building was a wedding cake and on the inside a jewellery box, with its abundance of gilt and enormous chandeliers. The people had made an effort to fit into the glorious setting. As we mingled with a crowd dressed in the finest French couture, I was very glad that I was wearing my new Parisian dress and my diamond earrings – a twenty-first birthday present and the only diamonds that I owned.

While Steven went to buy a programme, I took the opportunity to soak up the atmosphere and imagine how it might have been almost a hundred and fifty years earlier. Were the women who surreptitiously eyed each other in their Chanel and Dior actually descendants of Augustine's contemporaries, obsessed as they were with their Indian silk shawls?

Though Augustine had not lived long enough to see the opening of the Palais Garnier, I still felt something of her spirit as I took in the scene. The human instinct towards display had not changed over generations. I thought she would have enjoyed the evening's programme. We were going to see *Carmen*, which had its premiere in Paris. All the great tropes of the romantic opera were there. The poor girl, with beauty and charm that project her beyond her lowly station. The lover. The rival. The jealousy. The horrible death.

I also felt I understood some of Augustine's awe at her own first opera visit. With its ceiling painted by Chagall and all those rows of golden boxes, the Opéra Garnier made Covent Garden look rather dowdy. Steven had somehow got us a box to ourselves. I settled into a small hard chair that forced me to sit upright and pay attention. It brought to mind Augustine putting on a display for the Vicomte, showing off her best assets at the behest of Clemence and Arlette.

As the lights dimmed and the orchestra struck up the overture, Steven leaned across to whisper something in my ear. The feel of his breath on my bare shoulder was unbearably intimate. When he straightened up again to watch the action below, I pulled my jacket around my shoulder like armour against the feelings I was beginning to realise I still had for him. Though, intellectually, I thought I had come to terms with the reality that Steven and I were not right for each other, it was clear that my body had yet to take the news on board.

Later, while onstage Carmen lay dying, I couldn't help but feel a little melancholy. I dabbed at my eyes with the corner of a paper handkerchief, hoping to save my mascara. Steven noticed and when I had put the handkerchief away, he reached over and squeezed my hand to comfort me. I let him continue to hold my hand until the curtain fell. It was a curious sensation; both natural and awkward. When the applause began, I was able to remove my fingers from his without it being too obvious. I clapped hard.

'I didn't think you were so sentimental,' Steven observed when I was still dabbing at my eyes as we made our way outside.

'Neither did I,' I said.

He helped me into my coat and put his hand on the small of my back to guide me through the crowds. I noticed several women with the telltale bright eyes of someone who has been weeping.

'What now?' was the question on my mind when we were outside and walking back towards my apartment.

'We should get something to eat,' Steven said.

I had food at home and I'd told myself I would not stay out late, not with Steven, but now it came to it, I changed my mind. I didn't see why I shouldn't stay out with him. It wasn't as though I was in any danger. I knew him as well as I knew my siblings. And, I had to remind myself, it wasn't as though I had to worry about anyone else being upset. Not Marco Donato, for sure. Why shouldn't I let the evening carry on?

I told Steven I'd love to have something to eat.

'Great,' he said. 'I know just the place.'

He took me to a restaurant called 'I Golosi', an Italian place that was a deli by day. The staff seemed to know him and he chatted in easy Italian as they led us to a table at the back of the shop. The sound of spoken Italian touched my heart again, as did the list of food on the menu. There were plenty of specials that I'd only previously seen in Venice. Sardines in *saor* had been a favourite of mine. I loved the contrast of the sour dressing and the sweet juicy raisins.

As Steven studied the menu, I took the opportunity to look at him more closely. My memory of our last night together in London was one of horrible anger. I would never have guessed we would meet again in Paris and that I would feel this happy to be in his company. Then Steven told an anecdote about how he came to know this restaurant. He'd first been there to celebrate a colleague's birthday. I found I was relieved that he'd been there with a group of people and not on a date.

'It's nice,' I said honestly. Our table at the back was very private. There were many places in Paris that claimed to be intimate and romantic but there were few that actually were. This one genuinely was.

We ordered our food and Steven ordered a bottle of wine, despite my protests that I had to work the following day.

'Tomorrow's Sunday,' he observed.

'Then maybe I have to get up early to go to church,' I joked.

'So you'll need something to confess,' said Steven, as he filled my glass.

I laughed.

Later, while he was telling me an anecdote about his time in Paris so far, I thought about our first proper date, back in London. I was just twenty-one. I remember how thrilled I had been when he took over and picked up the wine list. It had made him seem so sophisticated. I had spent that evening in a state of intense anticipation. It wasn't that I was waiting for our first kiss – we'd already had that, in Steven's office at the end of a tutorial that took us from being student and teacher to lovers and equals. But when Steven and I were first together, any time spent outside the bedroom seemed like a bit of a waste. I couldn't look at his lips without wanting to kiss them. I couldn't look at his hands without wanting to feel them on my bare skin. After we made love for the first time, the longing only intensified, because now I knew for sure what he could do.

Our first proper date had been in an Italian restaurant. I'd ordered some spaghetti but liked the looked of Steven's dish more. He fed me a forkful across the table. It was so erotic. He never took his eyes off mine and I felt the jealous gaze of the people on the table next to us, who were having an altogether less interesting time. I felt sorry for the woman who would be going home to lie awake on one side of the bed while the man pretended to sleep on the other.

Now the boot was on the other foot. There was one other couple in our room at the back of the restaurant. They couldn't have known each other for very long, I thought. Or maybe they had. In any case, they couldn't get enough of each other. They both leaned forward over their little table. Their arms were entwined as though they were about to embark on some amorous arm-wrestling. From time to time, they both stretched forward as far as they could and their lips met. They whispered words into one another's mouths.

Steven caught me looking at them. He smiled at me. It was a smile that said he understood exactly what I was thinking.

We'd been like that too. Unable to take our hands off each other even long enough to eat. We had been so passionately in love we would have laughed at anyone who suggested that one day we might not know what to say to one another. That one day, we might have lost the trust we took for granted. Or that we might have tarnished our tender lovemaking by deciding it was boring and we needed to introduce something, or rather someone, else into the equation.

I started to feel hot with anxiety. What was I doing in that restaurant, sitting across a table from Steven Jones? Who was I kidding when I told myself that we could just have a nice uncomplicated meal together? So much had gone on between us and so much had been left unsaid at the end. I picked up the pepper mill and put it down again, quickly, having felt the flash of an urge to throw it at him out of anger that he'd brought us to this moment of limbo. It was all because of him.

Suddenly all the pain and humiliation of the past year seemed to be pressing down on me. If Steven and I hadn't broken up, I would not have become involved with Marco. And if I had not become involved with Marco, I wouldn't have made such a fool of myself in Venice. I wouldn't be so confused and angry and unsure of what to do next.

I felt such envy for the woman on the table next to me. She seemed to be cherished. Why hadn't things turned out like that for me?

'Are you OK?' Steven asked.

He reached for my hand across the table.

I gave him a strained smile. 'Thinking about the opera,' I said.

Steven's expression told me he didn't believe me. He knew what I was really thinking.

'I'm sorry,' he said.

There was a sincerity in those two little words that almost had me crying.

'It's OK,' I said.

He continued to hold my hand.

Despite the amorous couple, it was Steven and I who closed the restaurant that evening. We were the last people to leave by a long way. The staff hovered discreetly. I wondered if Steven was thinking the same as I was. Once upon a time, we would have taken the hint and left, knowing that we had a place to go to, but there was a sense that leaving the restaurant would have to signal the end of the evening. There was no question of going dancing or even for another drink. We'd have to go our separate ways. Me back to my stark white designer palace, Steven back to the place on the Left Bank he had rented for his stay.

My place was on the way to his.

'Can I come in?' he asked when we got there.

Muddy-headed from all the wine and the lonely feelings stirred up by the kissing couple in I Golosi, I didn't say no.

Steven followed me up the twisting staircase to the apartment. He leaned against the wall while I fumbled for my keys. When I finally got the door open, he came through it right behind me, his crotch against my buttocks, almost as though he were shoving me inside. He kicked the door shut behind him. I turned to warn him to be quiet for the neighbours, but before I could protest about the slamming door he started kissing me.

30

I didn't try to stop him. All evening the tension between us had been building .We'd talked about everything under the sun except 'us' but we were haunted by unfinished business. So there we were, about to finish it. Or were we just starting something else?

As we kissed, Steven danced me backwards into the living room and up to the edge of the huge white sofa. When the back of my legs made contact, I fell onto it, pulling him down with me. We were still kissing. At the same time Steven was undressing me and undressing himself. He struggled to find the carefully hidden zip on my new LBD. I helped him out.

He stood again up to pull off his trousers. He grabbed my hands and lifted me to stand in front of him. He soon stripped off my smart black dress, leaving it in a heap on the floor, which somehow seemed like where it was always destined to end up. He unfastened my bra with one hand – he was always an expert when it came to undoing brassieres – and tossed it so that it landed on a table lamp. My knickers ended up nestling in one of the twin arrangements of camellias. The white arrangement. White for 'available tonight'.

'You know,' I observed as Steven busied himself with rolling off my stockings, 'I think red camellias were meant to signal that Mademoiselle was not accepting guests because it was the wrong time of the month.'

'Are you not accepting guests?' Steven asked me. He looked up. His eyes were glittering with wickedness. I could not resist. I didn't want to.

'I think I've already accepted you,' I said.

I took Steven by the hand and led him into the bedroom, to the big white bed with the fresh sheets that I had not imagined sharing. Though perhaps subconsciously, as I'd changed the linen, I'd known that was exactly what would happen. I'd set the scene deliberately.

We were both entirely naked by now. There was such intensity in Steven's eyes as he looked at me arranged on the pillows. It made me a little nervous, but it also made me long to have him take me there and then. He clambered on top of me and took both my wrists, holding my hands on either side of my head. He studied my face.

'You're so beautiful,' he said. 'I thought about you every single day we were apart.'

His words made my stomach flutter but before I could bat the compliment away, as was my habit, his lips were back on mine, kissing me hard. I opened my mouth to let in his tongue, which writhed against mine. The taste of him was more delicious to me than anything we'd drunk that night. We'd always had great chemistry.

He let go of my hands and I immediately ran my fingers through his hair. I gently scratched his back and bit his shoulder while he nuzzled my bare neck. I relished the feeling of his bare skin under my fingers. I traced the freckles, almost forgotten. I felt the scar on his side where he'd fallen off his bicycle as a child. I knew every inch of his body so well. I was surprised and relieved to find that nothing had changed. He felt the same. He smelled the same. He moved in the same way.

It was as though we were two dancers, stepping back into a routine we had practised so many times. We moved as one, without interruption or awkwardness. I let myself be led and he responded in turn to my own moves. Stroking, kissing, caressing.

I soon opened myself up to him. I folded my legs round

him to lock him in tighter. When he made his first thrust, I felt a sense of relief and release.

We roamed all around the bed, changing position every few minutes. When he took me from behind, we both watched ourselves in the mirror on the wardrobe door. I was surprised by the way he had made me look. My hair was wild. My eyes were dark, with my pupils so dilated. I looked hungry with desire and so did he.

He came when I was on top. It was a position that had always worked well for us and especially for me, because I could control the intensity. At the same time, he could touch my breasts and massage my clitoris so that as he drew nearer to his climax, so did I. When we were most in tune with each other, we could come at the same time. Those moments were precious and spectacular.

It was the first time I had actually had sex since Steven and I were last together back in London. Since then, every encounter I'd had had been imaginary or virtual. I'd had nothing but a love life of dreams.

I had forgotten about the feel of two bodies slick with sweat. I had forgotten about the smell of sex, which lingered in the air when I came back from the kitchen with two glasses of water. I had forgotten how warm a bed became when two people were sharing it. Climbing back beneath the sheets, I moulded my body to Steven's, curling round his back and tucking my thighs tight against his. In the time it had taken me to fetch that water, he had turned over and fallen asleep. I had forgotten that part of it too.

But this was real. This was not some ridiculous virtual assignation. This was flesh and blood and sweat and semen. It was messy and complicated – not least because I'd just made love to Steven without resolving anything first – but it was also so very, very real.

31

Paris, 1840

Arlette let it be known that I would receive the Vicomte in private at her house the following week. When the day came, she let me wear a green silk gown that she'd grown a little too big for. It wasn't of the very latest style but Arlette said that was actually a good thing in the circumstances. The Vicomte knew quite a bit about fashion – for a man – and if I was going to be his consort, he would want me to be dressed in the very latest styles. Of course he'd have to buy them.

Entertaining the Vicomte was an excruciating experience. Not only did he gurn at me like a gargoyle from Notre Dame, he was half deaf and made me repeat everything I said a dozen times before he nodded vaguely and returned to gazing at my tits. The thought of his hands following his eyes made me feel faint with disgust.

But Arlette was right that the Vicomte's vileness was matched by his generosity. The day after his visit, he sent me an Indian shawl and instructions that I should meet with the best seamstress in Paris who would make me a dress for every day of the week. I was dumbfounded. Elaine was envious enough to spit! Arlette patted me on the hand and said, 'You see. You're a natural!'

A natural what? A whore? I am ashamed to admit that I was very happy to have the dresses, but I knew that I had taken the first step on a path I did not want to follow. The Vicomte wanted to see me in my new dresses, of course. And later he would want to see me out of them. What would I do then?

Fortunately, Arlette and Clemence were both shrewd businesswomen. They assured me that the very worst thing I could do was give in to the Vicomte too quickly. The dresses that seemed so expensive to me were nothing to a man of his wealth. If I gave myself to him now, he might even have been disappointed to think he'd bought me so cheaply. If I held out, he would pay out. They were right.

The next time the Vicomte visited, he brought me a gold brooch shaped like a cherub. He invited me to see another opera as his guest, with Arlette as chaperone. Other outings and presents followed. Arlette took the valuable gifts from me and had them sold. Half would go into my bank account and half into hers, to cover the expense of keeping me now I was no longer a maid.

At the same time, now that I was dressed like a woman of fashion and attended the opera or the theatre almost every night as the Vicomte's guest, I started to attract other suitors, including a politician and a famous newspaper editor. Arlette managed their visits and their donations towards my upkeep. I could not believe how much they were willing to spend on me. If one man sent a bouquet, the next would send two. There were evenings at expensive restaurants and weekends in the country. When the politician bought me a silver sugar bowl, the newspaper editor sent a silver milk jug. The Vicomte sent a silver coffee pot, two candlesticks and two spoons.

Arlette turned everything into cash, explaining to the men that I was an incredibly devout girl who insisted on selling their gifts to provide hot meals for the poor. That made them even more generous. The poor newspaper editor, who was not as wealthy as the other men, was almost ruined by the competition. As it was, his wife threw him out when she discovered he had been using her family money to buy me trinkets.

The Vicomte, however, still seemed closest to winning the right to go to bed with me. I heard him discussing his entitlement with Clemence one evening when she joined us all for dinner.

'Do I have to?' I asked Clemence.

'By now, you probably do.'

When the 84-year-old Vicomte died in his bed that very night, I thanked God for his mercy.

Unfortunately, he was soon replaced by another wealthy beast.

32

Shortly after the Vicomte's sudden death, Arlette was visited by the Duc de Rocambeau. I had not seen this man before, though I knew him by reputation. The whole of Paris knew about de Rocambeau. He was wealthy beyond imagination. His servants called him a tyrant.

I was upstairs in my room when the Duc arrived. I had planned to spend the afternoon repairing some old stockings, but Arlette sent Elaine to tell me that I was required downstairs and that I should make sure I looked my prettiest. Cursing my bad luck, I dressed quickly and had Elaine help me with my hair. Within fifteen minutes, I was in the salon. I curtseyed to the Duc and awaited an introduction, but rather than tell me his name, the Duc merely stared at me, as though seeing a ghost. He stared so hard that after a while I began to squirm a little and even Arlette gave a nervous laugh.

'This is my cousin Augustine,' she told him. 'But you look at her as though you've already met.'

'I don't believe we have,' he said. 'And yet at the same time I could swear I know her very well.'

'From a past life?' Arlette suggested, clapping her hands together. She was fond of the dark arts since she met a gypsy who said Arlette had lived in Egypt as a queen.

'No. From a painting.'

When he said that, I felt dizzy. It could only have been one painting.

'I saw a charming nude in the window of a junk shop in the Marais,' the Duc explained to Arlette. 'It was fairly crudely executed and very badly framed by someone who had no idea what he was doing but I fell in love with it at once. It's such a wonderful composition. The girl is sitting on a bed, covering her most private treasure with her hand, but she looks out of the canvas so brazenly, it makes even a man of my experience shiver at the thrill of taking that hand's place. If I didn't know this girl was your cousin and thus an entirely respectable young woman, I might have thought she was the subject. It's really quite remarkable.'

Arlette and I shared a knowing look. Arlette knew all about the painting and Remi's visit to the pawn shop.

'How I would love to meet that girl,' the Duc continued dreamily.

'Won't Augustine suffice in the meantime?' Arlette asked.

It seemed I would suffice indeed. The Duc was smitten. Like the Vicomte, he asked if he might see me in private. Arlette assured him it could be arranged.

'He is far wealthier than that old twit de Chanteduc,' said Arlette after de Rocambeau left us. 'If you get this right, you'll have more money than Marie Antoinette!'

The thought of giving myself to the Duc was scarcely better than the thought of going to bed with the Vicomte. He was not quite so old as de Chanteduc had been, but de Rocambeau was still at least three times my age. He had the look of someone hard and mean. His face was thin and long and his eyes bulged out of their sockets. His fingers put me in mind of a skeleton's bare-bone hands.

'But oh, he's so rich!' was all the other women would say when I voiced my reservations.

Arlette and Elaine speculated on what the Duc might give me in return for my favours. Arlette had already mentioned to him that I needed a new wardrobe for the summer.

'I'm certain he'll have picked up on my hint.'

Elaine hoped he would buy me a little dog. But that would just be the start of it. The Duc had bought one of his previous mistresses a house in the country and an apartment in the best part of town.

As it was, his first gift to me was far more valuable than any of us had dared hope. All because I let him think he'd taken something absolutely priceless from me.

It was Arlette's suggestion. She made it while she was braiding my hair in readiness for the Duc's next visit. She put her hands on my shoulders and regarded me in the mirror with the grave and loving expression of a caring mother, about to impart advice to her dear daughter on her wedding night.

'You've had only one lover,' she said. 'And given how short he is, I don't suppose Remi Sauvageon is hung like a donkey. Or even a goat.'

'Arlette!' I protested, but she continued.

'So the Duc will never know you're not a virgin if you don't tell him otherwise. Let him assume your purity and pay for it accordingly.'

I blanched at the thought.

Arlette squeezed my shoulders.

'It's not such a terrible thing. He will still want to have you if he knows you're not a virgin, but he will not be prepared to pay nearly as much. You need to think of it as doing him a favour. He will be happier and you will be happier too. You'll certainly be richer if he thinks he's the only one to have had you. You remember what to do, don't you? Be a good actress. Make sure you wince when he tries to put it in. Just re-enact the first time.'

I told Arlette that my actual first time had not been anything like the horror she described. It had been tender. I had not been scared. It had not hurt a bit and there had been no blood either.

'No blood?' said Arlette. 'Well, that's sometimes the case. But it won't do for the Duc. We'll have to engineer it so he comes to you at the right moment in the month.'

'You mean . . .'

Arlette nodded. 'It's all in the timing.'

The very idea turned my stomach.

'Think of yourself as an actress, my dear. Real life played out on a stage would seem much too small to be true. Thus you must create true drama around your first time with de Rocambeau. It's what I did when I went to bed with him myself and I'd had five lovers before he got anywhere near me. But men will believe what they want to believe. So make a fuss. Be sure to cry. I promise you it will be worth it.'

I started to cry for real then. Arlette had me stand and pulled me close.

'Hey, hey. It's not as bad as all that. There are worse things than becoming the mistress of a duke. Put on the green dress and make yourself beautiful. Be courteous and polite but hold yourself a little aloof. Get into the part, dear Augustine. You are a sweet and fearful virgin. You have never allowed a man to touch you. You still hope you might avoid your terrible fate.'

'I do!' I cried.

'Yes, that's good,' said Arlette, mistaking my genuine distress for play-acting. 'Let him woo you. Even a man as rich as the Duc likes to feel he has worked for what he has. You must make him think you have the right to choose but that your desire for him has overwhelmed you.'

If only I did have the right to choose.

'Hurry, hurry.' Arlette clapped her hands. 'Your visitor will be here in an hour!'

The Duc arrived exactly on time. Without the benefit of wine, such as we had drunk at our previous meeting, he seemed a little nervous. But his nervousness was not like Remi's. When Remi was nervous, he became quiet and intense. The Duc was the opposite. He talked and smiled too much. His teeth were big and yellow and his smile was not his best expression; he looked far better when he was being stern. But that afternoon, he seemed determined to play the friendly uncle. He enquired after my upbringing in Brittany. I found it too sad to tell him the truth of my childhood, which had been wonderful until the day Papa was lost at sea. I didn't want to share any of my early joy with him lest it be tainted. Instead, I weaved a story. I told him my father was an apple farmer and my mother was a milkmaid. I vowed there and then that the Duc would never see my father's painting. He might be able to buy every other part of me, but he would never own my heart.

After an hour had passed, Arlette came to show the Duc out. It still amazed me that we whores had to go through the dance of propriety too. I heard them talking in the hallway, negotiating another visit. The Duc wanted to come back as soon as possible; he said he could come back that evening. Arlette told him that was out of the question and suggested instead that he return in three days' time. I knew why she had picked that day. Oh, friendly moon.

So three days I had left to remain faithful to the memory of Remi. Three days to think of myself as a good woman, loyal and true. Three days of longing for Remi to rescue me from my fate.

No rescuer came. On the day of the Duc's next visit, I woke early. Arlette and Elaine were as excited for me as two good women might be for a young girl about to take her first communion. They dressed me in a white dress patterned with tiny rose sprigs.

'You could definitely go to church in that frock,' said Elaine.

I would rather I had been dressed in black and heading to my own funeral.

33

The day after Steven took me to the opera was a Sunday. There was no need to get up early. Neither of us needed to be anywhere in particular.

I rolled over and looked at Steven's familiar shape in my Parisian bed. I reached across and took a curl of his hair between my fingers, gently stretching it flat. Then I tiptoed my fingers along his shoulder. I heard him sigh quietly, suggesting that my touch had broken through his deep sleep.

He turned to face me and opened his eyes. He kissed the tip of his finger then touched it to my nose, as though to transfer the affection. It was an unexpectedly tender gesture.

What did this mean? Were we back together? Was our unfinished business ongoing?

Had I been unfaithful to Marco? There was no point thinking like that. Marco had dismissed me, making it clear that all he wanted was to be left alone. I owed him nothing, but I couldn't help feeling a little sad. It was a peculiar feeling. It wasn't so long ago that I was convinced of my undying love for Marco and now I was in bed with someone else. But it wasn't just any old someone. I had spent the night with the man for whom I would once have done anything.

'You look so beautiful in the mornings,' Steven told me. 'Even with your eyes all screwed up like a baby mole's.'

'What?' I swatted him lightly. Then I wriggled across the bed to be closer to him. Burying my face in his shoulder made it easy to hide the confusion and slight anxiety I actually felt.

Steven made breakfast. He was not exactly a keen cook, but when it came to Sunday mornings he was King of the Kitchen. He produced a sumptuous feast from the meagre offerings in my fridge. We ate our breakfast in bed. He fed me fingers of toast dipped in egg.

Afterwards, we made love again. This time it was less urgent, a little lazier. It was several kinds of wonderful. He made sure that I came first. He licked me and caressed me until I thought I would die from the pleasure. Then he fucked me slowly and deliberately, accompanying each stroke with murmured words of adoration and desire. When he came, I started to come again, responding to his ecstasy like an echo.

As we lay entangled in each other's arms, the sun bathed us in its summer warmth through the open window. It felt like a sort of blessing.

Later, in the shower, I felt remarkably relaxed. It was as though I had slipped back into being an earlier version of me: the one who was happy with Steven in London and who would have laughed to think I could get involved in such a tortuous situation as had sprung up in Venice when this was what it could be like. Was I being offered the chance to have such simple happiness again?

Steven and I spent the whole of that day together. As promised, he gave me a tour of his favourite parts of the city. We walked all the way to the Jardins de Luxembourg and beyond there to La Coupole, where we had lunch surrounded by the best of old Paris, who fed tidbits to the *sac-a-main chiens* they carried everywhere.

Steven walked me back home again. We held hands all the way.

'I won't stay,' he said when we got to my apartment block.

I nodded.

'Got to teach a class of American exchange students first thing.'

I understood.

'But it's my birthday this week,' he continued.

'I haven't forgotten.'

'Want to take me out?'

'I suppose I could. What would you like to do?'

'There's this club I've always wanted to go to.'

Steven must have noticed my expression change.

'It isn't that kind of club,' he said quickly. 'No one takes their clothes off. At least, no one in the audience. You must have heard of the Crazy Horse?'

I nodded. The burlesque club was one of Paris's most famous attractions.

'OK,' I said. 'Let's go there.'

Alone in the apartment again, I lay down on the bed where Steven and I had made love four times in twenty-four hours. The sheets wrapped me in his aftershave. I closed my eyes and began to drift into sleep. I felt myself rocking, rocking, rocking, as though on a boat on a calm sea. In my dream, I opened my eyes. I was lying on cushions in the *felce* of a gondola. But I was alone.

Had Steven's returned banished my masked lover for good?

34

Paris, 1840

On the appointed day, the Duc arrived exactly on time, as was his habit. When Elaine let him in, he bounded into the hallway as though he were the family dog, eager to greet his mistress. As Arlette had instructed me, I made sure I was coming down the stairs as the Duc walked in. In the white dress, with my hair braided with matching grosgrain ribbons, I was as ladylike as any girl the Duc might have met in his official social life. I might have been his daughter, even his *petite fille.* I was certainly young enough.

'How ravishing you look, my dear! You are as perfect as a freshly opened peony.'

He thrust a bouquet of white roses into my trembling hands.

I thanked him and showed him through to the salon.

Elaine offered the Duc some tea. He said he had no need of it, but I was desperate to forestall my fate for just a little longer. I said that Elaine should bring me a large pot.

'Very good,' said the Duc. 'A girl should not be thirsty.'

But after just ten minutes, I could tell the Duc was getting impatient. He kept asking whether the tea shouldn't be cool enough to drink by now? Perhaps I should add some milk to speed the process? Wasn't it terribly fashionable to take tea with milk in the English way?

I spun it out for as long as I could, as though five minutes more might make the difference. What was I expecting to happen? A volcano to wash the house away in a river of red-hot lava? After twenty minutes, the Duc took the choice out of my hands.

'I do not have time for conversation this afternoon,' he said, suddenly regaining his composure and speaking to me like the servant I was. 'Mademoiselle, you have had enough tea. We have some business that I should very much like to conclude.'

I blushed hard.

'Of course,' I said. 'Please follow me.'

I took him upstairs. Of course, I could not entertain the Duc in the *chambre de bonne* where I spent my lonely nights. Arlette had had Elaine change the sheets on her bed so that I could take the Duc there instead.

The Duc knew where to go. He pushed open the door and ushered me in. The curtains were already drawn, though it was still early afternoon. Elaine had filled the vases in the room with white camellias. She had heard about Marie Duplessis and thought I could benefit from the motif. I grew to hate camellias after that day.

The Duc took off his coat without asking me whether I minded. I sat down on one of the chairs by the fireplace and folded my hands in my lap. It being summer, the fire was not lit. I felt cold and I was shaking. Though the Duc was there by invitation, as far as I was concerned, I was a young woman about to lose her virginity by rape.

'Not there,' he said. 'Come and sit next to me.'

He had loosened his cravat and sat down upon the bed.

'Actually,' he said. 'Perhaps you could take off my boots first.'

Once in that bedroom, he was a beast. I got down on my knees and started to unlace his boots. Pulling them off, I got an unpleasant whiff of hot feet. I tried not to look disgusted. Unable to resist my maid's instincts and perhaps hoping to buy just a few more seconds, I took the boots and the Duc's jacket and arranged them on the valet stand next to the cheval mirror, where many a man of note had checked his reflection after visiting Arlette.

'Hurry up,' the Duc said harshly. 'We don't have much time. I have a dinner to attend.'

I scurried back to the bed. He patted the mattress and I sat down beside him.

The first touch of his hand upon my cheek made my entire body shudder. Goosebumps appeared all over my flesh.

'You're such a pretty thing,' he said.

'I'm very glad you think so, sir.'

Though my words told the Duc that I was flattered by his attentions, my body would not countenance a lie. My stomach churned and gurgled loudly.

'Sounds like you need something inside you,' said the Duc. 'Perhaps I might have something for you here.'

He patted the front of his trousers, where an erection was already tenting the fabric. It looked big. Arlette had told me that the Duc was as well-blessed physically as he was in land and riches. I saw now that she was not exaggerating.

'Sometimes he left me so sore, I couldn't sit down for days,' she had warned me.

I sat rigid and petrified. The Duc took my hand and placed it on his crotch.

'Bet you've never felt one of these before.'

Idiot man.

I simpered, as Arlette had instructed. I wanted to tell him that he was disgusting and he should go home to his wife. But even had I dared to say something so bold, I would not get the chance. He covered my mouth with his. I half-gagged as he stuck his tongue down my throat and waggled it as though he was trying to count my teeth.

At the same time, he squeezed my right breast like a housewife squeezing an orange. He was not gentle with me in the least. He undid the front of my bodice so that he could put his hand on my bare flesh. He found my nipple and pinched it hard. When I cried out, he gave a little snigger.

'What lovely little titties you have,' he said. 'Even better than the girl in the painting.'

He was too lazy to undo all the laces in my bodice and he ripped the white dress in his eagerness to get my other breast out. He slobbered over them, sucking them like some obscene overgrown baby. I felt my stomach contract in horror as he pulled on my teats.

'Lovely, lovely,' he murmured. 'And never been touched.'

Oh, had he known! I tried to block out the horror of the moment by thinking about the way Remi kissed me so differently. When Remi put his mouth to my breasts, I was transformed with delight. With the Duc sucking at me like a monstrous incubus, I felt sick to the very depths of my soul.

Worse was to come. Still sucking on my breasts, the Duc began to search for a way beneath my skirts. I was wearing a particularly complicated petticoat and I could tell that it frustrated him. He cursed under his breath as he failed to find a way in. Growing impatient, he pushed me back onto the bed as though I were a jointed dummy and devoted himself to getting passage to my knickers. He threw my skirt over my face and put his hand over my Venus mound. He rubbed at me through the fabric of my undergarments.

'I can tell you like that,' he said, as I tried to escape his horrible attentions. His touch was as arousing as the thought of stroking a rat.

But at least it meant that, despite Arlette's instructions, I did not have to pretend to struggle. I wanted to get away from that man more than anything in the world. If I could, I would have run from the room screaming and not stopped until I threw myself into the Seine. But he was so much bigger than me and so much stronger. And he was not afraid to use his strength against me. The harder I struggled, the more excited he seemed to become. I could tell he was enjoying it. He did not want me to be entirely meek. He wanted me to resist his advances. He liked to use force to part my thighs. He did not want me to give myself to him. He wanted to take my virginity by force.

His cock was – as I had ascertained when he showed me the bulge in his trousers – far bigger than Remi's. It was angry-looking, too. All red around the tip and already seeping with arousal. When it was free from his trousers, he instructed me to take it in my hand. I would rather have grasped an iron rod straight from the fire, but I did as he told me.

'See what you have aroused in me,' he said. 'You are a bad girl and you will be punished for what you have done.'

'No,' I begged him. 'No. Please don't!'

In the end, growing tired of my struggling, he flipped me over onto my belly so that my face was pressed into a pillow. Then he pulled my legs apart again and pushed into me without mercy. At first he stabbed blindly but then he found my sweet spot and, stretching me wide with his fingers first, entered me triumphantly. He fell upon me heavily and began to heave and thrust.

'See?' he hissed in my ear. 'See what happens when you make me so excited? You're excited too, eh? I can tell.'

I was not aroused in the least and it felt as though his monstrous member was tearing me apart. When I cried out in pain, he took that as encouragement and continued to thrust and thrust harder. The more I protested, the harder he pushed. My face was in the pillows. I thought I might start to suffocate.

It will be over soon, is what I told myself. It will be over soon.

I counted in my head, one jab at a time. He was so excited. He could not go past a hundred, I was sure. He would not be able to control himself. But he did go past a hundred. At a hundred and twelve he withdrew, but only to turn me over so he could stare at my breasts as he rode me. Bang, bang, bang. He fucked me so hard that the bed knocked against the wall. My eyes drifted up towards the ceiling, to the tiny hole through which I had received my education. I wondered if Elaine was up there even now, seeing how I handled my new role.

Two hundred, two hundred and one.

Four hundred and seven . . .

At last the Duc exploded into me with an enormous bellow. It was so loud and so startling that I did not have to pretend my distress. I cried out as he collapsed on top of me, squashing the breath right out of me and scratching my neck with his beard. He was oblivious to the fact he was suffocating me with his gross, old man's chest. At last, he grew soft and rolled off me again. My tears would be contained no longer. I sobbed openly. I sat up and clutched a sheet to my breast. The sheet below me was stained with blood just as Arlette had planned. Seeing it, the Duc smiled broadly, but then he remembered himself and stroked my face in a gesture of pity for my loss.

'Be quiet, my darling. Do not cry. You have given me a very great treasure today. I shall make sure you are recompensed.'

I continued to cry.

'Today lovemaking must seem to you to be a brutal thing, but you will grow to like it just as much as I do. I have never met a woman yet who did not come to beg me to do to her what I have done to you.'

I stared at him. He was repellent and I did not care if my eyes showed it, but he did not notice. He was too busy telling me what a great lover he was.

'Oh yes,' he said. 'One day soon you will find yourself waiting by the door for me to arrive, so eager to let me have you that you'll start unbuttoning my tunic in the hall.'

He took my chin between his thumb and forefinger and made me look at him. He held my face there until I offered him a smile. It was now that I needed the skills of an actress.

'I must go,' he said. 'My wife is expecting me this evening. She has invited her sister to dine and I must play the part of the good husband. The evening will be interminable,' he continued. 'But now that I have our little secret to think about, I will be able to bear any amount of talk about hairstyles.'

'I am glad,' I said.

'Oh yes, you have given me plenty to think about. I shall be thinking of your sweet soft skin as I carve the lamb this evening. With every sip of wine, I will think of the taste of your tender pink lips.'

He kissed me slowly. I think he thought it was romantic.

It seemed like an age until he had finally gone. The moment the door closed behind him, I ran to the jug of water that Elaine had prepared for me. It was almost, but not quite, cold. I washed myself thoroughly. I scrubbed myself until I was sore. The jug wasn't enough. I begged Elaine to help me draw a proper bath. I only wanted to get rid of the smell of him. Vile man. All that talk of how he would think of me while he was dining with his wife! I wanted nothing more than to put him out of my head for ever.

Arlette returned from the opera a couple of hours later. She called me into the salon and asked me how the evening had been.

'What did he give you?'

The Duc had given me a pearl as big as a blackbird's egg. When I showed Arlette she laughed and clapped her hands.

'You clever girl!'

'How much do you think it's worth, Arlette?' asked Elaine.

Arlette picked up the pearl and held it between her thumb and forefinger. She turned it this way and that, as though she were a jeweller. When it came to it, she had probably handled more jewels than most of the professionals in Paris. She knew what she was talking about when it came to diamonds, rubies and emeralds but pearls were her very favourite of all.

'I have never seen anything quite like this. See how it glows red and pink in the firelight. The surface is completely without flaws. It must be priceless. Did he tell you anything about it?'

'He said it came from Italy. It was once the property of the most notorious lesbian in Venice. The Duc's father ripped it from her hands when Napoleon took the city.'

'She must have been a very special lady to have such a pearl. It's worth millions of francs in my view. And now it belongs to the most wonderful young woman I know.'

Elaine raised an eyebrow.

'You will have your own pearl soon, Elaine. If you can only learn to be a little more ladylike.'

Elaine lifted her skirts and blew a raspberry.

'This is wonderful,' Arlette turned back to me. 'You have captured the poor man's heart. I know he could not believe his luck when he heard you were a virgin. I can't believe our luck that he believed you!'

I took the pearl with me to my room and set it on my nightstand. If Arlette was right, then as soon as I could, I would sell that pearl and use the money to leave this life.

I was glad that I had deceived the Duc. He deserved it.

35

Steven's birthday arrived and, as promised, we were going to the Crazy Horse.

The Crazy Horse is a Parisian legend. The Moulin Rouge and Les Folies Bergères may be on every daring tourist's ideal itinerary, but when it comes to exotic dancing that might actually be considered faintly erotic, the Crazy Horse has the market cornered. It was Steven's first choice when it came to finding somewhere to celebrate his birthday and I didn't refuse. I found I was as keen to see behind the doors of the famous club as he was.

That Wednesday night, I met Steven on the Champs Elysées and we found our way to the address. From the outside, it looked faintly seedy. It was in a basement. We made our way downstairs and a waitress showed us to our seats. I'd booked a table near the stage and a bottle of champagne. I'd had no idea at the time of booking quite how close to the stage our table would be.

The waitress opened the champagne – which was named 'Tsarina', in a suitably romantic way – and poured us each a glass. Steven toasted me. I toasted his birthday. He seemed very pleased with his birthday treat so far.

After about fifteen minutes, the show opened with a pastiche on the changing of the guards outside Buckingham Palace. I was shocked that there was no real preamble to the nudity. The girls were wearing bearskin hats and little else. I was mesmerised by how similar the girls were; the eight women on the tiny stage were as alike in height and body shape as octuplets. I had heard that the girls at the Folies Bergères were weighed before each performance and that straying outside a very narrow band of acceptable size could result in dismissal. The same policy must have applied at the Crazy Horse.

Not only did the girls look astonishingly similar, they moved as though they were puppets controlled by one long string or like parts of a large clock. Tick tock tick tock. No one out of step.

I glanced at Steven. He settled back in his chair. He lifted his champagne to his lips and watched the action on stage.

Each tick-tocking step revealed a little more. Beneath the tiny skirts that circled their waists, the girls wore skimpy black triangle-shaped merkins, so that they even had matching pubic 'hair'. When they turned to the side, and you could see their buttocks, it was clear that the attention to detail continued. Their buttocks even jiggled in time.

'What do you think?' Steven whispered.

I told him I thought the show was surprisingly tasteful.

The classic costume of the exotic dancer, the tiny lingerie and the sky-high shoes, had never looked so classy. I suppose it helped that the shoes were Louboutins and the tiny costumes were being worn on bodies so sculpted and toned. Their perfection made the whole thing seem slightly unreal.

A lone girl came out onto the stage next. She was dressed in nothing much, as had been the rest of the dancers, but her long limbs were covered in body paint that emulated the stripes of a tiger. Her set looked like a cage. But the bars of the cage were not metal; they were made of some kind of elasticated rope, which enabled her to use them as a sort of trapeze.

As she wrapped herself in the ropes, even at one point allowing one of them to go round her neck, I felt myself growing unaccountably anxious. I glanced at Steven again. His focus was fully on the stage. I could see the intensity in his eyes that let me know he was turned on.

The girl danced as though her life depended on it. She embodied the caged animal with nothing to hope for, who expended the last of its energy in an attempt to break through and escape. Though what was on the other side?

While Steven watched the dancer, my mind was suddenly elsewhere. Marco was a caged animal. For whatever reason, he felt he had to be hidden away. By trying to persuade him to leave his confinement, was I putting him under unbearable stress?

On stage, the girl made one last attempt to escape her bonds and ended the routine in a beautiful attitude of despair. When the music stopped, she collapsed dramatically against the set, her chest heaving powerfully with the exertion of her acrobatics. Another curtain came down before we could see her untangle herself. The air of mystery was maintained.

We finished the bottle of champagne as the dancers went through their paces. Some of the routines were playful. Others looked painful. Everything was completed with a polish and professionalism that, for me at least, somewhat lessened the erotic potential.

I wondered if Steven felt the same.

'Thank you,' he said. 'That was the best show I've seen in Paris so far.'

'A bit different from *Carmen*,' I agreed. 'Those girls are so amazing. How do they find so many dancers with exactly the same body shapes and sizes?'

'Dedication,' said Steven. 'Now. Your place or mine?'

I told him that I had an early start. It wasn't entirely untrue. Greg Simon was keen to see some more material and I had promised him a more up-to-date synopsis by the end of the weekend.

'OK,' Steven kissed my hand and flagged down a passing taxi. He stood on the corner and watched me as I was driven away.

Back at the apartment, alone, I was haunted by the memory of the dancer in the cage. Her desperate thrashing had reminded me of Marco, trapped by a psychological cage of his own making. But she also reminded me of myself. Her physical discomfort echoed my own mental state. On one level, my situation was clear-cut. Marco had not contacted me since I returned from Venice. He had not initiated contact since I left Venice the first time round. I had forced my way into the Palazzo Donato a second time and he had eventually asked me to leave. There was nothing left to hope for as far as he was concerned. Steven, on the other hand, was only to keen to see more of me. It should have been a no-brainer. There was no need for me to continue to mourn Marco Donato. I could have ended that night in Steven's arms. But much as Steven was on his best behaviour, attempting to remind me of the man I had fallen in love with, his affectionate attention was somehow falling short.

I wanted the man who could move me without laying so much as a finger upon me. I still wanted the man who had seen me differently and drawn me with such tenderness. I still wanted Marco.

36

Paris, 1841

How quickly life can change. Last February, I shivered in a garret with nothing to my name but the clothes I stood up in. Twelve months later, I had more clothes than I could ever have wished for and all of them in the very latest fashion. As a young girl, I had always wanted an Indian shawl of my own. Now I had ten. They were matched to my outfits. In fact I had so many I had grown slightly blasé about them, draping them over chairs as though they were old blankets. When the Duc bought me a small dog to keep me company when he wasn't around, I let the puppy have an Indian shawl to line his basket.

When it came to diamonds and pearls, I had enough jewels to fund a campaign in Prussia, including a tiara by Monsieur Fossin as expensive and beautiful as anything the Empress Joséphine might have worn. I had my own house – not quite the Champs Elysées palace that Arlette and Elaine had predicted but a big house as different from the room I had once shared with my mother as Heaven is from Hell. I had a cook and two maids. I had my own carriage and my own man to drive it. I had my own horses – two lovely chestnut-coated beauties. The

Duc told me he had chosen them because they matched my hair.

But the question on everyone's lips when a kept woman walks into the room is what exactly she has to do to keep her position. Well, believe me, I worked as hard for my riches as I had done when I took three jobs to keep Remi and me in our miserable garret.

I was expected to be available to the Duc at all times. He would arrive unexpectedly, in the middle of the day or the middle of the night, and I would need to be ready to receive him. Contrary to Arlette and Elaine's wild hopes when I first took the Duc's fancy, I was not allowed to fill my house with friends and feed them fine wines on his budget. He told me he did not want to have to cross paths with anyone he had not personally invited.

So most of the time I sat alone and entertained myself with embroidery or arranging and rearranging the flowers in my room. The Duc bought me a piano but I did not know how to play it. From time to time, I tried but the ugly sounds I wrought from the instrument were worse than no sound at all. Even my little puppy would run from the room when I opened the piano lid.

My life was quite different from Arlette's. How enviable her situation seemed! She might have had money worries from time to time now that her looks were fading, but her house was always full of friends and laughter. I lived in a mausoleum, taken out from time to time like a doll.

Oh, how he wanted me to be like a doll. Arlette had explained to me that what the Duc loved most of all was a naive young creature he could bend to his will. He did not expect me to be cultured or witty with him. I had only to look sweet and appear excited when he arrived to see me. In return, he would give me diamonds like a grandfather gives his daughter sweets.

Except I didn't only have to smile and seem happy, of course.

Much as he loved to dress me up, the Duc loved to undress me too. And the more layers he stripped away from me, the less a gentleman he became. He liked to bend me around his manhood as though I was a sapling. When he had finished with me, I would be scratched and bruised. He especially liked to see bruises on the inside of my pale pink thighs.

And there was worse. One night the Duc told me to dress up, for we were going out together. Ordinarily, I did not mind going out with the Duc, because it was far less onerous than staying in. At least if we were in a restaurant, he could not insist on pretending to suckle from my breast. Or expect me to sit on his prick for hours on end, while he pinched my nipples and slapped my cheeks. My favourite evenings with the Duc – if any of them can be called favourites – were those when we went to a theatre and a restaurant. The Duc would always order wine for me and I found alcohol to be a wonderful elixir for deadening both physical sensations and emotions. Sometimes, if I was very lucky the Duc would drink so much that he would not be able to get an erection, or, best of all, fall asleep in the carriage on our way back to the house.

But that night we were not going to a restaurant. The Duc instructed the carriage driver to take us to the Forêt de Meudon, fifteen miles or so outside the city, where a friend of his had a country estate. I had heard of the man in question. He was someone that Arlette would not allow over her threshold. When I asked Elaine why Arlette had such a strong aversion, Elaine shuddered and said, 'She's not the only one.' But they didn't elaborate and now I was on my way to the man's house without a proper understanding of the horror that would come.

During my time with the Duc I had felt miserable most of the time and degraded on a daily basis, but I had never felt especially frightened. Still, I felt anxious as we passed through the iron gates of the Château Meudon. The path was bordered on each side by dense woodland. I had the strange sensation of being watched from behind the trees.

At the end of the driveway, the Duc himself helped me down from the carriage. I could tell that he was excited. He was smiling his terrible smile.

A footman let us into the house, but I knew immediately that this was not going to be like any dinner party we had attended together before. While we stood in the hallway and another servant helped us with our belongings, I heard the sound of raucous laughter, followed by anguished shrieking, before a naked woman shot out of a doorway further down the corridor, with a half-dressed man in hot pursuit.

I held back. I was startled and instinctively alarmed by the woman's obvious distress.

'Come along,' said the Duc, offering me his arm.

'But—'

He took my hand and placed it on his forearm. He smiled at me, all teeth.

Part of the role I played for the Duc was that of an innocent, but when he wanted me to do something that did not appeal to me in the least, he was not above reminding me that I was not in fact a princess but a common prostitute. I had an awful feeling that I would have to face that truth again if I asked to be excused from the gathering.

37

It was an orgy.

If a newspaper editor, such as the one who courted me so extravagantly he almost lost his wife and his house, might have seen the men in that salon, he would have cried out in delight at the story he could write. As I glanced round the room, I saw half the most important men in France. There were politicians, soldiers, aristocrats and landowners. I held my fan to my face as I looked round. I thought perhaps I even saw our country's leader, with a young woman sitting in his lap.

There was so much naked flesh on display. Though the footmen who let us into the house had been dressed in a smart uniform, beyond the heavy studded doors it was an altogether different matter. None of the staff here were clothed, although they were adorned, in ways that made it obvious which of the naked bodies were guests and which were there only to serve their desires. They all wore collars, of the kind you would put on a dog. Of the kind I refused to put on my own dog because they seemed so very barbaric.

The Duc accepted a glass of champagne from a young woman, letting his eyes travel down her body without any sense of shame. As she turned to serve someone else, he slapped her on the bottom.

I took a glass of champagne for myself, hoping that its magical medicinal qualities would do their work on me quickly. I did not see any woman I recognised in that room. No fellow courtesan. I longed for a friendly face who I might interrogate as to what the evening would hold.

The party's host was touring the room, greeting his friends and admiring the women they had brought with them. I watched as he took some girl's chin in his hand and turned it this way and that as though he were admiring a horse he might buy if she were the right price. He squeezed one of her breasts as he talked to her lover. I was surprised he didn't lift up her skirt to check what was beneath.

My only hope was in the Duc's jealousy. Since we had become lovers, he had been adamant that I should not associate with any man other than him. I certainly could not, as Arlette often did, entertain male friends without a chaperone. I prayed that the Duc would be equally horrified by the thought of any other man touching me here.

Indeed he was.

'Are you not going to share your girl?' the host asked him.

'Not with you,' said the Duc. 'Not with any of you poor fools. We are here merely to observe.'

'Voyeurs,' said the host. 'What fun you'll have.'

'Perhaps we'll pick up some ideas,' the Duc added with a laugh that turned my stomach.

There was to be entertainment in addition to the naked servants. The host clapped his hands and bade us to sit down on the stiff-backed chairs that encircled the room, just as at any smart Parisian soirée. There were not quite enough seats, however, and so the Duc insisted I sat upon his knee. He held me in place a little too tightly.

The host clapped his hands again and a young man entered the room. He was dressed in an Arabian costume. He carried with him a long curved sword. After he had impressed us with his juggling tricks for several minutes, a young woman joined him. She too was dressed as something from Arabia. Her face was veiled.

They danced together for a while. Their *pas de deux* was as beautifully choreographed as anything I had seen at the ballet. They acted their love for each other so well, it could only be because it had its roots in the truth.

I relaxed just a little. Perhaps the evening would not be so awful as I had thought. The dancing was tasteful. But then the boy used the sword to carefully slice the girl's clothes from her body. Three swishes of the sabre and she was naked as the day she was born.

Now the attention of the room was firmly on her and her alone, the female dancer took up a position in front of the host. She danced close enough that he could reach out and stroke her bosom. Then she stepped away and leaned over backwards, making of her body a bridge. In that attitude, she undulated as though she had fewer bones than the rest of us.

And with each undulation she produced, from her vagina, a golden ball.

The audience was delighted. The Duc applauded raucously. The dancer skipped towards him and laid him a golden egg of his own.

Then her partner rejoined her. They moved together again. The girl avoided the sword by the smallest distance every time her partner turned her round until, suddenly, the young man seemed to be about to run her through. I flicked open my fan; I couldn't bear to see what happened. But quick as a flash, he turned his sword and, holding the blade, thrust the handle right up the girl's vagina. The assembled women all gasped in horror. The Duc cheered loudly. As finales go, it was a horrible one. I was relieved, of course, that the girl was not sliced in two, but her humiliation stung me as keenly as any real cut.

The girl stayed on her hands and knees, panting, with the sword sticking out of her like a tail, while her dancing partner accepted the applause of the audience.

'I liked that,' said the Duc. 'I think I would find the sight of you with a handle in your pussy most becoming too.'

I quickly excused myself.

Later that evening, I found the dancer in one of the bedrooms. She was alone, making repairs to her hair.

The girl said her name was Celeste. She wasn't French. I could tell that at once. Her accent was as exotic as her dancing. She was from Hungary. Her parents were itinerants, who came to France every year for the grape harvest. This year they had left her behind.

'My lord took a fancy to me while I was working in his vineyard. He offered my father more money than he'd ever seen if he could keep me here. My ma had just had another baby. One more mouth to feed. It made sense to leave me here in France.'

'And do you miss your family?' I asked her. I knew how badly I missed mine.

'Not really. I thought it would be better to be here than under the same roof as my papa. At least he couldn't fiddle with me any more. But it turns out my lord is even worse. Wants to do everything my father did to me and then some. There's days I can't hardly sit down.'

I remembered Arlette, talking about the Duc.

'But I tells myself that it keeps a roof over my head and I hope my pa has spent the money on my new baby brother.'

'You're a good girl,' I said.

I felt so sorry for her. She was clearly very young. Younger even than I had been when Arlette found me in the Bois de Boulogne. But her whole life had been one of misery and debauch. I, at least, had my happy childhood to look back on when I found myself in the depths of despair.

'He has a dungeon here,' Celeste said then, dropping her voice to a whisper. 'Back in his grandfather's time, they used to throw thieves and beggars in there. Now he uses it for himself. It's like his playroom.'

'I can't imagine.'

'You don't want to imagine,' Celeste assured me. 'I can tell you it ain't nothing good.'

She lifted her skirt and showed me her backside, which was criss-crossed with thin bloody lines.

'See?'

'My God!'

I winced at her pain. She must have covered the marks with make-up when she danced.

'You must escape here,' I said.

'How am I ever going to do that? I've got nothing. I've got no money. I haven't anywhere to go.'

'Here,' I said, taking off an ear-clip. 'Have this. It is worth enough for you to rent a small cottage while you try to find honest work.'

Celeste held the earring in her hand. Her eyes widened as she looked at it.

'This is real, ain't it?'

'Of course. Don't part with it for less than five thousand francs.'

'I'd better hide it,' she said. And with that, she popped the earring straight up her vagina. The opposite of her golden ball trick.

I grasped her hand. 'Get out,' I said. 'Please leave as soon as you can.'

Soon after that, I told the Duc that I was feeling unwell. I was surprised and very relieved when he agreed that we should go back to Paris. Later I would discover it was only because he was tired of having to defend me from the attentions of his friends. He wanted me naked and submissive for himself. That night he had me in a thousand ways.

I do not know what happened to that poor girl, Celeste. Of course, I have an idea but I put it from my mind. I did not want to think that I might have done something more to save her from her fate, as Arlette had saved me from freezing to death the year my mother died. In reality, I could have done nothing more than offer to take her place.

38

Just four days after Steven's birthday came my own. I was turning thirty. A momentous occasion for any woman. At thirty, my mother had a husband and two children. She had a mortgage on a four-bedroomed house and a family dog called Winston. At the same age, my own life was remarkably ungrounded. I had nothing to keep me anywhere, if I was honest. I had no mortgage. No husband. No babies. Not even a pet. It goes without saying that the thought of turning thirty without any of those things in place gave me pause. What should my life look like?

As it was, it didn't look too bad that morning. I woke up in a wide white-sheeted bed to find the summer sunlight pouring in through my window. My sister had texted to remind me that I was getting old. Mum and Dad called shortly afterwards with more traditional, positive best wishes.

Steven had been back in London overnight. He said there were things he had to do there, though he did not elaborate. He told me that he would be back in time to take me for dinner, however. That was something to look forward to. I was glad he did not seem offended by my leaving him on a street corner after our night at the Crazy Horse.

As I dressed for the day, I looked at myself in the mirror. How had the last year changed me? I didn't think I looked significantly older, though I hoped that my time in Venice and Paris had left me looking a little more sophisticated. I had finished my thesis and got myself a paying job. There were, however, definitely other things I wished I might have achieved.

At seven that evening, Steven arrived. I opened the door. He stood on the doorstep with something hidden behind his back. He looked excited to see me. He gave me a kiss and thrust another bouquet of camellias into my hand. But he was hiding something else as well.

'You need to sit down first,' he said. 'I hope you've had a pedicure recently.'

'What do you mean?' I asked.

'Just sit down and close your eyes.'

I took my place on the sofa and did as I was told. I heard the sound of Steven opening a box. I heard the rustling of tissue paper and started to peep.

'Keep your eyes shut.'

'What are you doing?'

'OK. You can open them now.'

Steven knelt before me like Prince Charming in *Cinderella*. Like Prince Charming, he was holding out a shoe for me to try on. Unlike Prince Charming, he was holding a shoe that looked more like a medieval torture contraption than an elegant glass slipper. Steven flipped the shoe over so that I could see the trademark red sole. It was a Louboutin.

'After you admired the girls' shoes at the Crazy Horse the other night, I thought you ought to have a pair of your own.'

'Gosh. Wow.'

'Happy birthday.'

He handed me the shoe. It was insanely high. It had a slight platform sole, but what was more striking was the strapping that would bind my foot and half of my leg with it.

'Let me put them on you,' he said.

How could I refuse? I stretched out a leg. Steven gently fitted my foot into the body of the shoe and began to wind the straps round my leg.

I was suddenly reminded of the underwear he had once bought me.

'You look like a goddess,' he said. But in the sky-high shoes, I felt like a goddess who couldn't walk. Steven held on to my hands as I wobbled to my feet.

'Your legs look amazing.'

It was true that the heels had given me muscle tone where previously I'd had none. The height of the shoes forced my feet into the most ridiculous arch. The shoes were cut low at the sides to reveal my suddenly vulnerable instep. I could see that they were beautiful, but there was something a little sinister about the degree to which they changed both my posture and, subsequently, the way that I moved. I had to take small steps. Subservient steps. Like a geisha.

Some might have said they were dominatrix shoes. I certainly couldn't imagine doing anything more than issuing orders while I was wearing them.

'I'd say that they're limo shoes,' I joked. 'Except I think I would have to be carried even to the limousine.'

'You don't have to wear them anywhere except in bed,' Steven assured me.

'I thought we were going to dinner?'

'Dinner can wait,' he said. 'Can't it?'

Holding me by the wrists, he began to kiss me. It wasn't long before we were back in the bedroom. He pushed me down onto the bed. I was still wearing the shoes.

He lifted my legs so that my calves were resting on his shoulders. My feet in the air looked like they belonged to someone else. Indeed, Steven seemed to be acting like he was someone else. There was none of the tenderness that had accompanied our reunion after the opera. Instead, he was moving me roughly. It was as though he didn't like me very much.

I struggled to sit up.

'I can't do this,' I told him.

Steven looked suddenly angry.

'I don't understand what the problem is. You were happy enough to go to bed with me when we came back from the opera.'

'That was different.'

'How? I thought we had put what happened in London behind us.'

'It's just that . . .' I glanced at the shoes. 'I don't know. I don't think you see me in the same way any more. Since that night at the club. You want me to be someone I'm not. I don't want you to think about the girls at the Crazy Horse while you fuck me.'

'Who said I would be?'

'You bought me the outfit.' I tried to make a joke of it.

'It's just a pair of shoes.'

'I don't know. They remind me of the underwear you bought for that night at the sex club. It makes me uncomfortable.'

'They weren't meant to be comfortable.'

'I mean emotionally uncomfortable.'

'You're nuts, Sarah. You read too much into things. I thought I was getting you something special. They cost enough.'

'And I'm very grateful but . . .'

'Forget it.' He was already standing up. 'This isn't going to work. I'm going home.'

'Steven.'

I couldn't hobble after him in the stupid bloody shoes.

What a day, I'd had. I could hardly call it my most successful birthday ever.

Getting ready for bed, I looked at the Louboutins, sitting next to their box in the corner of the bedroom. I walked over to where they lay in their expensively tortuous beauty. Given the choice between the shoes and going barefoot, I knew which one felt more like me. I put them back into their box and put the box in the wardrobe.

But they were only shoes. Designer shoes that any number of women I knew would have gone crazy over. The whole point of Louboutins was their slightly sluttish edge, wasn't it? The echoes of the dancing girl in Pigalle. Perhaps I did read too much into things. Like I read too much into Marco.

I sent Steven a text message. 'I'm sorry,' I wrote. 'I wish things had gone differently.'

'Me too,' Steven responded. 'Me too.'

But I think we both knew that we would never be able to put ourselves back together again.

39

Paris, 1846

My life with the Duc continued in the same vein for about four years. I was his most precious creature and he guarded me jealously.

One thing had changed, however. I did my best to please him because I had one eye on the future now. I knew it would not be very long before another, younger woman caught the Duc's eye. In the meantime, I must gather all the wealth that I could. When I first became the Duc's plaything, I had not asked him for anything at all, but let him choose what he wanted to give me. As the years passed, I was no longer so coy. Each time he visited, I prattled about the latest fashion in hats or dresses. More often than not, he would insist that I have whatever I needed to make me look acceptably chic. He would give me the money to pay a dressmaker. I would salt the money away and hope that he never asked to see the bonnet shaped like a church bell or the dress with the Ottoman sleeves. Whenever he gave me a piece of jewellery, I would appraise it with a usurer's eye. One pair of pearl earrings equalled three years in a small house near the Bois de Boulogne.

Arlette laughed when I told her what I was doing.

'I thought I would do the same,' she said. 'Just a couple of years with the Duc and I would be set up for the rest of my life. I'd never have to work again. But you'll get used to it, you wait and see. After the Duc has gone, you'll still want new Indian shawls. You'll still want to go to the opera. Take all that you can, but don't think you're saving for retirement. After the Duc there will be someone else. If I were you, I'd start flirting with the next poor fellow.'

That was far more distasteful to me than the idea of a life of poverty. After my time with the Duc and our visits to his horrible friends, I would sooner have spent the rest of my life in a convent than with another man. Except perhaps one.

What about Remi? He still haunted me. After I saw him at the Opéra Comique, on the evening that had changed the course of my life for ever, I had tried my hardest to put him from my mind. But of course it was impossible. Not least because the Duc insisted that the painting Remi had made of me – the one that had inspired his desire – took pride of place in the salon. He had replaced the simple frame with another, altogether more ornate frame that made the work inside look even more humble.

I hated that painting. When the Duc looked at it, he saw a naked body to which he had access day and night. When I looked at it, I remembered the long hours it had taken to create the painting. I remembered Remi's soft eyes when he gazed at me. I remembered how proud he had been to capture my likeness so well. But he had captured more than my likeness. He had captured my love for him too.

But what use was that love now? Arlette had informed me that Remi was engaged to be married. She had heard it from Charles the poet, who had begun to visit her again now that his own marriage was growing stale. I decided the painting had to go.

'I dislike that painting,' I told the Duc one afternoon, when he had had his pleasure and I knew he would grant me whatever I wished for just a little while. 'I know you are fond of it because it resembles me and you credit it with in some way bringing us together, but I have grown tired of looking at that woman. I worry that people think she is me and thus anyone coming into this house may think he knows what I look like naked.'

'I like to make them jealous,' said the Duc.

'I don't want just any man to know what I have under my clothes. Or even to speculate.'

I was surprised to see the Duc nod to himself then.

'Perhaps you're right, my little flower.'

'I'm glad you think so.'

'You should have a portrait of your own and you shall wear the best clothes when you pose for it. But whom shall I choose to paint it? He must be the very best.'

'Thank you.'

'Everything in my life must be the very best,' the Duc continued. 'That is why I chose you.'

'May I have the painting taken down?' I asked.

'Best wait until we have something to replace it.'

The Duc seemed very pleased with himself when he returned the following evening. He told me he had spoken to his most cultured friends and they had helped him to choose the artist who would best do justice to my many assets. He was especially excited, he said, to hear that this new artist's work was very similar to that of the painter who had captured me in my youthful nudity.

I should have realised when he said that what was going to happen next.

'The artist I have chosen is Remi Sauvageon.'

I felt myself grow pale.

'You do not look pleased, my darling.'

'Oh, but I am,' I half-choked on the words.

'I should hope so. I hear great things about him. He is quite the most sought-after artist in Paris these days. I had to offer to pay him three times what he is worth in order to secure his services as quickly as possible.'

'Does he know who he will be painting?' I asked.

'I told him to show up here at the house tomorrow. I also told him not to tell anyone he's coming here. I want your portrait to be a huge surprise.'

I could imagine how awful a surprise it would be for Remi. As awful as it had been for me, I hoped.

'Look happy, dearest,' the Duc exhorted me. 'Let's go upstairs and you can practise some poses. I thought perhaps I would tell him to paint you as a goddess, but which goddess shall you be? Diana? No, you are not so warlike. You are not round enough to be Ceres.'

It was not long before the Duc ran out of goddesses. None of them, it seemed, would properly suit me. Still, the Duc chose my clothes and he chose my pose. The following morning, I dressed in red silk and awaited my beloved's arrival.

Pierre, my manservant, announced Remi shortly after ten o'clock. I composed myself and maintained my composure by balling my hands into fists so tight that my fingernails cut into my palms. With the Duc beside me, I must not betray the slightest emotion at the sight of my lost love. It must be as though Remi and I had never set eyes on each other before. I could only pray that my first and only true love would be so discreet.

40

When Pierre opened the door, Remi bounded in with the energy that I remembered so well. He made straight for the Duc, hand outstretched in greeting, a slight duck of his head to show his deference. He didn't even glance in my direction at first. He was the perfect serf, wanting to show his respects to the master. I might as well have been a prized greyhound. Until the Duc gently directed Remi's attention towards me and I lifted my face.

Oh, Remi's expression said it all. I knew it at once. He was as moved as I was. The moment existed in an instant, but I saw he was shocked by the frisson that still passed between us after so much time estranged. He struggled to find the words.

The Duc looked at him quizzically.

'My goodness,' said Remi.

'Do you not think your subject worthy of your art?' asked the Duc.

'On the contrary,' said Remi. 'I am wondering how I may do justice to such a beautiful face.'

To the Duc he gave no hint that he had already done me great justice, though his eyes flickered from my face to the unsigned portrait that hung over the fire. The way his eyes opened slightly wider showed me he knew his own work.

'Well, I shall expect you to do your very best,' said the Duc. 'I shan't pay for anything less! Now, do you have everything you need in here? Is there enough light? Will you need props? I thought that Mademoiselle du Vert would sit in this chair here, with her fan slightly open on her lap and . . .' The Duc began to smile at his own ingenuity. 'My own face shall be painted in the folds of the fan. A subtle touch.'

Insofar as a mark of ownership can ever be subtle, I thought.

The Duc asked me to show Remi the fan, which already had his face painted upon it by a far less skilful artist.

'Very clever,' said Remi. 'It is a good idea to keep your face somewhere the young lady can see it all day long. Women tend to be terribly forgetful.'

How they both laughed at that.

Oh, the next hour was so painful. It seemed the Duc would never leave us alone. I had not realised he was so interested in art, or rather in the celebrity that followed the artists of Paris these days. The Duc wanted to know about Remi's associates. 'Was it true that So and So . . . Did What's-his-face really . . . Have you heard of Monsieur Blah . . .'

Remi played the part of the jolly bohemian, regaling the Duc with lurid tales from the underbelly of the city. The more he said, the more I began to hate him. Remi played the part well but I knew the truth. He could no more live a life of happy poverty than the Duc himself might have done. Remi was soft. He was an impostor. When he glanced at me, I was glad to see him look slightly ashamed.

'Well,' said the Duc. 'I must leave you to your work. How long will it take? I want to reveal the portrait at a small party in four weeks.'

'It will take as long as it takes,' said Remi.

The Duc nodded. I expected him to protest that Remi was in his employ and should make sure the painting was ready on time, but he didn't. It was odd. I had never seen the Duc subservient but subservient he was in the face of art and artistry.

The Duc left, kissing me on the forehead as he went.

When the door was closed, Remi and I stared at each other. He did not step closer to me and I did not move from my seat.

'You look well,' I said eventually. 'I am glad to hear your painting is gaining recognition.'

Remi continued to stare.

'The Duc's patronage makes you the best in Paris,' I prattled on. 'Since he will not bother with anything less than the best.'

'So what does that make you?' Remi asked suddenly. 'The best lay in France?'

I turned my face away from him as though I'd felt a blow.

'I suppose I should have known you'd come to this. Arlette must be very proud of you. I bet she couldn't wait to pair you off with some rich old prick when she had you back in her grasp. "Augustine du Vert." Was changing your name Arlette's idea too?'

'What was I supposed to do?' I hissed at him. 'After you left me all alone on the Rue de Seine? You said you loved me! And then you left me. You chose the easy life in Guerville over my love. You left me with nothing but the clothes I stood up in while you went back to the bosom of your family like the milksop you are. Unable to live without your comforts, your restaurant meals and your nights at the theatre. Or was it just an excuse to be rid of me? Less than six months after you left, you were back in Paris. Sitting in the stalls at the Opéra Comique with your friends again. You weren't so desperate to be parted from me that you came to find me first.'

'But I did,' said Remi.

'When?' I said. 'When did you come to find me?'

'Only two weeks after I left you.'

'I don't believe you.'

'I came back as quickly as I could. I was taken ill from exposure on the way to Guerville. As soon as I was better, I went straight to the Rue de Seine and hammered on our door. You'd gone. Some vile old woman had already taken our place. Then Jeanne-Marie sent me to Arlette's house. I ran all the way. And all the time I was running, I imagined scooping you into my arms and carrying you away from there. I was ready to defy my father. I knew that the moment he met you, he would understand why we could not be parted. But you had already forgotten about our love. Elaine told me you'd found someone else. You gave up on me just like that.'

He snapped his fingers.

'You told me to give up on you! In those horrible letters. When you sent me the money.'

'What letters? What money?'

'The letters telling me we were from different stock. The money to buy me off.'

'I never sent you any money. Nor any letters, except the one to tell you I would be back with you the minute I was well.'

'You sent me a letter telling me it was for the best that we broke off our relationship and a promissory note drawn against your father's account. Don't you remember?'

'What?'

'I have never been more insulted in my life.'

Remi looked suddenly furious.

'Don't you see? My father wrote those letters, while I lay ill in bed. He must have copied the address from my letter telling you I would be coming back and destroyed it before sending you a message of his own. I would never have deserted you.'

'Your father wrote the letters? Why should I believe that?'

'We have an identical hand. Look!'

He pulled a piece of paper from his jacket pocket. It was a letter from his father. A friendly letter full of fatherly concern for his son's progress in Paris. The handwriting was indeed very like Remi's.

'When I recovered from my hypothermia, I told my father I was going back to Paris to marry you. I should have wondered why he seemed so unconcerned. He knew you would not be waiting for me.'

'No one told me you came to the house,' I said. 'Do you think for one moment that I could possibly have forgotten you so quickly? You should have begged to be let in and waited until I appeared.'

'I thought I deserved your disdain.' Remi stared at his feet. He was as a small boy, deeply ashamed. When he looked up again, something in his expression had changed. 'But you acted on my father's letters with alacrity. As Elaine confirmed. You could not have accepted to be this man's concubine if you really loved me. I should have known you were a whore when I met you at a prostitute's house.'

'Why are you being so cruel to me?' I wailed. 'I was devoted to you. You were the only man I ever loved. I would have loved you for the rest of my life. I gave you my virginity and you left me to fend for myself and yet you accuse me of being a whore? It is you who made me a whore, Remi. The alternative was to starve. Don't tell me you would have starved for me.'

Remi's shoulders slumped and he was once again the broken man who had set off in the snow to beg his father's assistance rather than face hunger with me.

'I have been punished for my cowardice a thousand times,' he said. 'The sight of you with the Duc burns my eyes. Every day we've been apart I have thought of you. I will be punished until I die for what I did when I left you alone in the snow.'

'I do not blame you for your weakness. But in turn, you must not blame me for having accepted the Duc's protection. Just as you have chosen to marry a woman I understand to be the heiress to quite a substantial fortune herself.'

'I do not love her,' Remi burst out. 'I love only you. Augustine, you must understand. That has not changed at all.'

'Oh!' I was distraught.

'This is hopeless. Hopeless!' Remi wailed. He threw a piece of charcoal across the room. 'I cannot be expected to go through this torture. I cannot be so near you and yet not have you for myself.'

Taking his sketchbook with him, he left me at once.

That evening, the Duc noticed a change in my mood. I always tried my best to be light and gay in his presence, but now that Remi was back in my life, I just couldn't pretend.

'You are listless, my petal,' said the Duc.

I told him it was due to a novel I had been reading, in which a girl and her sweetheart are kept apart by the most terrible circumstances.

'You girls and your novels. I do not think you ought to be exposing yourself to such nonsense. Why don't you take up sewing? Sewing never made anyone sad.'

The Duc seemed to have forgotten my humble beginnings as a seamstress.

My sadness did not discourage the Duc from making love to me. He started by kissing away my tears in the manner of a mother comforting a small child, but he soon grew tired of that and forced me to accept his tongue in my mouth. After that, his mouth wandered down my neck towards my cleavage. He pushed my breasts together and thrust his tongue between them. I continued to cry but if he noticed, he ignored it. He was bent on nothing but his own pleasure now.

He undressed me, throwing my gown over the back of a chair and ripping my chemise in his impatience. I did not say anything, although since I had made my plan for an escape, his tendency to rip things hurt me far more, as I would be less able to sell the clothes when I was no longer in his favour.

That night, however, I was very much in the Duc's favour. My low mood and my heartfelt tears had filled him with desire for me.

More than ever, I felt like a puppet in the Duc's strong arms. I let him pull me this way and that. I let him examine the secret places of my body more closely than any doctor. He asked me to call him 'Papa'. As soon as he was hard enough, he forced his way into me, not caring that I cried out in pain because I was not ready for him. I knew only too well that my anguish did not make him more careful; it made him more determined to have his ecstasy. I braced myself as he hammered into me again and again, grunting and swearing like the pig that he was. When he came, I wanted to scratch his face off. Instead, I balled my hands into fists again and promised myself that I would not have to bear this awful situation much longer. I would run away. I would ask the cook to sell some of my things. If I offered her a cut of the proceeds, she would keep my secrets, I was sure.

The Duc did not have to leave me quickly that night, alas. He wanted to stay beside me and tell me all about his latest social triumph and complain about his wife. I knew what to do. I nodded along, but all the time my mind was elsewhere. It was with Remi, back when we were happy together in the garret.

I was terrified I would never see him again. I lay awake all night long, praying he would change his mind.

When Remi returned in the morning, as if nothing had happened, I felt for once that fortune might be on my side.

41

Greg Simon, the producer who had been my main point of contact for the Augustine project, was coming to town. He wrote to tell me he would be arriving in just a couple of days. When I got his email, my first instinct was to panic. Since breaking up with Steven for a second time, I had indulged in something of a wallow. I was sure he would want to stay in the apartment, and it was a mess. After all, the production company was paying for the place and it was big enough for both of us.

But when I told him that I would have his room ready for him, Greg told me not to bother. When he was in Paris, he liked to stay at Le Bristol. Since he would only be in town for a couple of nights, he wanted to make them luxurious. On that subject, he continued, perhaps, after our meeting, I would care to join him for dinner at Macéo on the Rue des Petits Champs?

The restaurant was right opposite the Bibliothèque Nationale. I didn't have much else on my agenda. I told him I would be delighted.

I had wondered what Greg Simon would be like. Naturally, I'd googled him the first time I heard his name. He was a seasoned Hollywood professional. He'd made several shows that I'd actually heard of. In his photograph, he looked like any American professional of a certain age. His hair was neat. His smile was big. He could have advertised anything from hair loss products, to toothpaste, to life insurance.

When I met him in the flesh, I'm glad to say he did not look quite so plastic.

He had booked a corner table in the restaurant. As we were shown to our places, Greg explained to me that Macéo, now a chic spot popular with the businessmen from the nearby Bourse, had once been the site of a high-end house of ill-repute. The elegant restaurant's windows looked out onto the back of the Palais Royal, originally a palace built for a cardinal, where casinos and brothels had proliferated after the revolution. Later, the novelist Colette had been a frequent visitor. Her gift to the proprietor in her day – a pickled melon – still had pride of place in the quiet spot where we were seated that night.

'I love all this history you Europeans have,' said Greg. 'I just wish the plumbing wasn't quite so antique.'

I laughed at his self-parody of the American abroad.

As we talked about the project so far, I began to feel excited. Calum Buchanan – one of the most sought-after young stars in Hollywood – had signed on to play Remi Sauvageon. His name had brought millions in funding in the past few days. A contract had been signed while Greg was in the air over the Atlantic.

'This is the best news but alas, there's just one condition,' said Greg. He took another gulp of wine as though to steel himself to tell me what that condition was. 'He wants to pick the actress who plays Augustine.'

'Is that a problem?' I asked.

'It is when he wants me to audition a complete unknown. Here. You've been living and breathing Augustine du Vert for the past few weeks. You should have a good idea what kind of girl could play her. Tell me what you think.'

He reached into his folder and pulled out a black and white headshot. He passed it across the table to me.

Unknown to Greg she may have been but the girl in the photograph was not unknown to me. It was the girl behind the mask who had been the catalyst for my first break-up with Steven. I knew her all too intimately. The girl in the picture was Kat. I could only stare at her familiar snaggle-toothed smile.

'English teeth,' said Greg. 'No offence. She'd have to get those fixed. Having said that, maybe it doesn't matter so much if she's going to be playing a nineteenth-century whore. I don't suppose they were all that hot on orthodontics back then.'

'No,' I agreed. 'I don't suppose they were.'

As I traced the outline of Kat's face with my finger, one of Colette's maxims came to mind. *Look for a long time at that which pleases you and longer still at what pains you.*

'But she's pretty enough,' Greg continued. 'And there's something kind of timeless about her face.'

'What's her experience?' I asked.

'She did a load of adverts when she was a teenager.'

That explained why I thought she'd shown confidence way beyond her years when we met at L'Infer.

'She's done some short films. Nothing full-length. Certainly not as a lead. The one good thing is that she'll be cheap.'

I passed the photograph back.

'It's quite a risk, isn't it, expecting someone so inexperienced to carry a film?'

'You're not kidding. But Calum made it a condition that we find something for her to do. With a bit of luck, by the time I've seen her he'll have started dating someone with a proven track record. Someone who can actually act.'

'When are you seeing her?'

'She's coming to Paris tomorrow morning,' he said.

42

Paris, 1846

Who would have thought that being in Remi's presence again could bring me so much pain? When the Duc was with us, or when Pierre or one of the other servants was in the room, Remi was perfectly correct. He would make small talk and entertain us all with his stories. The moment we were alone again, the torture began. Now I knew he had not just abandoned me that winter, my heart softened towards him all over again. I forgave Elaine too. I knew she had only been trying to protect me by sending Remi away – she had heard about the horrible letters and believed, as did I, that they were from Remi's hand – but what happiness we had missed as a result. What terrible paths we had taken instead.

Then, one day about a week after he began to paint me, Remi announced that he could take no more. He clasped my hands and beseeched me.

'I have to be with you. I want you to be my wife.'

'But what can we do? You are to be married to someone else and even were you not, I have fallen so far, you could never possibly acknowledge me as your woman in public.'

'I can and I will. I am not the frightened provincial boy who fled Paris at the first sign of hardship any more, my love. I am the most sought-after artist in this city. The most fashionable people in Europe want me to paint their mistresses, their wives, even their horses . . . I must get more practice at horses.' He laughed at the thought. 'The situation is very different this time, Augustine. I will be able to support you. Not quite like this.' He waved his hand around the room. 'But . . .'

'I don't care about this,' I assured him. 'This place has never felt like my home. I was happier in our little garret than I have ever been in this gilded cage. I should be glad to be away from it. I hate all this fanciness! Give me the man I love and a simple wooden rocking chair and I should be the happiest woman in the world.'

'Then we'll do it.'

'How?'

'We shall run away together. We could go now! The Duc will not be back this evening. By the time he realises you've gone, we could be on the other side of La Manche.'

I would have done it. I would have left the Duc right that minute. I would have packed up only the things that were truly mine: my old bone comb and my father's seascape; and run away with joy in my heart. But moments later, Remi was not so ready to put our plan into action.

'Wait. I am being ridiculous. We cannot leave quite so quickly, my dear little bird. However romantic it sounds to run away with nothing but the clothes we're standing up in, we will need something to live on until the scandal dies down. The Duc has said he will pay me the first instalment for the painting tomorrow. When he has done that, we will have the funds to rent a little cottage for a year. It will be modest but it will be warm.'

'And we will be so happy there!' I said.

He took both my hands in his.

'Yes. Yes. We will be so happy there.'

Then he smothered me with kisses.

We did not waste any time. Having sealed our new pact with a kiss, Remi and I retired to the day bed. We rolled and giggled just as we had done in our youth. In Remi's hands I was helpless and helplessly happy.

'Stay with me,' I said.

The Duc would not be back that night. He was far away from Paris. He had been concerned I would miss him, poor fool, but in fact I was filled with elation at the thought of being without him. I would be spending the night with my true love instead.

'What about the servants?' Remi thought to ask when we were both already naked.

'They are loyal to whoever pays them,' I said. 'I have more than a little money in a box beneath my wardrobe. I will make them a gift and the Duc will hear nothing, I promise.'

I trusted my servants. I had overheard them gossiping in the past. The cook said she felt sorry for me, saddled with such a cruel lover. She would not begrudge me a little happiness. Pierre the manservant, who was in love with the cook, would look to her for his opinion on the matter.

Momentarily putting on my dress again, I went down to the cook and told her I would have a guest for dinner.

'Very well, mademoiselle,' she said. The glint in her eye told me she approved.

How sweet it was to make love to Remi again. After so many years of being tossed around like a doll stuffed with rags by the Duc, it was simple ecstasy to be back in his arms. When we kissed, we were connected in many more ways than the simply physical.

Remi's body was so beautiful. Perhaps he was a little heavier now that he was a famous artist and could afford to eat and drink all that he wanted, but otherwise he was little changed since we last lay together in the Rue de Seine. He assured me that the same was true of me, though I knew that unhappiness had robbed me of my appetite and made me thin. It had also stiffened my shoulders so that I might have been carved from a block of wood. Only when Remi kissed me so tenderly did I feel my body relaxing in his embrace.

How happy I was to see Remi's manhood, bobbing up to greet me like an old and trusted friend. I was only too delighted to fall on my knees in front of Remi's penis and take him into my mouth. The growing sense of his arousal was wonderful to me.

To have him inside me again was pure bliss.

Later Remi caressed the most secret part of me and I came just as I used to. And I cried, but for the first time since the Duc took my second-hand virginity, I was crying with happiness. With Remi back in my arms, I felt complete.

With the Duc, I never reached that place where I found my own pleasure and during the long dreary years with him, I had given up on finding pleasure for myself when I was alone. With Remi back in my life, it was as though I was waking from a long winter.

The next morning when I woke, the sun was shining brightly like a blessing but my darling Remi was already gone. In his place, he had left a note on the pillow. He promised me that he would devote the rest of his life to making me the happiest woman in the world. Once he had prised me from the Duc's clutches, we would never again be parted.

With his note pressed to my bosom, I stepped lightly through the house. I had a smile for everyone and they had smiles for me. When I was dressed and settled in my salon, I did not insist that Pierre move my chair so that it faced away from my likeness any more. Now that Remi was back, I could remember the love with which he had painted me with soaring happiness.

Later in the day, my mood dipped just a little. The Duc would soon return from the countryside and he must not see me changed. He must think that I had spent the previous evening alone, pining for his company. I hated the thought that I must continue to deceive him, but I knew Remi was right; he must be paid before we could make our escape. I had already decided that I would not take any of the jewels the Duc had given me when I ran away. If I took nothing, he would be less likely to try to find me, as he surely would be able to if I tried to sell any of the distinctive baubles.

'And how was your day with the artist?' the Duc asked when he returned.

'It was dull,' I lied. 'I hate to have to sit still for hours on end.'

'But did he not entertain you with his conversation?'

'He had nothing to say that interested me.'

'Good,' said the Duc. 'If he tried to steal you from me, I would have his brushes stuck up his arse and used as a wick to set fire to him.'

I must have grown pale; the Duc apologised for his coarseness.

'But of course, you are not so silly that you would ever run away from me, my darling child.'

He took my left hand by the wrist and kissed my palm. I flinched as I remembered how Remi had kissed me in exactly the same spot so very recently. And then I felt triumphant. This would all be over soon.

43

It had been less than a year since I last saw Kat, but in that time she had changed quite a bit. When we met at L'Infer, she was nineteen years old and Steven's student. Though she had incredible confidence for someone so young, she was also kittenish and eager to please, living up to her name. As soon as I saw her walk into the lobby of the Bristol, I knew that she was considerably more sure of her worth now, although she was still only twenty.

The doormen fell over themselves to help her, though she was carrying only a tiny paper bag of macarons. I didn't think I would have attracted so much assistance had I been dragging in a trunk the size of a coffin. Kat was wearing a slim-fitting denim jacket. She handed it to another member of staff, who carried it off to the cloakroom as though it were a mink. Underneath, she wore a summer dress, diaphanous and elegant and, though it was just a scrap of fabric, obviously very expensive. The perks of having a movie-star boyfriend, I supposed.

As Kat chatted for a while to the concierge, I took a moment to examine her more closely. I wondered if Steven knew about the elevation in Kat's status as far as men were concerned. Perhaps he didn't even know she'd left university to become an actress. After all, he'd been in Paris for several months. I wondered then if Kat had visited him here.

Greg Simon came down into the lobby. You wouldn't have guessed for a moment that he had any reservations whatsoever about being forced to consider an unknown for the biggest role in his film (or second biggest, as he'd wryly pointed out to me. Now that Calum was on board, there was every chance that the film would shift focus to the painter rather than the prostitute). He greeted Kat warmly. She air-kissed him on both cheeks with a nonchalance I could never manage. Kat certainly would never bump noses, as I always seemed to end up doing. They chatted for a short while: weather, traffic, macarons (Kat showed him the bag from Ladurée), before Greg motioned that they should make their way to the bar where I was waiting.

'Kat Adams, this is Sarah Thomson. Sarah has been developing the script. I thought it would be interesting for you to meet her since she knows Augustine du Vert as well as any of us. She's a bona fide historian. Didn't you study history, Kat, before you gave it all up to risk your sanity in the movie business?'

'I did,' said Kat. She put her hand out to shake mine. Her eyes did not betray the slightest sense of recognition. Perhaps she did not recognise me – after all, we had been wearing masks when we met – but surely she would have put two and two together when she heard my name and my profession. How many historians called Sarah Thomson were there? Or perhaps Steven had meant so little to her, she'd genuinely forgotten that before she came along, he had a girlfriend called Sarah.

'I've been reading up on Augustine ever since Calum mentioned he'd signed to play Remi Sauvageon,' Kat told Greg. 'She's such an interesting character. It's incredible the amount of wealth those courtesans amassed. I was reading about one – La Paiva – whose lover built her a palace on the Champs Elysées. Can you imagine? What's the equivalent today? I suppose it's becoming Hugh Hefner's number one bunny.'

'Even Hugh's married these days,' said Greg.

Greg and Kat settled into an easy conversation about the lives of the *grandes horizontales*, as the very best of the courtesans were called. I didn't feel I could add very much. Though I had never encountered Kat during her time at university, I could see why Steven had offered her a place on his course. She was intelligent and widely read. She was keen to know as much as she could about whatever subject you cared to introduce her to.

'Sarah, we've been doing all the talking,' said Greg after a while. 'Perhaps you could tell us a bit more about how you envisage Augustine?'

'She was very much a romantic at heart but she did not give her love easily. Though she gained a reputation as one of the wickedest women in Paris, it was largely unfounded. She actually had only two lovers her entire life: the Duc who gave Augustine her fortune and, of course, Remi Sauvageon.'

'I find it fascinating that she let him come back to her, after he'd been such a jerk, leaving her alone in the garret while he went back to live in comfort with his family,' Kat interrupted.

'Whoever said love is rational?' I asked. 'I can think of plenty of modern instances where a woman has forgiven a man who seems to be one hundred per cent rat.'

'I wouldn't do it,' she said, with a confidence that made me sure she had never really been in love. She had no idea what it was like to be humbled by your feelings for another person. I knew then for certain that she would come to no harm if her relationship with Calum didn't work out. It would barely touch her. Kat was no Augustine. She was more like Arlette, moving from one man to another, making sure that each move was in the upward direction. Captivating Steven had almost certainly helped her in her first year at university. Charming Calum had launched her into the stratosphere. I imagined their first meeting – she said they'd met in a gym. The poor bloke probably didn't know what had hit him. And now he was willing to risk putting her in a movie that could make or break his career without ever actually having seen her act? Kat certainly had some skills of seduction.

'I would never let go of my pride like that,' Kat continued.

'You'd be surprised at the things you're prepared to let go of when you really love someone,' I assured her.

'No,' she said. 'That's not my idea of love.'

Kat left after forty-five minutes. She had a meeting with a model agent in town. Yes, even though she was a good four inches shorter than the average catwalk model, Kat was trying her hand at that too. It seemed there was nothing she couldn't do – or rather, nothing people didn't think she could do – now that she had Calum's seal of approval.

Greg and I were left alone.

'What do you think?' asked Greg. Before I could answer, he told me, '*I* think she is absolutely charming. She's got a timeless look about her. I can totally see her in a recreation of the dress Augustine's wearing in the portrait. I could see her in just about anything, to be honest. I don't say this very often, but that girl's got star quality. Maybe Calum wasn't just being led by his libido after all.'

'She certainly seems to be very switched on,' I agreed.

But I was still confused by the way Kat had not shown the slightest hint of having met me before. I started to wonder if it was a deliberate dig at me, reminding me that I was insignificant. Perhaps she had liked Steven more than I suspected and he'd told her when he wrote to me while I was in Venice, asking me to reconsider our split.

Whatever Kat's reason, I was glad I would not have to spend too much time with her, if any. I could probably get through the rest of my life without ever having to see her in the flesh again. Though Greg had offered me the opportunity to write the first draft of the actual script, he had warned me at the same time that it was very unlikely I would get more than one go at it. He was already looking for what he referred to as a 'name screenwriter'. It was just as important as getting the right actors on board. Perhaps more so, because there were very few actors who had the skill to make a bad script into a great movie. They were only as good as the words the screenwriter put into their mouths.

Still, despite the caveats, I was grateful for the opportunity and the money that came along with it. It was more than I would earn in a year as an academic.

'Of course,' Greg continued, 'she'll need to do a screen test and the casting director will have to take a view, but as far as I'm concerned, Kat's got my vote. I've seen pictures of her with Calum. It looks like they've got chemistry. This could be dynamite.'

'She'd certainly make a good Arlette,' I suggested. 'She has a knowingness about her.'

'No. She's not old enough for Arlette. She can do the ingénue,' Greg insisted.

'Well, if she can't, then perhaps Calum will be happy if she plays Arlette instead, is all I'm suggesting.'

Greg nodded, but I knew he wasn't really taking much notice of me. He had succumbed to Kat's magic. Why wouldn't he? After all, I knew what it felt like to be on the receiving end of her gale-force charm. It was not something any mortal could hope to resist.

'I'll fix up the screen test. Do you think you could write a scene for her with Calum? It would be useful to see what their chemistry's like. Weird thing is, I was always convinced he was gay. I guess he's just very good at the casting couch.'

I thought about that on my way back to my apartment. What a cut-throat world it was, if you could only get ahead by pretending to be whatever the producer standing in front of you wanted. Straight, gay, submissive. What's your pleasure?

44

Later that evening, my mobile rang. My French mobile. So few people had the number that I barely recognised the ringtone. When I eventually picked it up, after it had rung three times, I didn't know the number on the screen. I pressed answer.

'*Bonsoir*?' I said tentatively.

'Sarah, it's Kat.'

'How did you . . .?'

'Get your number? Easy. I told Greg I'd like to talk to you about Augustine. Get more of a feel for the character before I fly to LA to do the screen test. Greg was delighted to hear I'm taking the role so seriously. I think it's in the bag. I have a feeling Greg would give me anything I asked for right now.'

She laughed. Her laugh was slightly cruel.

'So,' I said. 'What do you want to know? From the conversation we had at the Bristol, I'd say that you've read pretty much everything that's ever been published about Augustine. I'm not sure how much I can add. It's all down to your acting skills now. And they're pretty good, I have to say.'

'Thank you.'

'Certainly no one would have guessed that you and I had met before. You played the stranger brilliantly.'

'What should I have done instead? Said, "No need for the introductions, Greg. I've already brought Sarah to orgasm in a seedy London sex club?"' She laughed again. 'I was trying to spare your blushes. Though I have to say, I was pretty surprised when I saw you. I didn't think we'd ever meet again. Not after you ran off to Venice.'

'I didn't run off to Venice. I had a research project to finish. I'm a historian. Seems like you've given up on that.'

'I only picked history because it was my favourite subject at school. I had no intention of seeing it through if something better came along, and something better *has* come along.'

'Calum?'

'You could call it that. I call it the chance to be an actress, which is what I always wanted. Look, I didn't call you up to trade insults over the phone. What are you doing tonight? Do you fancy meeting up for a drink?'

It wasn't the question I had expected. Part of me wondered why she would ever think I might want to go for a drink with her. She must have known on some level how difficult I had found my split from Steven and that I blamed her for being the catalyst. A larger part of me was both flattered and intrigued. I found I wanted to know more.

'OK,' I said.

'I knew you'd say that.'

'Does anyone ever refuse you?'

'Not often,' she admitted.

'So where shall we meet? Do you know Paris at all? I can recommend a few bars near to your hotel. There's a place called the . . .'

'I know Paris pretty well,' Kat interrupted. 'Why don't you meet me at Willi's on the Rue des Petits Champs? Dress up.'

When I arrived at Willi's, Kat was already at the bar, chatting to the handsome older guy behind it. She had changed out of her elegant floral frock into something much more edgy – a tightly corseted number that even I recognised as an Alaïa original. She beamed when she saw me.

'We meet again,' she said, kissing me on both cheeks. 'Nice dress,' she added. Her lips curled to tell me that she recognised it and was amused by the memories it brought to mind. I had inadvertently put on the dress I wore to L'Infer.

'I didn't know what would be appropriate,' I said.

'Oh, that dress is totally appropriate. You could wear it anywhere. Dinner with the in-laws. A sex club . . .'

I shook my head to warn her not to go there.

We drank a bottle of wine and shared a plate of cheese. The conversation was not as awkward as I had expected. Kat really did seem serious about preparing for her screen test. She was deadly serious about becoming an actress. Inspired by her enthusiasm, I told her more about Augustine than I had planned to. But then, Kat had a way of getting you to give up more than you intended. We talked until the bar staff started to clean the tables around us.

'Come on,' said Kat, when one of the barmen swept the floor around her feet. 'I know another great place nearby.'

We walked – slowly because of Kat's heels – around the corner to the Rue Thérèse. There didn't seem to be much going on there, but Kat drew my attention to a plain, blue-painted door next to a large plate-glass shop window hung with a venetian blind.

'This is it,' she said.

'Really?'

She pushed the door open. Beyond that first door was an anteroom, as plain and uninspiring as the waiting room of a minicab firm. It had a hatch just like a minicab firm too, but that was shut. There was no one to greet us. I wondered if Kat had got the right address.

'This is where they decide whether or not we're sexy enough to get into the club itself,' she told me.

'How will they do that?'

'It's like a holding pen. We're being watched. See?'

Kat looked up into the corner of the little anteroom where a CCTV camera was focused down on us. She gave it a little wave.

'Take your coat off,' she told me. 'Show them what you've got.'

I thought about Clemence and Arlette encouraging Augustine to show her shoulders at the opera.

'I don't know . . .' I began.

'Come on,' said Kat. 'This place is fun and not everyone gets to see inside it. Don't you want to know more about the real Paris?'

Maybe it was the wine that made me agree with her. I shrugged my coat from my shoulders. Kat, meanwhile, preened for the camera like a young hopeful on *X Factor*. She had all the moves.

After about half a minute – though it seemed much longer – we heard a buzzing sound that indicated the inner door was opening. We were through.

'What is this place?' I asked my new friend.

'Just a club,' said Kat. 'You'll like it. They stay open until late. Lots of famous people come here.'

'What's it called?'

'I'd tell you but then I'd have to kill you.' Kat laughed. 'Come on.'

It didn't seem like much of a place. It was dark and old-fashioned. Kat found us two stools by the bar and ordered two glasses of champagne. A whole bottle duly arrived. The barman explained that it was courtesy of the man in the corner. We peered to see him. He was quite ordinary looking. He wore a suit with a white shirt, unbuttoned at the neck. Kat raised a glass to him before she turned back to me.

'Cabinet minister,' she whispered.

'What? How do you know?'

'I'm interested in French politics,' she said. 'My mother is French. I lived here until I was eleven.'

That explained her ease with the door staff at the Bristol. Kat was a bilingual flirt.

In the dim light, Kat looked even more beautiful than before. No matter what I'd thought of her before, I could see the star quality Greg talked about. She knew her power and her potential. I wished I could have absorbed some of it too. I especially wished that I'd had her confidence when I was her age. It was a rare thing for someone so young to appreciate the mesmerising quality of youth.

We wouldn't want for a drink that evening. Even as the barman was upending our empty bottle of champagne in the ice-bucket, another shadowy figure was signalling across the room that our next drink should be on him. Kat received these favours with grace and poise. I would have spluttered and insisted on paying my own way, insulting the giver because I was not sure I deserved the gift. Kat was not like that. She was a true descendent of Arlette Belrose and Clemence Babineaux. She understood how to turn beauty into wealth.

I suggested as much to her.

'I read about Clemence Babineaux when I was just fourteen,' she said. 'And I was fascinated by her. The power she exerted over men was immense. But she was exploited too. When she was just a child. I think you have to hate men more than a little to take such cruel advantage of them. When it came to finding love, she ended up with a woman.'

'I didn't know that,' I said.

'She was tired of all the thrusting.' Suddenly, Kat placed her hand on my knee. 'You know, I didn't make love to you just because Steven wanted me to. I told him that afternoon that if I didn't actually fancy you, I wouldn't be able to do it. I may be a great actress but even I can't fake enough enthusiasm to go down on another woman if she doesn't turn me on.'

'I suppose I should be flattered.'

'You should. You've got an amazing body.'

She stroked the bare part of my thigh beneath my hem.

'There's something else about you too. You have a sort of buttoned-up intensity. Like Charlotte Rampling in *The Night Porter*. As soon as I saw you walk into the club, so upright and brittle, I knew that if you could ever let go of your inhibitions you would be dynamite.'

I stared at Kat. She looked right back at me. She didn't care if I seemed discomfited.

'It was a challenge I could not resist,' she continued. 'Getting you to come undone for me.'

'I did it for Steven,' I said. 'I was at that club because I thought it would save our relationship. I let you touch me because I knew it would turn him on and I thought that the sight and the memory of it might be enough to keep us together.'

'You may have started out doing it for Steven, but I don't think you really believe it ended up being such a one-sided transaction. You enjoyed it. If you hadn't let yourself enjoy it there's no way you would have come and I know you weren't faking it. I could taste you.'

I was transported back to that night at L'Infer. I saw Kat dressed in her silly kitten costume: leather basque, red velvet cape and the cats' eye-shaped half-mask that drew attention to her perfectly shaped mouth, outlined in scarlet lipstick.

Kat took her hand from my leg and sat up straight. I watched her take a sip from her drink, with its salty rim, and lick her lips clean afterwards. At the same time, I thought of her mouth upon my body. I focused on the lipstick mark she had left on the glass. When I looked up again, Kat was studying me with a half-smile. Then she glanced over my shoulder.

'Oh,' she said. 'Looks like the party's started.'

Right behind us, another very straight-looking man in a suit had his tongue down the throat of a much younger girl. Her dress was open and her small pert breasts were exposed.

'Prominent member of the socialist party,' Kat told him. 'I met him here last year.'

'What kind of place is this?' I asked, realising too late that Kat had brought me to another L'Infer.

'Want to join in?' she asked me.

'No,' I said. I felt too hot all of a sudden. I started to get up.

'I know you still fancy me,' said Kat, catching my hand. 'And I fancy you even more now that I've got to know you properly. Why don't you just let go for a while? No one here is going to judge you. No one knows you. What happens in here will remain our secret.'

She pulled me close to her with surprising force. She took my head between her hands and kissed me hard on the mouth. It was as though she had flicked some kind of switch inside me. I immediately felt everything below my navel begin to soften and start to vibrate. Kat's kiss was as powerful and exciting as any kiss I'd received from a man. But I couldn't take it further. Just as forcefully as she had grabbed me, I pulled away.

'This isn't my thing,' I told her. 'I ought to go.'

'What's stopping you from letting go, Sarah?'

I walked out of the club before she could stop me.

45

When she realised that I wasn't coming back, Kat followed me down the street. I heard her clipping along behind me. She caught up with me at a crossing.

'I'm sorry,' she said. 'I didn't mean to upset you.'

I shook my head. 'It's OK.'

'No, really. I shouldn't have done that.'

It seemed unlike Kat to worry so much about offending anyone. I guessed she was worried that I had more sway over the casting of the Augustine movie than I actually did. But when I could bring myself to look at her, I thought perhaps I had been too harsh. She did look genuinely concerned.

'It's not about you,' I told her. 'There's someone . . .'

We sat down together in a small scruffy park so that Kat could have a cigarette, and I found myself telling her about Marco. At least, I told her a heavily edited version. I didn't say we hadn't actually met.

'So that's how you got this job,' she said when I finished.

'What?' I didn't understand her.

'Marco Donato is the guy bankrolling the movie.'

I just stared at her.

'You didn't know? Greg Simon told my agent. My agent wanted to make sure I wouldn't get stuck with the bill for flying out to LA, so Greg reassured him that the money is all there. Marco Donato. Cruise liners. Has to be your guy, doesn't it? Apparently, this is his pet project.'

I felt a bubble of emotion growing inside me, though I

didn't know whether it was excitement or anger. At last the bubble came out as a laugh.

'Did I say something funny?' asked Kat.

'You've made my day,' I said.

'If you didn't know,' said Kat, suddenly worried, 'then perhaps I wasn't supposed to tell you.'

'You definitely weren't supposed to tell me,' I said. 'I don't suppose Greg thought we'd end up drinking two bottles of champagne together after he'd gone.'

'Or kissing . . .' said Kat.

'He definitely wouldn't have thought that.'

'So, why didn't your friend Marco tell you this was his film?'

'Perhaps he thought it might put me off. Look, I've got to go but before I do, I want to give you something.'

Kat tilted her head expectantly. I think she may even have puckered her lips. I shook my head, got out my phone and a pen and copied down a number onto the back of her cigarette packet.

'If you want some more company this evening, I'm sure Steven will be very glad to hear from you.'

I couldn't get home fast enough after Kat told me the news. Marco must have set up this whole film just to make some kind of contact with me. It was too much of a coincidence that Greg Simon had approached Nick Marsden about the research job. He must have known Nick would recommend me. The job was always mine.

'Get out of this one,' I argued with Marco silently as I hurried home through the quiet streets. 'Now try to tell me that you didn't want me back in your life. Tell me you didn't plan for me to turn up in Venice all along.'

I ran up the stairs to my apartment and opened my laptop before I had even taken off my coat. I didn't want to wait a moment longer than I had to.

Dear Marco,

I've just had a most interesting evening. Are you familiar with Kat Adams? Well, you should be. She's about to get a part in your movie.

Marco, I know that you put up the money for the development of Project Augustine. I'm guessing it's not a coincidence that the research job spec ended up on my desk. And knowing that I would jump at the chance of working on a film and that I would take my role very seriously, you must have known that eventually my research would lead me back to your door. Why insist then that you had no idea that I would return to Venice and that you certainly wouldn't have encouraged me?

Perhaps you'll explain to me why I'm wrong and tell me once again that you have no interest in me whatsoever. Or perhaps, for once, you'll tell me the truth.

Yours,

Sarah

I pressed send. Let the fireworks begin.

46

Paris, September 1846

The thought that Remi and I would soon be together again sustained me through the long winter nights. Though I began to suffer a slight cough, for the most part I felt as vibrant as I had done in my childhood. I was even able to be a little more affectionate towards de Rocambeau. Though the man was a brute, I was soft-hearted enough to hope that no one – not even the Duc – would be hurt when Remi and I made our escape. Despite the brutality with which he had sometimes treated me, I sensed that de Rocambeau had, somewhere in his selfish heart, a little place for me and he would miss me.

Oh, and he would be embarrassed too. A duke does not lose his lover to an impoverished artist. Or even an artist who can provide her with a decent bourgeois living, as Remi said he would be able to do when the portrait was completed and the Duc paid up. Yes, Remi had decided, we would now have to wait until the painting was done before we did our flit. The fee would keep us both comfortably for a year. Plenty of time for the scandal to die down.

What dreams I had about the life that Remi and I would make together. I drew a little picture on a piece of paper that Remi left behind one afternoon, of the cottage

I imagined we would have. It might be modest but it would be comfortable. There would be fruit trees in the garden and flowers round the door. Inside, I would have a big wooden table where one day we would share meals with our beautiful children. Remi would have a studio in the house too, where he could continue to paint the portraits that would assure his place in history. Upstairs would be our bedroom with our very own double bed. Clean sheets and deep pillows. We would lie there in bliss for hours on end. As I thought about that, I felt the familiar tingle. I was so happy.

Then, one afternoon, I had an unexpected visitor.

'There is someone here to see you,' said Pierre. He handed me a calling card. The name on the card was 'Sauvageon' – the name that always warmed my heart – but the initial was not 'L'. It was 'C'.

'Send them in,' I said.

I was still expecting my visitor to be Remi, though surely in that case, Pierre would have told me that 'the artist' was on the step, or even just let him find his own way in, as he had done several times that week. I smoothed down my hair and arranged myself by the fireplace. I grew more nervous as I heard my visitor's footsteps on the stairs.

If a Sauvageon who was not my beloved Remi was visiting me, then it could only herald bad news. Remi was meant to be with me that afternoon. Was this C. Sauvageon here to tell me why Remi had been detained? Had there been an accident?

Standing by the fireplace, dressed in my silk dress and my Indian shawl, I was suddenly as fearful as that little girl in the garret, waiting for her lover to come back from the snow. I put my hand on the sketch in my pocket as though it were a talisman, but I could not shake my feeling of foreboding.

Pierre drew my attention to my visitor's arrival.

'Mademoiselle Christine Sauvageon.'

'Christine Sauvageon?'

'That's right, Mademoiselle du Vert. I am Remi's older sister.'

Christine Sauvageon gave me a small curtsey.

'Thank you for seeing me without an invitation,' she said.

'It's a most unexpected pleasure,' I answered by the book. 'How may I help you? Would you like to sit down? Would you care for some tea?'

'I will sit down,' she said. 'But I will not be having tea. I do not intend to take up much of your time.'

'Oh but you must stay as long as you like,' I said. 'I have nothing to do this afternoon except wait for Remi to arrive.'

I was incredibly nervous. This could be my future sister-in-law – *ma belle-soeur.* As she arranged herself on the chair opposite mine, I imagined this as the first of many meetings. We would become great friends. One day we might even sit opposite each other like this with our babies in our laps. For all these reasons, I loved Christine Sauvageon right away. She so closely resembled her brother that it was hard for me not to fling my arms round her and kiss her familiar cheeks. But she did not regard me with the love I knew Remi had for me. Instead, she kept her dark eyes on her gloved hands as she began to speak.

'Mademoiselle du Vert, I know that my brother is in love with you. And I believe, having heard him speak of you at some length, that you are worthy of his love.'

Her words were thrilling to me, but she continued.

'You were not born to such wealth as surrounds you now and I understand the awful circumstances that have brought you here. I have been lucky enough to enjoy the love and warm support of a father for all my years, and I would not judge you for the choices you have made in the absence of a father's guiding hand. It cannot have been easy to find yourself an orphan at such a tender age.'

I nodded my agreement.

But she carried on and the tone of her message started to change. 'I am not one of those women who considers that your kind is only to be reviled. I pity you and, in a strange way, I admire your courage. Seeing you here, I can also understand how you have bewitched my brother. I had heard talk about your beauty but you are far more lovely than I might have believed. I suppose I had expected you to show some sign of the life you have led on your face.'

'Debauchery is not quite like the smallpox,' I laughed.

Christine did not laugh with me.

'My brother loves you with all his heart and for that reason he is prepared to throw away everything to be with you. Believe me, Mademoiselle du Vert . . .'

'Call me Augustine . . .'

'Mademoiselle du Vert, believe me, if my brother follows through his silly plan to run away with you, he will lose everything. It goes without saying that my father will disown him. His poor fiancée will be left humiliated. And my sister and I will have to abandon all hope of making our own decent marriages.'

She sniffed into a handkerchief.

'Surely not . . .'

'You know I speak the truth. But I know I cannot expect you to be swayed by the news that our father would be devastated and my own heart would be broken. For there is a man I love as dearly as you love my brother and he in return loves me ardently. He has asked for my hand but should you allow Remi to cause a scandal, my beloved will have no choice but to let me go.'

I reached out for her hand, hoping to show her that I cared very much.

'It cannot be as serious as that,' I said.

Christine Sauvageon glared at me.

'My beloved is a good man from a good family. I would not have him sully their name by association with . . .'

'With me?'

I sat back in my seat. I was beginning to like Christine Sauvageon less and less. Having seemed so modest and shy at first, suddenly she was a tigress.

'But if my predicament and those of my sister and Remi's blameless fiancée do not move you, then for pity's sake, consider the consequences for Remi himself. At this moment, he can think of nothing other than a future filled with happiness for the pair of you, but imagine how your lives will be, in a couple of years' time, when the initial glow of love begins to wane.'

I began to protest.

'For all women know that our charms will not be with us for ever. No sooner have we reached the peak of our beauty than it begins to fade. Imagine then, how happy

Remi will be, when you are old, to live with you in a cottage, working at some menial job to support you and your children.'

'He would not have to work at a menial job. He would be painting.'

'Painting whom? Do you think the Duc De Rocambeau will give you and Remi his blessing? Do you think he will make you a dowry? If you leave de Rocambeau for Remi, he will do his utmost to ruin my brother. He will ensure no one ever commissions a painting by Remi again.'

'I am not going to take a thing with me,' I said. 'So de Rocambeau will have no reason to come after me and no reason to try to hurt your brother.'

'You honestly believe that leaving your jewels will be enough to calm the Duc's rage? He will be humiliated and he will humiliate Remi in turn. Remi will find he has no customers and he will be unable to paint. If he is unable to paint, he will be unhappy. Desperately so. You know I speak the truth.'

I was assailed by the memory of Remi complaining he could not paint through that cold winter six years earlier as surely as if Pierre had opened a window and let a frozen blast in.

'Augustine, if you love my brother, you must release him of the obligation to be with you. As much as he loves you, he loves his art more. Yes, most of all he loves his art. You cannot ask him to choose you above painting. Please, Augustine.'

Suddenly, she fell to her knees in front of me and grasped both my hands, holding them tightly as she continued to beseech me. I knew she was thinking largely of her own stake in my dilemma – the effect on her own marriage prospects – and who could have blamed her? I knew what it was like to love.

'I cannot leave here until I have your promise.'

The passion of her pleading set me coughing. I had been coughing quite often in the week leading up to her visit, but now it was uncontrollable. I felt as though my ribs were breaking with the force of it. Christine had to release my hands so that I could cover my mouth.

She looked about to find a glass of water. I shook my head at her. Water would not stop this cough. When I took my handkerchief away from my mouth, I saw the blood spots. Christine saw them too. Her eyes widened in horror. We did not need to discuss their significance.

'A moment of happiness for a lifetime of discontent,' she said at last.

'I think you had better leave,' I said. I pointed towards the door.

After Christine Sauvageon had gone, I asked Pierre to call for a doctor. I had access to the best medical care in Paris; the Duc took my health almost as seriously as that of his horses. The doctor arrived within the hour. I described my symptoms and he listened to my chest. He examined the inside of my mouth, my ears and my eyes. He prescribed some poultices and bed rest so that when Remi arrived to continue with the painting that afternoon, Pierre had to tell him I could not receive him.

The turn in my health was not the only reason I could not see him. Much as Christine Sauvageon's words had hurt me, I knew I could not dismiss her logic out of hand. If, in that moment, I did not care whether the entitled little mademoiselle was able to marry her true love, her insistence that the Duc would ruin Remi haunted me. Remi lived to paint. Long before he met me, he had chosen art as his true mistress. Without the ability to support himself by painting, he would be miserable and he would hate me for it.

And if the doctor was right, then what point was there in asking Remi to give up anything on my behalf? The signs all pointed towards consumption, the disease which had taken my mother. Despite the doctor's best ministrations, I could suddenly feel the shadow of death upon me. 'A moment of happiness for a lifetime of discontent.' Christine Sauvageon's words rang in my ears.

After a while, I asked Pierre to bring me my small writing case. He set it up next to the bed and I began to write the most difficult letter of my life.

47

I cried as I wrote to my lovely Remi. My dear, flawed, cowardly Remi. Once upon a time, we might have built a life together, he and I. When I was well and he was not so used to luxury. Perhaps I should have fought for him then. I should have walked out to Guerville in my tattered old boots and made his father see that whatever he had heard, I was a decent woman, worthy of his son's love and his family's respect. But I had taken a different fork in the path and Remi had not had the faith to pursue me after Elaine sent him away. We had missed our moment and now I must let him go for ever.

I did not want him to hate me, and yet that seemed to be the only way to cast him off right then. He must not make any foolish gesture to try to win me back. I was not so strong that I would be able to resist. If he let me shrug him off now, he might rescue his engagement, keep his commissions and go on to live a happy life as the artist he had always wanted to be. Christine Sauvageon could marry her man from a good family. Their little sister might make a match with a Duc as a wife and not a concubine.

But the most important thing was that Remi should always be able to paint.

I wrote . . .

September 17th, 1846

Dear Remi,

How lovely it has been to have you in my house these past few weeks. How exciting and romantic it was to make a plan to run away together. But also, how very foolish. Just a few days ago, I started to give the plan my proper consideration and could hardly believe what an idiotic notion I'd put into your head. You and I, together in a garret again? Even a cottage? However would we stand it?

The truth is that we are not the young lovers we once were. Life has changed us both. In some ways for the better, in other ways most definitely not. Back then, when we met, you were a sketch artist and I was a virginal housemaid. Now you are on the point of becoming a great painter and I am a notorious courtesan.

I would not have chosen to take this immoral path, but my position comes with compensations that I would find it too hard to give up at this stage in my life. I am writing to you from a bed piled high with silken pillows, dear Remi. A manservant has brought me this writing case and will soon return with my supper on a little silver tray. Once upon a time, I scrubbed until my hands were raw. Now I need never lift a finger except to ring a bell that will bring my own maid running to me at once.

And then there is the Duc. For all my complaints, I must admit to you that I have a great affection for him. He has been kind to me and through his kindness I have been able to have the sort of life I might only have dreamed of. If I were to leave him, he would be devastated. The poor soul is trapped in a hopeless marriage and I am the one comfort he has.

I am sure you will be surprised to get this letter but I must ask you not to try to make me change my mind. I have already thought long and hard about our situation and I cannot be persuaded. Please, think of me with kindness, Remi. I am sure that when you are married and surrounded by your beautiful children, you will appreciate that I was right.

Affectionately yours,

Augustine

How he would hate me when he read those words! How I hated myself, though I knew they were not true. But I could not tell him the real story, that I feared he would lose his livelihood for me and that after only a little time had passed, he would realise he had paid more than my love was really worth to him. I could not bear to be the one who robbed him of his dreams.

'Should I wait for an answer?' Pierre asked me.

'No,' I said. 'Please don't.'

When the Duc arrived that evening, I pretended to be happy and well. He commented that I looked a little red around the eyes. I told him I thought perhaps it was the smell of the oil paints that had given me a reaction. I would be very glad when the painting was finished.

'In fact,' I said. 'I don't think there is any need for me to sit for the artist any more. He has only the folds of my skirt to finish now. The paint gives me a headache and what's more, I am bored.'

'The artist bores you?'

'He talks about himself all the time,' I said. 'Please ask him to finish the portrait without me.'

48

Twenty-four hours after Kat's revelation, I had heard nothing from Marco, but reading about Augustine's decision to let Remi go made something clear to me. Marco might well have come to a similar decision: that to ask me to be with him was too great a sacrifice. But I was not Remi Sauvageon.

I had to go to Venice again. If Marco was not going to engage with me remotely, then I decided I would stand in the courtyard of his house and shout at the top of my voice until he came downstairs and met me: face to face. I might have to stand in that courtyard for a year, but I would see him.

I wrote one more time before I booked a flight.

Marco,

I know that you were at the ball that night in February. I know that you were the man in the library. Bea surprised you. You panicked and left.

Bea told me about your injuries and she told me how she reacted to them. I hope you believe me when I say that had I got to the library first, things would have been very different. My feelings for you are from the inside out.

I want the chance to know you properly. Surely my persistence is proof enough of my sincerity? You've said some pretty unkind things to me in the past, Marco, but I'm still here and I'm still saying that I still want to know more. I don't care if you're not the man in those silly pictures on the Internet. It may have been those photos that first intrigued me, but it's your mind, your intelligence and your humour that really hooked me in.

I'm coming back to Venice. I won't be staying at the Bauer this time, since I'll be travelling on my own money rather than yours. I've booked a little *pensione* in the Dorsoduro. I will be there from tomorrow morning until Saturday. That should give you plenty of time to find a minute or two to meet me alongside your 'business' commitments.

Please don't say 'no'. You were brave enough to find a way to bring me back into your life by getting me a job on your movie. Now, be brave enough to bring your feelings and your face out into the sunlight again.

Sarah

The next day was agony. On the one hand, I wanted Marco to write and tell me that my decision to go to Venice was the best news he had heard in years. On the other hand, I was comforted by the lack of response, because I did not really expect Marco to be delighted by my sudden insistence that he give me one more chance. In those circumstances, nothing was better than an outright refusal to see me.

Still, I don't think twenty-four hours ever felt so long and then, when I got to the airport, I discovered that my plane was delayed. I sat right next to the scheduled gate, refusing even to risk getting myself a coffee in case I managed to miss the flight when it was finally called.

When the plane eventually boarded, almost two hours late, I found myself seated next to a handsome Italian man in perhaps his late thirties. He seemed keen to engage me in conversation. I told him that alas I had work to do, but really there was fat chance of that. I could think of nothing but Marco and the moment of truth that lay ahead of us. I opened a book and read the same page over and over again.

I gazed out at the clouds and counted the minutes. The flight couldn't pass quickly enough. I was so impatient to be with the man I loved. The man I was sure loved me in return.

I arrived in Venice at five o'clock. I did not even think about going to the hotel to gather myself before I went to the Palazzo Donato. I hustled straight for the water-taxis, almost pushing people out of my way in my haste to get into a boat and on my way. The water-taxi driver tried to make small talk. I told him that I would appreciate it if he would just concentrate on getting me to the Grand Canal post-haste.

I sprang from the boat onto the deck. I hammered on the door. Silvio, as usual, took his own sweet time. I hammered again. I shouted.

'Come on, come on.'

'Signorina Thomson?' Silvio was not expecting me but he didn't seem unduly distressed. 'You have come to visit the library? I didn't know you would be here today.'

'I haven't come for the library,' I said, not waiting to be invited inside. I squeezed past Silvio and headed for the courtyard garden.

'Miss Thomson! Please wait,' he called from behind.

Silvio tried to stop me but he was too much of a gentleman to try to restrain me physically in any real way. He made a half-hearted attempt to block me with his body but I pushed past him – rather more roughly than I needed to – and made straight for the library. Once inside, I went to the shelf that hid the secret door, pulled out the copy of *Beauty and the Beast* that triggered the lock and pushed hard.

He wanted me to find him. I knew that was the truth. Why else would he hide the secret door behind my favourite book? Had he been determined to keep me out, he could have locked his door, even barricaded it. But he didn't, and when I stepped into the corridor, the door to his office was already open. Marco was at his desk with his back to me. He did not even flinch.

I stood in the open doorway, catching my breath and wondering what I should do next. My grand plan to burst into Marco's house and push my way into his office had ended at the moment when I opened the door.

'Most people knock before they come into someone's office. I suppose you should come in properly,' he said. 'Close the door behind you.'

I stepped over the threshold and pulled the door shut, quietly so that it made barely a sound. I'd made enough noise as I barged through the house and now I felt rather foolish.

'So, you get what you always wanted at last. You get to meet me in the flesh.'

I was still out of breath.

Slowly, Marco got to his feet. He leaned heavily on the desk in front of him, giving the impression that the movement was difficult. He straightened up. He was tall and elegantly slim. He was wearing a silk dressing gown. His dark brown hair curled over his collar. I longed to reach out and touch it.

'Now I can only hope you think it was worth all the fuss,' he said.

There had to be a happy ending.

49

Paris, December 6th, 1846

Remi never replied to my letter. I was devastated. Though I had decided a total break would be the best thing – for him at least – I did not expect him to give me up so easily. But he did. The painting was taken from my house to his studio, where he finished it without needing to look at me. It was brought back to the house a week later. I could hardly bear to look at it.

Just as with Arlette's portrait all those years ago, Remi had not let me see his work in progress, insisting it was for his eyes only until it was absolutely finished. I knew how happy I had been while I was sitting for the painting – lifted up by the idea that soon I would leave the Duc and be with Remi for ever – so I was surprised to see that I seemed so very sad. It was as though Remi had looked into my heart as he applied the final brushstrokes.

The Duc didn't like it.

'You look miserable,' he said. 'Surrounded by everything I've given you, you look like a Breton fishwife after a bad sardine harvest.'

He glanced from the painting to me.

'You're starting to look like that in real life too. You're getting rather thin.'

I didn't feel much like eating. Since September, my cough had been getting worse. The servants at the house did their best to look after me, but it did not seem to matter what they put on the table; I was growing weaker by the day.

'You are giving in to your illness,' the doctor told me. 'You must spend more time in the fresh air.'

I had Pierre drive me around the Bois de Boulogne but I kept the curtains of my carriage closed. I could not bear to look out and see the whole of Paris carrying on as though nothing had changed. The city's indifference to my broken heart made the pain keener still.

Arlette, who was concerned, came to visit. Dear Arlette was the same as ever, full of gossip and laughter. She carefully kept off the subject of Remi, and the poet too, in case that should remind me of my lost love. Instead, she regaled me with tales of the general, who still visited twice a week, and Girodin, who had ended up in prison. Elaine was still in her service but not for much longer. She had captured the heart of a sailor and he intended to marry her when he returned from his next voyage to Mexico.

'I approve,' I said.

'See,' said Arlette, when she had been with me for an hour. 'Laughter is bringing the colour back to your cheeks. It's not consumption that ails you, it's heartache, and the best way to get over heartache is to let yourself be entertained. Come to the opera. Tonight. It's *The Damnation of Faust.* And, more importantly, Clemence Babineaux is going to be debuting her new hairstyle. You will laugh yourself half to death when you see her. She looks exactly like her new spaniel. Please come.'

Arlette held both my hands.

I agreed I would be there.

'Come back to life,' said Arlette.

That evening I dressed in the dark red gown that the Duc had bought for me only that week. Against my white skin, the effect was dramatic. I wore my hair in a chignon, studded with pearl- and diamond-topped pins. I wrapped pearls round my neck and hung diamonds from my ears.

My new maid, Natalie, nodded her approval.

'You look really lovely,' she said, as she wrapped a shawl round my shoulders.

I thanked her. She was a good simple girl, as I had once been myself. I hoped that her time in my employ would not corrupt her.

Pierre drove me to the Opéra Comique. I would be alone in the Duc's box that evening. Arlette would be with Clemence. We would all meet to go to dinner in Le Grand at the Café Anglais afterwards.

As soon as I'd started to dress for the evening, I'd felt a little better. Perhaps Arlette was right and all I needed to do was pull myself out of the doldrums by meeting with some dear old friends. By the time we arrived at the Opéra, I was quite excited. My reflection in the mirrors in the hotel lobby told me that no matter how I felt, I was still beautiful. I could see that in the regard of the other opera-goers too. I still made heads turn when I walked into a room.

I took my place in the Duc's box. I nodded to the familiar faces in the boxes to either side. I leaned on the velvet-covered rail to look down into the stalls, and to give the people in the stalls the chance to look at me.

That was, as Arlette had once told me, an important part of my occupation. The opera box was a shopfront; I should never forget that one day soon the Duc would tire of me and I would have to look for a new protector.

My eyes filled with tears at the thought.

Thankfully, the opera was beginning. In the darkness, I sank into my seat and listened to Faust's tale. I could not keep from crying when his darling Marguerite sang '*D'amour l'ardente flamme*' as she waited in vain for his return. I composed myself, however, before the curtain fell.

I told myself I must be happy, I must be gay. I must be entertaining at the dinner. The gaslights were turned up again. I looked across the theatre for Arlette. And that is when I saw him.

Remi was not alone. He had beside him a petite young woman, with blonde hair arranged in ringlets around her pretty, plump face. He was telling her something. She was laughing. She batted at him with her fan. I could tell she was in love with him. I could not see whether her feelings were reciprocated; he was half-turned away.

I could not take my eyes off him. My beloved was a stranger again. Then he stood to escort his young lady from the box and, in doing so, he glanced across the theatre to see me. His smile disappeared. He regarded me as though I were a beggar, trembling and covered in dirt.

He met my eyes for just a moment, but it was long enough for me to know everything. He hated me. He had cast me from his heart for abandoning our love and I would never be able to tell him why.

I left the theatre in a hurry. I told Pierre to take me directly home. I went straight to my bedroom where I had a coughing fit that seemed to last for hours.

I coughed until the candle on my bedside table had burned down. After that, I lay awake in the dark, feeling very small and scared. I thought I heard my mother's voice, telling me that it would all be over very soon. I cried for Remi and for the chasm that had opened between us. I tried to remember what it had been like when he smiled at me. I couldn't bear that my last memory of him might be of his eyes filled with such hate.

50

So, at last, Marco and I were going to meet face to face.

I thought I had prepared myself for this moment. I had considered the very worst and at the same time hoped for the very best, but right then I was scared and I was shaking. I held my breath. I thought that perhaps he was holding his breath too. He still had his back to me. I stared at the back of his head. I took in his thick dark hair curling over his collar. His square shoulders. His posture was relaxed. He was still holding a pen in his left hand, which did not seem to be injured. I had caught him writing.

'I don't suppose we can put this off for very much longer,' he said, laying down the pen.

'No,' I agreed. 'And just think, in a year's time, we'll laugh about how silly we were to take so long to get here.' I laughed. It was a high, nervous laugh. I was suddenly petrified.

'I want you to stay silent,' said Marco. 'When I turn round.'

I put my hand to my mouth. I bit down on my knuckles.

Marco turned.

His eyes were still the eyes of the playboy in the picture. They were still vital and engaging. I would have recognised him anywhere.

I pulled my hand from my mouth.

What was I supposed to say? It's not so awful? You don't look like you've been freshly pulled from an inferno? I could tell that he'd received his injuries many years ago. His skin looked tight and uncomfortable. In places it was shiny. His mouth drooped at one side until he smiled. It seemed like an effort but it also seemed genuine. I smiled back but stayed silent, as he had requested.

He stepped towards me. His beautifully cut shirt fitted him perfectly. It showed off a broad chest. A swimmer's physique. Except that his right arm hung awkwardly. He was trying to hide that hand.

I reached out and took his left hand in mine. It was the first time we had ever touched.

'You're still here,' he said.

'Of course I am,' I replied.

'You don't have to stay if you don't want to.'

'I do want to.'

We sat down side by side. I held his hand and took in the reality of him. I felt a thousand emotions rushing through me. Pity, fear, anxiety but also, just as strongly, delight and love.

'You look—' I started.

'Don't, *cara*. Don't. I don't want to hear any lies. You know that you shouldn't have come here.'

'I had to. You wanted me to! Why else fund a whole bloody movie? You could have sent an email.'

He smiled but this time it didn't reach his eyes. The magic of the moment when our eyes had first met was already being clouded by the thought of 'what next'.

'I was selfish,' said Marco. 'I should never have started this at all.'

'But you did and now we're here. You're looking at me and I'm looking at you.'

'I don't want you to look at me. Every time I look in the mirror, I want to stab myself in the eyes. This face is not who I want to be for you, Sarah.'

'It is who you are.'

'But I can't forget what I was.'

'Then don't look in the mirror. Look only into my eyes and see who I think you are. I love you. I don't care about a layer of burnt skin. It's what's underneath that counts.'

Marco rolled his eyes. '"It's what's underneath that counts."' He parroted my words back at me, in a silly voice that made me shrivel inside. Was that how he thought I sounded? 'Sarah, you have no idea how stupid that sounds to anyone who isn't perfect on the outside any more.'

'I'm not perfect,' I said.

'Perfect. Normal,' said Marco. 'You know what I mean. It sounds ignorant and patronising. It's easy for you to say it. It probably makes you feel good to think that you're so open-minded, you could consider loving a man so badly disfigured that even his own mother couldn't bear to look at him. But then you've always been like that.'

'What do you mean?'

'You've always got a kick out of caring for the underdog, haven't you? Like when you were a schoolgirl helping out at the hospital, trying to make that poor Italian boy speak.'

I was surprised to hear Marco refer to the story I'd once told him about my holiday job and the patient I'd become so fixated on: a young man recovering from a car crash.

'It made you feel important, didn't it, to think that you were the only one who understood. Do you know how many of those nurses tried to speak Italian to me?'

'It was you?'

'Yes, it was me. You must have figured it out by now. I was the kid who had the car crash. I was the rich guy who wrecked his Ferrari and killed the most important person in my life at the same time.'

'Marco . . . why didn't you say?'

'Perhaps it was an intelligence test. You bugged the hell out of me, you know.'

'I was trying to help.'

'You were trying to make yourself feel better. You were an unattractive, unsophisticated schoolgirl. I was the ideal boyfriend. Rich, Italian, couldn't talk back. And maybe one day I'd be handsome too. Well, guess what? I'm never going to be handsome again.'

'And I don't care about that.'

'Don't you remember our early conversations when you first came to this library? You often made reference to my looks. They matter to you, Sarah. They matter to anyone who's sane. Because they matter in the real world. How could we ever have a proper relationship? I won't go outside my house.'

'With me beside you . . .'

'With you beside me? You think that makes it better? When you're beside me, people will wonder why and they won't think it's because I've got a great personality. Or perhaps you're thinking I'll make you look better.'

'Marco, now you're talking shit. Please stop.'

Everything was going wrong. He pulled his hand away from mine. He stood up and walked to the window.

'The contrast between my hideousness and your beauty. Imagine it. And not only will you look beautiful, you'll look kind too. You'll probably find that you've never had so many offers from other men. There isn't a man on earth who isn't really looking for a nice kind girl like you.'

'Why can't you just accept that I love you?' I pleaded with him.

'And why can't you accept that I don't want to be loved? Don't they say that everyone ends up with the face they deserve? Well, I deserve to look like this. This,' he indicated his face, 'is a manifestation of my inner ugliness. It was caused by lust and cowardice.'

'Don't be ridiculous.'

'You don't know what happened.'

'Then tell me, because I'm finding it very hard to understand.'

'I think you had better go.'

'I don't care what you think,' I insisted. 'I'm staying. When I look at you, I see only the man I love and I love him because he has a good heart.'

'Sarah, *Beauty and the Beast* is a fairy tale. Here in the real world, monsters do exist and I am one of them.'

I tried to hold him but finally he pushed me off and I sensed that there was no point persisting for the moment.

'Go,' he said. I took my instructions and left.

But I couldn't let it go. Of course when I got back to my hotel room, I wrote another letter and I delivered it by hand. I pleaded with Silvio to be allowed back into the Palazzo but he told me he had his instructions. He asked me not to try to circumvent them. He did not want to have to get physical with me.

Despondently, I backed down and left Silvio to guard the door. He watched me walk away down the street. I had the feeling he wanted to say something to me. He didn't.

I spent an anguished night, unable to sleep properly. It would have been better had I been able to call on Nick and Bea, but I had not told either of them I was going to be in town, and with Nick at least, I had pretty much burned my bridges.

I tried to calm myself with the thought that this was bound to happen. I had surprised Marco. He wasn't ready. He would think about our encounter overnight and by the time morning came, he would be in a better state of mind. I'd just keep going back until he saw me again. I had to.

51

I must have fallen asleep at some point and as soon as I did, my dreams were with me.

My little room in the Dorsoduro was stiflingly hot, so I'd left the window open. The sound of water rippling in the canal outside provided a backdrop for my nocturnal fantasies. Sleepwalking, I crossed the room to the window.

Slow and silent, the gondola appeared.

I walked down the stairs and let myself out onto the *fondamenta.* The gondolier brought his craft near to the edge. He held out his hand to help me on board. I knew at once who had sent the boat for me. My masked lover was waiting for me inside the *felce.*

Except this time he wasn't wearing the mask and the face I saw was the face I had seen in the secret room earlier that day. The pain of the past was indelibly etched upon it, but the eyes that looked out spoke of hope for the future.

'Don't say anything,' I said before I covered his mouth with a kiss.

I felt his arms fold around me, bringing me closer, as his mouth responded to mine. When we were kissing, nothing else mattered. The only thing in the world was our connection. In the darkness, we were entirely equal.

His hands roamed my body. I unbuttoned his shirt. We didn't take our mouths off one another for an instant. I felt his cool fingers brush my nipples. I rested my hand on his chest, feeling his heartbeat beneath my palm. He cupped my breasts, gently squeezing their soft weight. I caressed his hard pectoral muscles. His hardness and my softness were perfectly matched.

I moved my hand to the front of his trousers and felt his erection stiffen further in response. His fingers were inside my knickers, finding me already wet and ready. Carefully, I undid his trousers and freed his penis. I moved so that I could take him in my mouth, delighting in the sweet, salty taste of him. He manoeuvered himself so that he was between my legs and pulled me down onto his mouth. I shivered with pleasure as his tongue flickered over my clitoris. I returned the favour in kind, sucking him in deeper, adoring him with my lips.

Just as my orgasm seemed inevitable, he lifted me away from him. I let him go and turned so that I was on top of him, looking down to where his face should be, obscured by the darkness of the *felce* in the moonless night. He put his hands on my waist and guided me down onto him. He slipped into me easily. No part of me tried to resist.

With his hands still on me to hold me in place, I started to move up and down. We were like two parts of the same creature. It felt so right to have him inside me. I wanted nothing else.

I moved upon him, faster and faster as the desire to have him fill me with his cum overtook me. His breathing echoed my movements. His fingers tightened on my hips. He started to brace himself against me, pushing up, up, up. He flooded me with his ecstasy and cried out as he came.

Afterwards, I brushed his cheek with the back of my fingers and felt the wetness of his tears.

'It's worth doing this,' I told him. 'It's worth trying to break through.'

He told me he felt the same way.

* * *

The following morning, there was a letter waiting for me at the reception desk of my scruffy little hotel. I recognised the curling hand at once and fell upon the envelope, tearing it open before I even left the desk. I read the letter in the middle of the lobby. It was a mistake. I should have known it would only be bad news.

> Dear Sarah,
>
> I can't ask you to be with me. Choosing me means choosing to abandon everything you truly want in your life. Don't kid yourself it would be otherwise. You should not have to compromise. You want to have an ordinary life. You deserve an extraordinarily ordinary love.
>
> It is better that we end this insanity now. Forget this house, Sarah. Forget me. Forgive me.
>
> Marco

52

7th January 1847

My dear Arlette,

I am writing to thank you for coming to visit me the other evening. I am sorry I could not see you, but since that night at the Opéra Comique in December, my health has taken a turn for the worse. I fear I may have taken an unnecessary risk when I came out that evening and now I am paying the price.

In truth, I think I may be about to pay the ultimate price. The doctor comes every afternoon and assures me I will soon feel better but I can tell by his expression that he is counting down the days until he loses another customer and the only way I will feel better is when I cannot feel at all. There is no poultice that will work for me now.

It is for that reason that I send Pierre to you with this package, which contains some personal items that I do not wish to fall into the Duc's hands.

First, I am entrusting this little picture to you and ask that when I am dead, you will make sure it finds its way to Remi. As you know, my father painted this seascape and it is my most treasured possession. I am afraid that if I do not pass it to you now, when I am gone, no one in this household will understand its true worth and it will end up on the fire. Remi, I know, will appreciate it.

I also enclose my diary, which you must pass to him at the same time. It contains the truth about our final parting. Explain to him that it is only safe he knows of the depth of my love for him now he cannot ruin himself in pursuit of it. He is not to blame his father or his sister. They did what they thought was best.

You asked me in December why I ever loved Remi Sauvageon. This diary will explain that too. When I look into Remi's face, it is as though I am looking into his soul. He has greatness. You can see it in his paintings. One day the whole world will understand. Be kind to him, Arlette. As you once said, 'He's just a man' and he was quite fond of you.

For you, my dear, dear friend, I am sending this pearl. You must remember it. The pearl that belonged to the poor Venetian lesbian robbed by de Rocambeau's father. Now it is yours. The Duc will not miss it and I know how well it will go with your hair. Better than it ever did with mine. Please think of me whenever you wear it and know that I treasured your friendship and guidance during the hardest part of my life far more than any jewel. There is another smaller pearl here for Elaine. She can do what she likes with it. I hope you will both come to my funeral. The thought that my grave might be unattended is as chilling as the touch of death itself.

But don't weep for me too long, my darling Arlette. I will be happy on the other side and I will always be thankful for the day you found me beneath that tree in the Bois de Boulogne.

With love,

Your Augustine

53

Six months after the death of Augustine du Vert from tuberculosis – consumption, as it was called back then – her name was already slipping from the memories of those who had called themselves her friends during the good times. Another girl had found her way into the Duc's box at the Opéra Comique. Some said she resembled Augustine, but in truth she was not nearly so gentle or fine-featured. When she laughed, which was often, she showed her back teeth. She had none of Augustine's natural elegance and modesty. She wore her jewels like she was the Duchesse d'Orleans' Christmas tree. Arlette and Elaine, regarding the new girl from the other side of the theatre, felt all the more keenly the absence of their dear gentle friend.

However, Arlette recovered enough to note that the pearls the new girl sported were no match for the pearls that the Duc had given Augustine. 'He doesn't like her anywhere near as much.'

'I still can't believe what you did.' Elaine shook her head.

'I didn't want it,' said Arlette. 'And *he* did not deserve such a precious gift as Augustine really left him.'

'But that pearl was worth millions of francs!'

'It was worth much less than Augustine's love. He will never understand that.'

'He might have understood if you gave him her diary.'

'More pearls before swine,' Arlette tutted.

* * *

The pearl that the Duc had given Augustine for her second-hand virginity now adorned the neck of Madame Remi Sauvageon, the former Mademoiselle Virginie Ducharmes. In a complete reversal of Augustine's last wishes, Arlette hid the diary and had Augustine's seascape properly framed and given pride of place in her salon. The tainted pearl she gave to Remi in the hope it might bring him bad luck.

But Remi Sauvageon's life seemed to hold nothing but good luck from that moment on. The Duc's patronage was just the start of it. To begin with Remi painted Augustine's replacement in almost exactly the same pose. She even wore the same Fossin tiara.

Soon Remi was exhibiting all over the world and the list of men and women he painted included princes and queens. He married the beautiful Virginie, daughter of a rich wine merchant from the south, and in time they had three lovely children, who would go on to have beautiful families of their own. He left behind him a vast fortune and, as a result, Remi's offspring would dominate the social life of Europe for decades. Many of them became artists in his footsteps, to greater and lesser degrees of success.

Augustine left nobody behind her. When she died, there was no family member left to tell. The Duc took back most of the gifts he had given her. In fact, as far as he was concerned, he took back everything. He did not know about the two pearls, the diary and the little painting of the sea.

Following Augustine's death, Arlette had a premonition of her own lonely death and adopted two orphans from the Marais to make sure there was someone to mourn her. It was Arlette who left a provision in her own will that Augustine du Vert's grave always be adorned with fresh flowers.

54

So, Marco had sent me away again. I went back to Paris, since I still had to move out of the apartment. I wrote to Greg Simon telling him I needed to be released from my commission and he should work out how much money I owed him. He told me that I need not worry about returning any of my advance; the work I had done so far was more than enough. I guessed Marco must have told him to say that.

I had a few things to do before I left the city. I went to the Musée d'Orsay. Now I knew that the painting that hung opposite Remi Sauvageon's portrait of Augustine was a portrait of Sauvageon's wife. Both Augustine and Virginie Sauvageon were painted wearing the same pearl, the enormous South Sea Island beauty that shone with the colours of the setting sun that had been the price of Augustine's maidenhead. The pearl which once belonged to the most notorious lesbian in Venice. I wondered if that could be my Luciana, who'd received the pearl from Ernesta, her courtesan lover. Had Luciana given up on men altogether after Casanova sprung her from the convent?

There was sadness in Augustine's eyes. I saw that now, while Virginie's expression shone with great contentment. Augustine's face was all angles. Virginie's face was plump with goodness and the happiness of a woman who had ended up with everything she wanted.

Before I left the city, I also went to see Augustine's grave one more time. I took my usual offering of peonies and found once again that someone had beaten me to it. Her grave was freshly swept and as neat and tidy as the memorial of a beloved sister, daughter or aunt who had been dead for just a few weeks rather than over a hundred years. I knew now that Arlette had made provision for Augustine's grave to be kept well, but I wondered if it was really possible that her instructions still had any influence more than a hundred and fifty years later.

Are there some women, like Augustine, who are destined to be unlucky in love? Could things have turned out differently? I thought of the generations of little Sauvageons who had enjoyed rich and happy lives thanks to their *grandpère*'s artistic talent, and then I thought of Augustine, who had no family to mourn for her and no family to lay claim to her story years later. It was what made her the perfect subject for a film, as Greg Simon put it, but it was still very sad to me.

Perhaps it was especially sad because it put me in mind of my own situation. Marco had made it clear this time that I was not to hold out any hope that we could have any kind of relationship. He was even willing to sacrifice any hope of friendship, since he did not want me to harbour any kind of fantasy that he might be softening in his resolve to stay alone for the rest of his life. I did not have to stay alone, however. I was getting to an age where my friends were getting together, two by two, like the animals trooping onto the ark. Several had children already. They were mapping out futures that encompassed whole generations, not just five-year plans. Marco warned me to waste no more time thinking about a phantom.

I stayed with Augustine for slightly too long. I almost missed my train back to England.

As I travelled back to London on the Eurostar, that last scene in Marco's office ran through my mind. I leaned my head on the window and remembered that moment – so full of possibility – when I burst into his office and saw him sitting on his chair with his back to me. Could things have gone any differently?

In my imagination, I stepped forward and put my hands on his shoulders. He reached up and took one of my hands in his. He turned to look up at me. His face was as it had been in all those old photographs, when he was the gilded youth with everything ahead of him.

He got to his feet and we stood face to face. He stroked a hand across my cheek and murmured something sweet in Italian.

We kissed and the love we felt for each other blossomed between us.

Marco was right. I had made a fool of myself and embarrassed him. We could not have a future. Even now I knew the truth, my fantasies inevitably harked back to the way he had been and not the way he was now.

The train arrived at St Pancras and I disembarked with a heavy heart. London was just another temporary stop on a longer journey. In just a couple of weeks I would be on my way to Berlin.

What would await me there? I had a research project to embark upon, again, and that would undoubtedly throw up some surprises, but what would happen beyond that? Had Marco Donato surprised me for the very last time?

Epilogue

In his bedroom in Venice, Marco Donato was deep in concentration, while his doctor carefully examined his skin for signs of improvement or deterioration.

'It's time,' said Marco at last.

'What?' His doctor came to see him once a month and the conversation was always the same. Yes, Marco was comfortable. Yes, he was looking after his skin. No, he did not want to consider the possibility of reconstructive surgery. 'Time for what?' the doctor pressed.

'Whatever you can do,' said Marco. 'I've decided I want you to do it. I've waited too long.'

'Because you have waited so long,' said the doctor, 'we might not be able to get the results you require.'

'Do what you can. I just want to be able to go outside without attracting too much attention.'

'Very well. And what's brought this on?'

'Doctor, you know not to ask.'

For Marco, his appearance had been an outward manifestation of everything that he hated about himself. He had caused the accident in which he'd been injured, and the way it had left him looking seemed like small recompense for having survived when his passenger didn't. But at last, Marco had a reason to want to move on from the past. He could only hope that his future would still be waiting for him when he did.

Sarah's thrilling and sensual love story continues with

Hidden Women, Book Three:

The Girl Behind The Curtain

Stella Knightley

Sarah Thomson and Marco Donato's complicated love affair continues – their passion is a deep one but both have been badly hurt before and are wary of exposing their vulnerabilities to the other.

Meanwhile, Sarah begins to research a new subject . . .

In Nineteen-Thirties Germany, Katherine Hazleton escapes her stuffy finishing school and runs away to Berlin in pursuit of an unsuitable man. Alone and penniless when her boyfriend deserts her, she is forced to become a hostess at a cabaret bar. There she reinvents herself as Kitty Katkin. Writing her own songs to accompany her risqué dance routines, Kitty is soon a sensation. She is in love with Berlin and her handsome musician lover, Otto. But Germany is about to change.

Will Kitty and Sarah find the love they truly deserve?

Coming out in September 2013 in paperback and ebook: pre-order now!

HODDER

Do you wish this wasn't the end?

Join us at www.hodder.co.uk, or follow us on Twitter @hodderbooks to be a part of our community of people who love the very best in books and reading.

Whether you want to discover more about a book or an author, watch trailers and interviews, have the chance to win early limited editions, or simply browse our expert readers' selection of the very best books, we think you'll find what you're looking for.

And if you don't, that's the place to tell us what's missing.

We love what we do, and we'd love you to be part of it.

www.hodder.co.uk

@hodderbooks

HodderBooks

HodderBooks